FORGIVE
OUR
IGNORANCE

THE FORGIVE ME FATHER SERIES
BOOK ONE

CAITLIN MAZUR

Book cover design by Daniel Eyenegho

ISBN 978-1-960864-01-7

❀ Created with Vellum

For my boys.
May you always challenge the status quo.

AUTHOR'S NOTE

This story takes place across New Hampshire and Vermont, with the Coutts commune established in what was once White Mountain National Forest and Coutts Peak established on what was once Mount Washington. For the sake of storytelling, some details of the landscape may have been altered.

Birds born in a cage think flying is an illness.

— ALEJANDRO JODOROWSKY

1

MAURA

MY HUSBAND'S voice did not belong out here. It most certainly did not belong to the figure I watched, aiming a gun at a helpless man.

For eighteen years I believed God walked with the faithful, helping them overcome fear so long as their obedience never wavered. A beautiful thought, but also a lie. Obedience wasn't steadying my breathing. It wasn't making it possible to move. This fear felt primitive. And it paralyzed me.

"We got no idea who you're talking about," said an older man. "We were just passing through. Honest."

I pressed my shoulder up against a dirt-crusted dumpster, fingers grasping at the sharp edge to peer around. The obscure figure with Andrew's voice stood in the middle of a paved road, clothed in green armor and a helmet, flanked by two identically dressed figures of similar height. All of them held large, black guns aimed at three people with their arms tied behind their backs.

Their gaunt faces peered up at the armored men from where they kneeled on the hot pavement.

"I know she's here!" the familiar voice yelled, shaking something in his free hand. I squinted, trying to make it out, and my heart dropped when I realized the armed figure held my canvas scavenging bag. I squeezed my eyes closed. "Did you take her?" the voice demanded. I tried to study the tone and inflection, the edge of hysteria. Perhaps I'd thought wrong. Perhaps it wasn't him.

"No!" a young, red-haired woman cried. She knelt beside an old man with thinning hair and sunspots. "We haven't seen anyone!"

"Honest to God," the youngest of their group answered. He still had the markings of a teenager — a fresh spot of acne, uneven facial hair, and an edge of cushion around his cheeks slowly being carved away by his cheekbones.

"Shut up," the man who might be Andrew said. He threw the bag at them and it landed with a plop on the pavement behind them. Then, with a growl, he pointed his weapon across the line, prompting them each to wince as it swung inches from their faces. "You're no son or daughter of God. Sinners! Depraved souls! You are not worthy of his grace, nor mine!" He slammed the back of the gun down on the young man's face, and he crumpled with a pained moan.

The woman began to cry, mumbling to herself, as the bruised man struggled to get back to his knees. And though I saw terror pass fleetingly across his features, the elderly gentleman looked up, his fierce gaze fixed on the man with my husband's voice, as if he dared him to pull the trigger.

"Change your mind?" one of the not-Andrews growled, brandishing his weapon.

"No," the old man answered.

The helmeted figure in the middle turned away, shaking his head. Annoyance. Did Andrew shake his head like that? I tried to remember his unique look of disappointment.

He walked a few paces toward the dumpster, away from his obedient soldiers, who kept their weapons pointed at the prisoners. The building the dumpster leaned against shadowed his helmet, but as he pushed the visor up to reveal himself, there was no question. Disgust swam in those remarkable blue eyes handed down to all the Coutts' brothers. My heart sank. I would know the man I married anywhere.

Andrew reached into his headpiece with a gloved hand, wiping beads of sweat away from his upper lip before sliding it down again.

"Sir?"

My husband turned on his heel. "Take them," he ordered, pointing at the young man and woman. His pointer finger drew a straight line to a large black truck idling on the other side of the road. "I'll take care of *him.*"

Cold shock flooded through me. Had I noted a tone of glee in his voice? Surely not. But then again, anything was possible. I had never known Andrew to be cruel. He had been, through and through, a Coutts man of God. A devout follower of the Prophet. A paragon of our beliefs.

But I had also never known Andrew to have knowledge of Outsiders. Andrew and the Prophet told us they had searched for months, and there was no one left out here. If this was the truth, wouldn't he have responded to his captives existence with awe instead of anger?

The men acted immediately, forcing the two young people to their feet, guns pressed against their backs. They cast pain-filled gazes back at the elder, who continued staring up at Andrew.

"Please," the woman cried, even as she trembled from fear. "Please, just let him go. He's an old man—" The Hunter behind her slammed the long barrel of his weapon against her face and she gasped as a wound opened high on her cheek.

"Get moving," he ordered, pressing her onward toward the truck.

"Dad!" she screamed over her shoulder, neck at an odd angle. But even I knew it was hopeless, because I could see Andrew raising the gun, his finger resting upon the trigger, no note of hesitation in his stature.

"Please don't," the younger man said, moving sideways. "We'll go with you, just let him—"

The bullet sliced through the air, the sound so loud it set my own ears ringing, and I scrambled backward against the wall, stuffing my fist in my mouth in a pathetic attempt to muffle my cries.

No!

A scream pressed against my airway and I bit down on my knuckles to suppress it. Teeth sunk into my flesh, but no pain registered. I stared out toward the brick building enclosing me in the alleyway, trembling.

A thud came somewhere through my distorted senses and though I no longer looked at them, I knew the man had fallen back, dead. Screams followed — loud, guttural, and soaked in agony.

The world slowed. I squeezed my eyes closed, the revulsion inside of me bursting for release. Terror and confusion circled me like vultures. Try as I might, there was no semblance of sense in what I'd witnessed. Just pure, unfiltered horror.

Andrew. The man was a soldier of God. That's what Father had told me when he'd announced our marriage. He was a holy servant, a follower of the church, a devout disciple of the Lord. I had been lucky to marry him — even Mother had said so. He was chosen. Picked to fight in the battle between good and evil. He upheld our morals. He was Father's confidant.

But this? Killing a defenseless person?

This was *unforgivable*.

"Get in the truck," my husband yelled through the young man and woman's anguished cries. I pressed myself harder into the corner of the building and dumpster, desperate to stay hidden, terrified of what might happen if Andrew caught me now. My heart beat in my throat, pounding against my dry airway.

Tires squealed against the pavement as the trucks took off toward a distant destination. I pulled my head back to find the sky. Through my blurred vision, I found it as cloudless and beautiful as ever. But it felt so unnatural, so undeserving, after what I'd just seen.

As the sound of the truck faded, I forced a low, guttural shriek to God above. How did He let this happen? How could my life unravel so quickly? Was everything I'd ever known to be true a lie?

I succumbed to my tears, grief consuming me until I couldn't breathe. I choked on my distress, struggling to cough, to find my way back to a steady breath. Nausea rose in my belly, and in a final act of defiance, my stomach contracted and I retched.

Sour bile splashed across the pavement, forcing me on all fours. I stared at the contents of my gut — the only tangible thing to focus on. The sick caused by the senseless murder caused by the husband who had defied God.

It didn't make sense.

I remained doubled over, coarse asphalt digging into my skin as I watched my wet vomit trail through cracks in the concrete. And when I turned my head, I saw the old man's blood in the distance, doing the same.

2

MAURA

ONE WEEK EARLIER

"Bow your head and pray for salvation."

"Amen."

The chorus of prayer echoed through the church. I pulled my knees back from the padded kneeler, sticky from heat. My legs screamed to be freed from their position, but I persisted, thinking of Job, eager to push past the pain. To show discomfort in this moment of prayer would be foolish and downright disrespectful. I had sins to atone for.

Forgive me, Father. Save me from my sins. Grant me divine eternity in your Kingdom of Heaven.

I squeezed my eyes tighter, just to make it really stick.

"My children." A booming voice filled the room, its familiarity forcing my gaze to a broad mahogany stage toward which our pews faced. The white wall behind it reached two stories high, decorated with a polished wooden crucifix hung beneath a large, framed photo of our Prophet, Peter Coutts. Sunlight spilled through identical rose-colored windows on either side.

The Prophet, who was both my biological and spiritual Father, stood before a handsome altar, a wide grin painted across his expression. He raised his arms above his head in a sweeping gesture, motioning us to stand.

"I call you together today to, once again, celebrate our good fortune," he continued, as the crowd got to their feet. "The Lord rewarded us in the world's darkest moments with life and prosperity. With good health! With opportunity! He's put into our hands the responsibility to carry forth our obligations until he returns to bring us home to Heaven."

"Amen!" a few people shouted. My heart thudded as I gripped the pew in front of me. The thrill of the Prophet's sermon clutched me in a tight grip of holiness. We were special. We had made it. God had saved us.

"The almighty Lord sent great plagues to this Earth," he continued, clutching his microphone as he strode across the stage to address each corner of the church. "Killing billions, damning the Jezebels, the unclean, ridding Earth of the Devil's influence. And who has He left? Who has He trusted in these end days to continue His legacy? Who has He chosen to save and protect?"

"Us, us!" Eager chants filled the space. "He chose us!"

I nodded with absolute certainty, fixated on Father.

"He chose us!" The Prophet yelled, his eyes wide and wild. "He *chose* us. Only us! Oh! How blessed are we? And we go forth and do his work and wait for the Day. The

Day of Reckoning. The Day He will come to save us all
and lead us into the Kingdom of Heaven."

"Amen! Amen! Amen!" more shouted. "Amen!"

I joined them.

THE SKY GAVE no sign we were the last people left on
Earth. That was the beauty of it, really — the certainty
that the sun would rise and set, even when everything else
was chaos. This morning, the backdrop looked as if God
Himself had shaken out the clouds for us, His most
devout servants — the ones He'd saved from his most holy
wrath.

We spilled from the mouth of the church, down steep
marble steps, and onto a paved lot filled with sleek coach
buses. The sour stench of sweat lingered in the summer
air. Even up on Coutts Peak, a summit that had once held
snow year-round, the heat still found us.

The church's nave roof stretched high to the heavens,
anchored to the towering mountain rock behind it. Decades
before I was born, Coutts men had built upon the foundation of old observation towers, carving flying buttresses and
pinnacles from stone, tunneling aisles and entrances, chis-
eling ornate sculptures to grace our holy place of worship.

The peak overlooked our mountainous region with
rolling, green hills and steep, purple summits, shadowed
by distant clouds. Our commune's land stretched over a
thousand miles across these lands and continued to
expand as God saw fit. I faced west, confirmed by the
distant cluster of vase-shaped cooling towers. Steam

billowed from their mouths — the sign of clean nuclear energy powering our holy commune.

"Maura!" A pair of familiar hands gripped my arms.

I turned chin-to-shoulder to smile at my sister. Physically, Morgan could have been my twin; one year younger, with sun-kissed skin, tight black curls, and bushy brows. While I'd inherited our dark-skinned Mother's dimpled baby face, my sister mirrored Father's more chiseled jawline, which she held clenched as she released her grip on me.

"Another *glorious* day," Morgan said.

"Don't be ungrateful."

She frowned. "Right. There's nothing more I want to do than wash dirty laundry all day. Praise God!"

I jerked my head toward my sister, eyes wide and heart hammering, before glancing over my shoulder. We were far enough away that nobody would've heard Morgan's blasphemy, but I glared at her all the same. God had heard. He'd heard every defiance she'd ever uttered, which, recently, had been many. Since my marriage, Morgan had become the eldest daughter in Mother's household, meaning she was next in line to be married off. She resented everything about it.

"Quit it," I hissed. "Someone'll hear you."

"Let them," she grumbled, toeing the grass at the edge of the pavement.

"Morgan!"

"Maura!" she mimicked, her eyes narrowed. "You can't tell me you're looking forward to another afternoon of scavenging."

I pursed my lips.

"Thought so," she said.

"It's not so bad," I lied.

"Mm-hmm."

I refused to play her games. I had an example to set as a new, high-ranking wife with a job in the community. No matter how boring it was, I would be grateful.

"There's no use in complaining, Morgan. It'd do you some good to take pride in your role."

"Spoken like a true Coutts."

I opened my mouth to retort, but stopped. A hush fell over the throng of people outside; a couple hundred, I guessed. Monday morning was a light day of worship, as the children were already in school. The crowd parted toward each side of the steep staircase. All faces turned inward, some standing on tip-toes to get a good look.

Our Father, the almighty Prophet, descended, wearing a crisp gray suit, the massive, four-story church a mere backdrop to his presence. He nodded with ease as he passed the congregation on the stairs, pausing every so often to shake a hand, wave, or flash his wide, sweeping smile. Father was a tall, sinewy man with a crew cut and a prominent nose, giving him a shrewd composure. Even watching from a distance, my heart swelled with pride. We were all God's children, but I was one of Father's *true* biological daughters. And that meant something.

I glanced sideways at Morgan, who had gotten a piece of hair stuck in her mouth. She spat it out, her attention focused on patting it back into place. I frowned. Morgan rejected the idea of being a proud Coutts daughter. Whereas I made an effort to participate in our community, Morgan found her duty to be meaningless and forced. Although I was no longer part of my old family, I still worried about what kind of trouble her defiance would get her into.

"Maura!" My name rang out across the parking lot. This voice I knew, but was disappointed to hear.

Andrew Coutts was a heavier version of Father, with the same silver hair and blue eyes that blessed all the Coutts brothers. His weight dulled any sharp edge he might have had, making him appear less intimidating, which wasn't always the truth.

"Hello." I forced a smile as he hurried to join us.

We married just before the great plague, but I still hadn't found comfort in the man I called my husband, although I'd known him for all of my life. Morgan theorized it was because he was thirty years my senior, but I knew through hard work and servitude, my feelings would change. Or so I hoped.

"Darling," he said, wrapping his hand around my head to press his dry lips to my forehead. "Wonderful service, don't you agree?"

"Absolutely wonderful," Morgan agreed, a little too enthusiastically, as though she were trying to make up for her sinful words. My heart almost stopped. He hadn't meant the question for her, and, realizing her mistake, she clamped her mouth shut and looked at her shoes. I forced a placating smile at Andrew, who flashed her a skeptical look.

The Prophet frowned upon associating with our old families after marriage, even if it was only for a few moments. It didn't help that Morgan's reputation labeled her a miscreant. A little over a year ago, Mother had discovered her bed cold and empty. Father and his men searched the commune far and wide, but came up empty-handed. Weeks later, they rescued her, and she returned, bewildered, forbidden to describe what she'd seen. Her absence marked her as an usurper and Father sent her to the Island of Repentance where she'd stayed for months, missing our wedding.

Andrew's expectant stare lingered on me. "It was beautiful, as usual," I answered, filling the uncomfortable silence.

This seemed to please him, and he slipped his arm around my neck. "We should get going," he told me, as if Morgan did not exist. "Lots to do today."

I looked back at Morgan, hoping to catch her gaze, but she didn't dare look up again and I didn't dare say anything more to her as Andrew pulled me toward the walking path leading to our homes. Morgan wandered into the crowd and I glimpsed her joining my mother and siblings. A painful jolt of longing pierced through my chest.

"You know better than to be passing time with someone like *her*," Andrew said, his hand tight on my shoulder. "You belong to a higher status, Maura. We don't want to be setting a poor example now, do we?"

"No, sir."

"I'll be heading into the cities this afternoon." Andrew grasped my waist to fall in step with him. "But I'm mostly looking forward to our evening together."

I forced my smile, pretending to be very interested in the large rocks marking the sides of the walking path.

"Me too," I answered after a long pause. But something else had gotten Andrew's attention. His gaze lay on his cluster of homes coming into view as we walked.

These were the Coutts Estates — one of the highest

points on Coutts Peak, second only to our church. Living on the peak was important to Father; he wanted his holiest servants closest to God. Every male directly descended from the Coutts bloodline would house their families atop Coutts Peak or its associated mountains.

Outside the oak fence surrounding Andrew's massive property waited two women; my sister wives, Sister Abigail and Sister Joanna. Abigail was Andrew's first wife and matched him in age, with thin lips and greying red hair. She had worked for a few years as the Matriarch, the girl's purpose training leader, before marrying. Together, they had four children.

Joanna was Andrew's second wife; a tall, slim blonde woman with a sharp jaw and down-turned eyes. As she rotated, her swollen belly came into view, and I stewed with jealousy. Another new life would soon join our community. Joanna had already welcomed two others into the world, now aged four and two.

The pair of women let their gazes travel over my head, acknowledging Andrew as he released me from his hold. "See you tonight," he called over his shoulder, joining his wives at the estate entrance. I waved to no one as they turned their backs. The familiar feeling of otherness returned, as it often did when I walked the path to my scavenging duties. I was the only wife in my family with a job. The only one without a proper home. The only one without children. Without purpose.

———

THE AFTERNOON SHOWERED me in uncomfortable heat as I dug my heels into Sweetheart, our family's black American Quarter Horse. Together, we trotted along the east perimeter of my zone, a six-mile square that included seven looted homes, one dilapidated shed, two ditches, and a whole lot of trees. I knew because I'd picked through all of it at least three times this summer.

At first, I'd brought back bounties — bulging bags of my findings, clothes and seeds, blankets, paper, children's toys, and books. I'd even found a drawer filled with women's cosmetics and snuck Morgan a few new lipsticks to add to her collection. It wasn't all gold, but it was *something*. Tangible things to give me purpose.

But that had been back in June, and August was nearing its end. The past two months had produced nothing but meager findings, and my sister wives had rightfully reprimanded me. I was a new wife, and I still needed to pay my dues.

After the Outside had succumbed to the Great Plague, Father expanded our boundaries. My task as a Scavenger was to survey the land and any property on it to determine what we could use for the good of the commune; things like clothing, lumber, electronic parts, or automobiles. We were allowed to keep smaller things for our families, like food, toys, or approved books for trading, gifts, or our own enjoyment. Though we once had various methods of production for these items, Father had shifted labor to more essential needs in the past year.

We'd traded the last of my findings away weeks ago and it was becoming more and more obvious I was not pulling my weight within our family. Until the boundaries expanded again, I'd have nothing to show for myself. Truly nothing, as every pregnancy test Andrew provided me with had come up negative since we'd been trying to expand his legacy.

Coming home empty-handed day after day had taken its toll. I frustrated Abigail and Joanna even if they didn't say it outright. They resented the space I took in Andrew's bed and the amount of share I got as a new wife. If only they knew how eager I would've been to give it back to them.

Sweetheart halted as I pulled on her reins. The west side of my zone met the north at the corner of a large, rushing creek. Its water flowed southeast into unknown territory with a deafening roar. Across the way, past rocky shallows, a steep cliff backdrop stretched ten feet above the water. Lush trees scattered the top of the bluff, disappearing beyond my line of vision.

Sweetheart shook her mane out with an impatient neigh, hurrying me toward our favorite part of the afternoon. I swung my legs to one side of her saddle and landed with a *thump* in the grass. She nudged me with her muzzle.

"All right, hold your horses," I laughed, reaching for her bitless bridle to guide her alongside me as we approached the rushing creek.

The sun reflected on the river like diamonds, twinkling as the water raced along. A small breeze drifted through, cooling the drying sweat on my neck. For weeks, I appreciated the pure, untouched beauty of this place. But as my frustration with my duties grew, my appreciation waned. Luckily, out here, with only Sweetheart in my company, I could be as unappreciative as I wanted with no one knowing otherwise.

The creek marked a border. One I could never cross.

Not for an emergency, not for curiosity, not even if a meaty deer crossed my path. I was to return to base and let the Hunters take over. Only they could ensure my safety, which was of the utmost importance. Women were to be protected.

Better to be patient than a warrior, Father told me when I'd first gotten this job. *Better to have self-control than to capture a city.* I glanced at Sweetheart's empty saddlebags as she dipped her head into the creek. Patience felt like a punishment.

With a heavy sigh, I resigned myself to enjoy the moment of peace and took a seat in the grass. I leaned back on my elbows, turning my face toward the sun. Had I blinked, I would've missed the flash of light I caught from the corner of my eye.

My heart fluttered. I straightened, straining my neck higher, squinting as I scanned the top of the cliff. Something was there. Something new!

I tilted my head to the left, and sure enough, right between a cluster of trees, was something that looked like glass. I scrambled to my feet, trying not to lose the spot I'd seen. Another breath of breeze shifted the surrounding leaves. I strained my eyes through the sun's reflection on the creek, the corners of my eyes watering. There it was again. On top of the cliff, maybe a hundred feet away; glass, split into four even panes, connected to greening wood, well hidden beneath overgrowth.

A window.

My stomach somersaulted as I stepped into the shallows, allowing the water to run around the toes of my boots. How had I not seen it before?

I supposed I hadn't been looking up much, eyes glued

to the earth to find anything I might've missed. But this window meant *possibilities*. I glanced at Sweetheart, imagining bulging saddlebags, then back at my potential treasure in the distance. There was the border, sure. But who would know?

I lengthened my body as far as I could, stretching over the water, desperate to get a better look at the structure. The sun winked in the window as though it were taunting me. I pulled my shoulders back, hands on my thighs, squinting…

Just a bit further.

I stumbled, my feet tangling with the small rocks at the edge of the creek, landing on my knees and hands in a frigid, shallow pool. Instantly soaked. Flushed with embarrassment, I grunted as I pushed myself away from the water and onto steady legs. Beside me, Sweetheart munched on fresh grass, unbothered. I sighed, grimacing at the stains on my jeans. Abigail was going to be furious.

The sun dipped lower now, the edges of it touching the treetops in the distance, but the heat wouldn't give up that easily. I just hoped I'd be dry by the time I returned home.

"C'mon girl," I said, grasping Sweetheart's reins. "Let's get home."

3

MAURA

AN OAK FENCE marked the perimeter of Andrew's eight acres of land. Two wide, concrete columns greeted me at the entrance to the estate, each with his initials carved into the side. A sensor-driven light hid beneath tasteful landscaping surrounding the base of each. I gripped the far column and spun around, my boots clicking against the paved drive as I walked toward the homes.

To the left stood a three-bedroom modern farmhouse, painted white with black trim — Sister Abigail's home. Behind it loomed a two-story gray contemporary home with floor-to-ceiling windows and corners as sharp as its keeper — Sister Joanna. On the right was Andrew's six-bedroom lodge. With its rustic, dark-wood beauty, our husband's home was and always would be the masterpiece of the estate, the place where all his wives and children would gather every night to eat.

I was new to these luxuries. Despite being married to Father, my Mother was only seventh in line, which meant they built her a much more ordinary house at a lower elevation. It was a nice home and well taken care of, but reminded her of her place. Only the first three wives earned homes of honor within the Coutts Estates. I had been told many times just how lucky I was to be a third wife. I was now considered higher ranking than my own mother. Still, I could never dream about bossing other wives around like Abigail and Joanna sometimes did.

They would build my home on the estate too, that was, if I ever managed to get pregnant. For now, my place was at Andrew's home. I glanced at my canvas bag, which I'd filled with my meager findings: sticks for firewood, a handful of oyster mushrooms, and about three cups of elderberries picked from an overgrown bush. It wasn't nothing, but that's what Abigail and Joanna would think.

With a heavy sigh, I climbed the wooden stairs up to the front porch, entering the house through a side door. I emerged into a gray-paneled mudroom that held our winter things, shoes, Andrew's green Hunter suit, and garden tools. Sister Joanna would frown upon my mud-slathered boots, so I kicked them into the corner. Heaving my bag higher on my shoulder to hide my meager haul, I entered the hallway leading to the kitchen.

Slow roasting meat wafted through the well-lit room. Sister Abigail's doing, no doubt. Sister Joanna was a terrible cook. Neither turned to acknowledge me. Joanna sang a hymn to the gaggle of children sitting obediently at the long dining table and Abigail stood at the sink, up to her elbows in soapy dishwater.

"Hello," I announced my presence, placing my bounty on the marbled center island. Abigail glanced over her shoulder at the bag and frowned, before pulling her hands from the water to wipe them on a dishrag hanging from the oven.

"Back already, are you?" she asked, turning, her gaze landing on me. She gasped. "Look at the sight of you!" she roared. Her lined face purpled as she took in my mud-soaked jeans, dirty hands, and drenched socks. "An absolute disgrace!" She threw her hands up and down, gesturing at my unacceptable appearance. "Did you at least come back with something worthwhile?"

I looked at my socks.

"I'll take that as a no," she sneered, grabbing the canvas tote from the counter. Afraid to look up, I picked at my cuticles as Sister Abigail sighed in frustration. She pulled out everything I'd collected before sliding the bag back across the island at me.

"Put that away. And go clean yourself up, for heaven's sake! You're supposed to be a wife of this house, not a hog meant to roll in the mud."

"Yes, ma'am." I picked the empty bag up, noting no difference in weight.

Abigail's lip twitched as she considered me. "I hope you're not out there daydreaming on that horse," she said, after a moment's pause. I suspect she'd wanted to say something very different to me.

"No ma'am."

"Well, there's no excuse to return home with this little Maura. How can anyone expect you to run a household of your own if you can't even do this simple job?"

I hung my head. "Yes, ma'am," I said, pulling the tote closer to my chest. "I'm sorry."

"I don't want apologies," Abigail hissed, turning her attention to a large, steaming pot on the stove. "You have standards to uphold. Your failures reflect on this family. Fix it."

I nodded, shame blossoming in my gut. Abigail returned to her stew, and I hurried outside to hang the bag on the fence for tomorrow's scavenging. I suspected it wouldn't be any better. Once finished, I re-entered the mudroom, ready to head to the shower. But voices drifting from the kitchen kept me rooted to my spot.

"... believe it?"

"Andrew needs to address it." Joanna's high-pitched voice contrasted with Abigail's deeper tone. "It's clear she's not committed to the task. If she isn't bringing enough in, he should order her penance."

"Yes, but who knows if he'd even agree? He coddles her like a child."

"She *is* a child."

"She's not ready for this kind of marriage." Abigail's harsh voice sliced through me. "But what can we do? She's Peter's kin. Of course she's getting preferential treatment. I will *never* understand why he married that mixed-race outsider when he had his pick of so many willing, devout women."

"Abigail!" Joanna released a sardonic laugh. "Don't let Andrew hear you speak about his brother like that." I winced at her jovial tone.

As I leaned up against the wall, I wished I'd taken my time coming in. Feeling disliked is violently different from *hearing* you're disliked. Blinking back tears, I hurried from the mudroom, straight to the bathroom, where I could, at the very least, cry my shame away in peace.

ANDREW CLOSED the door behind Sister Abigail, always the last to leave, and watched her through the foyer window as she herded her children across the driveway. I stood in the hallway, hands intertwined behind my back, watching. With dinner and cleanup complete, there was only one last thing to do before bed.

My husband switched off the porch lights before rounding on me. Being alone with Andrew was still strange, not the way I ever imagined a married couple should be. But this marriage was the one Father had proclaimed, and I tried with every ounce of my being to be the wife God wanted me to be.

"Come," Andrew said, walking toward a pair of dark wooden doors with brass handles. Andrew's bedroom featured polished hardwood floors, a full sitting room with a stone fireplace, a California King bed, two walk-in closets, and a marble bathroom. Windows covered the entire room, overlooking his property and stunning mountain views beyond. Even in the moonlight, the view was breathtaking.

I followed Andrew through the doors, pulling them closed behind me. What happened in this room was always between the two of us, and I knew the routine down to every meticulous detail. Andrew was a creature of habit, so when he stopped in his sitting room, I froze.

I hovered by one of the velvet green chairs beside the fireplace, uncertain if I should sit or stand. Andrew took his time on the other side of the room, standing at a built-in bar surrounded by handsome oak bookshelves holding a variety of religious and philosophical texts. Bottles clinked, liquid poured, and Andrew turned, a glass of whiskey clutched in his grip. He ran his right hand over his face, then took a sip before sitting in a chair facing me.

Andrew kept his unfocused gaze on the floor while I leaned against the arm of the chair; a halfway point between sitting and standing. He took another sip, smacked his lips, and rested the drink on his knee. His blue eyes met mine.

"So, I spoke with Abigail this evening," he began.

Weight settled in my chest. I tried to search his face for any sign of what was to come. I thought of Abigail and Joanna's conversation, and for a moment, the room spun. They wouldn't have gone to Andrew over this, would they?

"Oh?"

Andrew's hand tightened around the glass. He sighed. "She tells me the last three weeks of hauls have been nothing but twigs and berries."

And mushrooms.

"Yes," I admitted.

"And why do you think that is?"

His eyes searched my own, but the question confused me. "The borders," I whispered. "They haven't extended them in weeks—"

"Have you been praying on it?"

I opened my mouth, then let it close again. "Well, yes."

Andrew cocked his head and raised his eyebrows. "Maura." He laughed. "Have you?"

"I'll pray harder."

"The Lord rewards His greatest servants," Andrew preached. "If you're struggling, perhaps you must change other areas of your life. Perhaps you must pray *harder*.

Serve *harder*. Remember," he said, "God is always watching. If he's punishing you, it means there is something within you that must change. He makes no mistakes."

"Yes, sir."

He stood and approached me like a lion stalking its prey. Though I knew his presence should've made me feel safe and loved, I wrestled with an uneasiness in the pit of my stomach. He paused before me, lifting my chin with a single finger, and leaned down to press his lips to mine.

I tasted the bitter liquor as his mouth grazed my own and I stiffened, surprised by the sudden affection. He pulled back, face only inches from mine, studying me as his hot breath rolled over me in waves. "I need you to do better," he whispered.

I swallowed the weight of his words, obediently nodding my head. If I couldn't measure up to what a Coutts wife should be, it reflected poorly on all of us. And what then? Was I doomed to be exiled? Demoted to a lower-status family? I had never heard of a wife underperforming as I had. Perhaps those punishments were too brutal to be uttered aloud.

Andrew pecked my cheek before straightening, leaving me to the bathroom to wash up. There, I fiddled with the wedding ring he'd given me a year ago — a simple gold band with an ornate *C* all wives received when marrying. Perhaps I did not deserve this privilege.

Perhaps you're just not cut out to be a wife.

The thought startled me and I swallowed it, scolding myself for bringing it into existence. I returned for my duty, face squashed into a pillow with Andrew's heaving, sweaty body behind me. I focused on a spot on the wall until he was done, trying to think of anything but my failures and what might come if I didn't correct them.

But even after the lights had dimmed and Andrew had fallen into heavy sleep, I stared at the dark ceiling, wondering *how* I could possibly do better.

That night, I dreamt of the window.

4

MAURA

I BOUNCED on the balls of my feet outside the church, peering through the thinning crowd. Andrew stood at the base of the stairs, arms crossed, speaking to a young blond man I didn't recognize. I longed to race to the buses that would carry me to the horse stables to start scavenging, but since we'd married, Andrew had insisted I wait for him to walk home.

Moisture rose from the ground, nestling in the air, making even the thin cotton t-shirt I wore uncomfortable. I squinted, shielding my eyes from the sun with my hand, my heart leaping as Andrew finally weaved through the crowd toward me. His features lit up as he found me, and I did my best to match his excitement.

"Hello, sweetheart." He grinned, his round face coated in sweat.

I gave an awkward wave, then clasped my hands together behind my back.

"Another fantastic service," he said.

"Oh, yes."

Andrew grasped my waist and began to walk. "Did you pray on what we spoke about last night?" He kept his voice low, lips hovering above my ear.

I stumbled before looking up at him. His stern gaze bore through me and for a moment, I wondered if he knew I'd been thinking about the window all morning.

"Of course."

He gave a nod. "Don't disappoint me, Maura. I would hate for you to require penance."

"I won't." But my heart ached with guilt. I did not deserve his faith. I still had so much to prove! If Andrew knew what I was thinking about doing, would he still be so pleased?

His lips curved into a smile and despite my misgivings, warmth spread through me. I longed for Andrew's approval, to impress him and the others. I wanted to feel needed and respected, like I'd earned my place in our family. A flush rose to my cheeks as I thought of over-hearing Joanna and Abigail.

We reached the fence where my sister wives stood, their attention on one another. Andrew paused before they were in earshot and turned toward me, wrapping a finger in my curls. "Bring back a good haul for us today," he drawled, his tone heavy. He was handing me responsibility without saying *or else*.

I nodded like a soldier off to battle, grabbing my canvas bag from the fence along the way as Andrew walked Joanna and Abigail up to the houses. I knew what I had to do. God had shown me that window. He'd wanted me to see it — why else would it have appeared in my moment of need? Despite the border restrictions, God had given me a gift, and it was up to me not to waste it.

With the window still occupying my thoughts, the mile-and-a-half walk to the large paved parking lot where a single bus idled, took almost no time at all. The bus that took us to the stables was the polar opposite of the sleek coach buses which carted people to and from church. The yellow frame seemed to sag over flat tires, ill-equipped to handle the rocky terrain. Still, somehow, the driver shuttled ten female passengers from here to the stables and back, daily.

I was always aware of being one of the youngest women on the bus. Though no one would admit it, they often gave scavenging duty to high-ranking barren women — first or second wives whose children had come of age and could not produce more. I tried not to think about it. Andrew had promised this was only temporary until I was with child.

Only one other woman near my age rode the bus. Eve had straight, jet-black hair and angular eyes. She was the closest person I could call a friend. We sat together every morning on our ride, sometimes making small talk, other times sitting in silence. But we never talked about pregnancy or the absence of it and for that, I was grateful.

The selfish part of me wished I would conceive before she did — something I tried praying away. It was a horrible thing to hope for. But every time I saw her in a seat, I breathed a sigh of relief.

Today, we sat in comfortable silence, bouncing along a small paved road that led us down the mountain. The hour and a half drive was a welcomed length as I mulled over what I was about to do. Breaking commune rules terrified me. But the threat of strict penance scared me more. It meant giving up my job as a Scavenger to be at

Abigail and Joanna's beck and call; or worse, being sent to the Island of Repentance. If I found just one valuable thing behind the window, it would hold me over a little longer, at least until the Hunters extended the borders.

Despite the morning heat, I broke into a cold sweat as we passed a large, glass-backed sign that read *JC Family Ranch*, named for my late grandfather. The white, C-shaped horse barn sat at the end of a wide dirt road. Both sides featured grandiose stalls for family horses each with its own dutch door facing outward. The bus stopped before the entrance, a two-story structure, complete with arched French windows. As I stepped off the bus, the air changed; a mixture of earth and manure stung my nostrils.

We clambered from the bus to the dirt, entering the main area of the barn, ponderosa pine lining every inch. In the middle of the circular room hung a colonial chandelier with unlit candles centered over a glass coffee table. Plush couches surrounded the space, an unblemished Oriental rug beneath it all. A stone fireplace stood on the left, untouched during the summer, not a stray ash in sight. A massive window on the far wall revealed the grazing pasture where two chestnut horses roamed.

"Good morning."

A voice teetering on the edge of adulthood echoed through the space. I crossed my arms as I turned to greet our group leader, Father's fifth wife's oldest son, Jeremiah. The teen wore a straw hat, a whistle around his neck, and held a clipboard in his hands. The barn and his role as Scavenger coordinator had been a gift from Father last fall when the young man produced the largest harvest we'd seen in years. Morgan, who'd worked in the gardens as part of her penance, complained about his reward for months.

He had help from dozens of us, and we got nothing but a few free tomatoes.

I wanted to trust Father's decision, but I had to admit, the boy's air of authority annoyed me. I hated the way he kept dominion over our zones and the shadow of a sneer that crossed his face each time I asked when he would extend the border. Somewhere in my subconscious, I knew it was wrong to blame him for my shortcomings, but I couldn't help it.

"Good morning," the small group of us answered. Jeremiah nodded before assigning our zones.

"Maura Coutts, Zone 16," he said, chewing on his fingernail as he glanced down at his clipboard. No surprise there. "And we haven't pushed the borders back yet, so don't ask," he added with an edge of annoyance. For the first time in a very long time, his response wasn't disappointing.

"Yes sir."

He narrowed his gaze before marking something down, continuing down the line of us. When he finished, he dismissed us to our duties. I skipped past him toward another pair of doors leading from the lobby into the stables, excitement bubbling in my belly. The hallway held rows of saddles and bridles, each labeled for their associated horse, along with buckets of grooming tools. I grabbed a bucket before heading to Sweetheart's stall.

Someone had cleared the stables hall floor of straw and feed. I counted six down on my left, unhooking the door latch to slip into Sweetheart's enclosure. The black beauty chewed in her trough, lifting her head to greet me.

"Hiya, girl." I ran my hand across her back. The barn had groomers, but I never skimped on brushing Sweetheart. The act of removing her dead hair and picking her hooves gave me a sense of satisfaction I cherished, especially these days. In an effort not to arouse any more suspicion today, I would maintain my routine.

I ran the rubber curry comb in circles across her coat, losing myself in the motion. I hoped she wouldn't be too angry with me for leaving her while I crossed the creek, but I had no other choice. Sweetheart often grazed on her own, especially when I had first explored, but I wasn't sure how she'd react if I was out of reach.

After the curry comb came the dandy brush, soft brush, and finally the hoof pick. Gently, I released her back leg, kicking a stray pebble away before I went to grab her bridle and saddle. With one last pull to tighten the straps beneath her belly, I tugged on her reins to guide her out of the stall.

We walked to the end of the row, sliding open the barn door to the pasture. My fingers shook as I gripped the saddle horn, secured my boot in the stirrup, and swung my body up and over Sweetheart's broad back.

It was time to change my luck.

WIND RUSHED past my ears as Sweetheart cantered through the woods, following a sparsely marked trail. Though scavenging had its downfalls, there was no denying the beauty of this journey. Tall pines provided generous foliage coverage, the sun's rays casting light across a mossy, pine-needled forest floor. I felt so sorry for the poor souls who'd died on the Outside. They would never get to experience this earthly splendor again, for they had sinned and did not repent. If only they had listened to Father.

We traveled at a slight incline until we reached a faded white marker stapled to a tree, which showed the start of my scavenging area. Sweetheart slowed on instinct, but I dug my heels into her side, encouraging her to keep pace. I leaned forward to caress her neck. "Not today, girl," I whispered. "Keep moving."

I pulled Sweetheart to the right, taking our familiar path to the creek. The overgrown grass had grown so high it touched my knees. We traveled past a large ditch, hidden well beneath clustered overgrowth, where I'd found camping gear back in June. I wrinkled my nose at the memory. It had been the first time I'd found an Outsider's corpse.

After some time, we reached a clearing and with a triumphant neigh, Sweetheart trotted toward our favorite spot. I smiled as she carried me, letting her reins slack in my hands until the ground got too soft. Pulling her to a smooth stop, I shifted my weight and slid off the saddle, pulling my tote over my arm.

The creek rushed past in a noisy symphony, its rapid movement likely prompted by the precipitation we'd gotten the night before. I kept my eyes on the muddy ground. Terror settled in my gut, prompting rolling nausea I fought to keep at bay. What if I'd imagined the whole thing? What if I'd seen wrong? Or, worse, what if it was there, but there was nothing to find?

I stepped to the creek's edge and closed my eyes,

focused on my breathing. Rushing water thundered in the background of my thoughts.

You can do this.

Could I?

You have to do this.

I opened my eyes and looked up, searching along the cliff's edge. Nothing had changed from the day before, but even though I'd made careful mental notes of what the window looked like, my memory failed me. And then I saw it, just as the sun danced across the glass pane. My heart dropped into my stomach. It seemed so obvious. How had I ever missed it?

I turned to Sweetheart. "Okay, girl," I said, running my fingers through her mane. "You go on and enjoy the day. I'll be back soon." Her lips rippled over her teeth as she sighed, then nudged me. I took a step back.

"Don't be like that," I told her. "I'll be fine." I placed my head against her long muzzle and gave her a small squeeze before turning toward the creek.

Adrenaline surged through my chest as I charted my course. A flat rock protruded to my left, water crashing around it in white peaks. Another boulder sat maybe two or three feet beyond, close enough to the opposite creek edge to make it at a long jump, if I could get on top of it. A steep incline, thick with dirt, trees, and brush, was about ten feet to the right of where I'd land. I could use them as holds to the top of the cliff, check out where the window led, and get back across in no time.

Easy enough.

With a deep breath, I plunged into the creek. Frigid water wrapped around my ankles, seeping into the tops of my boots and soaking my socks. The smell would be atrocious and Abigail would complain, but perhaps she'd overlook it if I brought back enough of a bounty.

I waded toward the first rock, water coming up around my calves. It'd seemed a lot closer moments ago. Determined, I forced my heavy feet forward. But as the water deepened, I struggled to place one foot in front of the other against the tide. The creek floor dipped, and I faltered, losing my footing in the harsh current. I leaned forward to catch myself, but freezing water rushed over me before I steadied, drenching the rest of my pants and part of my shirt. Engaging my core, I tried keeping my balance, but with nothing to hold on to, I fell sideways.

I kicked my feet as the water rose to meet my shoulders. My canvas bag slid from my arm, succumbing to the powerful flow. Within seconds, I was chin-deep, desperately swimming against the current. With a terrified burst of strength, I hurled myself forward toward the rock, but as hard as I tried to make up the ground I'd lost, I couldn't fight the water. The rock seemed to get farther away.

No.

My teeth chattered so hard it was becoming difficult to see. I squinted through the rolling tide, looking for the rock, rolling my shoulders with my arms outstretched to gain enough momentum to grasp it. Water splashed from all directions and as I sucked in my next breath, I inhaled water instead of air.

I couldn't breathe. The water burned my nose and throat, forcing my eyes closed. It was all I could do to stay afloat as I choked down cold liquid, searching for a breath to ease the pain in my lungs. But the water was relentless. Horror flooded through me as I strained my fatigued limbs to keep me from sinking. They felt heavy and uncooperative, like foreign appendages I hadn't yet mastered. I needed to get out of the water, find something to grab onto, or make it back to shore. But all I could see were surging waves as I dipped up and down against the tide.

In a final attempt to stay adrift, I pressed my toes down, hoping to find the bottom of the creek. But there was nothing. I slipped beneath the surface, water stinging my eyes, chilling me to the bone. Unable to see or breathe, I surrendered to the current, letting it carry me off, certain of one thing.

I was going to die.

5

ELI

A COTTONTAIL TREMBLED between the wire confines of my trap. I sat on a nearby rock beside my hunting rifle, pressing a damp rag against my scorched neck for some relief. Though summer was abundant with game and food for harvest, the sun was a goddamn bitch.

"Bad day for us both," I mumbled to my prey, running my fingers through my overgrown beard. It had been a long morning of bare traps and the prospect of returning to camp nearly empty-handed didn't thrill me.

As I sat relishing the first break I'd had in hours, a loud shriek cut through trees, high into the valley. I jerked toward the noise, heart racing. Quiet had permeated our land for so long that any sound of distress was a sure sign of danger. And here I was, out in the middle of nowhere, with nothing but a handgun and an inferiority complex.

"You hear that?" The rabbit's nose quivered as I watched her, waiting for another sign. I could run. Maybe I should run. But the scream came again; unmistakable this time.

My adrenaline soared, pushing me to my feet, the rag forgotten on the rock. I kept both hands on my handgun as I jogged between a few trees, reaching the edge of earth that fell away to allow space for the rushing creek. In this area of our hunting grounds, the water spanned almost a half-mile across, splitting the Coutts commune off from the regular world — our world. Or what remained of it.

To my left, the water roared downstream, swirling around rocks and branches as it chiseled its way through the earth. We knew to avoid this part of the creek. The strong current could sweep you under in seconds. We stayed on dry land and got our water from a much calmer brook closer to camp.

But that scream had undeniably come from somewhere near the water. A call of distress. Despite knowing the dangers, I squinted, keeping my breath steady as I searched the creek, the water's cream tips fading into murky green as it moved. No sign of life. Perhaps they had gone under — a thought, I'm sorry to say, that calmed me. It would be a terrible way to go, but it meant I wouldn't have to risk my life *and* I'd still be able to sleep at night.

I had no such luck. A wail coated in terror came again from somewhere on my left. I turned my attention, straining my vision. Rocks, water, leaves, broken trees, moss, and then finally — something out of place. A mop of black hair hugging a protruding tree branch for dear life. Their legs dangled in the creek, tugged forward by the strength of the rapids.

"Fuck," I said in a slow whisper. Of course it was me. Always had to be me.

For a moment, I froze. Part of me wanted to pretend I

hadn't heard, to take my rag and my cottontail and go back to camp without a word to my companions. But I knew I'd never forgive myself.

I squatted, unzipping my pack to place the gun in the topmost pocket before shifting to more closely inspect the situation. It was a young woman, chest-deep in the creek water, talking to herself. I stood to full height, regretting my decision to approach. Her fearful eyes caught my movement and even clear across rocks and water, her desperation was palpable. "Help me!" she screamed. "Please!"

Had this been a little over a year ago, I wouldn't have hesitated. Not for one second, like I did that day. I gave myself some grace. The world had changed. There were no more hospitals or doctors to visit if you broke your leg or got an infection. Now, those things sentenced you to a horrific death. One I had no desire to experience.

"Hang on!" I yelled, exasperated, examining the path forward. I made slow and careful steps beside the creek's edge, the fear of slipping weighing heavy on my every move. The young woman had somehow wedged herself between the broken branches of a dead oak. If nothing else, it looked like she had a good grip. I charted my pathway — slide down the cliff's edge, grab onto the tree base, and hoist her up to safety.

Or fall into the creek and die.

One quick glance at the ruthless water solidified my thought. The world spun, and I shook my head. Nothing like a life or death moment to keep your blood pumping.

"Don't let go!" I yelled, trying to sound confident as I moved toward the tree.

"I'm trying," she howled.

"I know," I shouted back, my voice already hoarse. "You're doing great. I'm going to try to get onto the tree so I can pull you up." I learned once communicating with someone in distress helped keep them calm. "Keep holding on."

"Oh, good Lord in heaven!" she sobbed. "Help me! Please!" I looked up just as she tried to readjust her hold, gripping farther up on the tree. The bark came away, and she fell back again with a terrified cry.

"I'm trying!" I answered, wishing she'd shut up so I could focus. She was lucky I was trying to rescue her at all. A smarter man might not have. One wrong step was all that kept me from a watery demise.

Don't think about it.

The uneven ground forced my ankle to twist in an awkward position as I tried to find my footing on the edge of the short cliff. I estimated the tree the woman hung onto was about three feet beneath where my legs dangled and considered my jump. Too much weight would split the wood. I needed to be careful.

"I can't hold it!" she screamed again.

"Hold on!" I yelled over the rushing water. "Don't you let go."

I pressed myself flat, my backpack acting as a barrier between my spine and the rock as I slid down the earthy cliff and onto the base of the tree. It shook and shuddered with my added weight, but I persisted, the trapped woman only ten feet away.

Steady now.

My fingers fumbled for a better grip against the slippery bark as I shifted myself up the trunk.

"Help me! Please!" she cried, voice muffled with water. Her nails dug into the side of the bark, scraping away the outer layer to reveal paler oak beneath. Once I had my bearings and was sure the tree wouldn't give, I inched toward her. Stretching myself out over the end, I grasped the tips of her fingers in a slippery grip.

"Okay," I called over the thunderous water. "I got you now. I'm going to grab your wrists," I told her, continuing to move forward. "You ready?"

"Yes!" she screamed as my hands found her thin arms. "Please!"

High on adrenaline, I hoisted, leaning back to readjust my grip, finding her forearms, then her biceps, finally grasping beneath her armpits to gain enough leverage to pull her in to straddle the trunk.

I heard the crack before I felt it. Our added weight had taken the fallen tree to the edge of no return. My heartbeat thrashed in my ears, somehow even louder than the creek below. My worst fear realized, and I was powerless to stop it.

I found her eyes — brown, wide, and terrified. "Hold on," I yelled. "The trunk—"

She reached for me, nails digging into my forearms. The back of the trunk snapped, sending us straight into the mountain water.

The tree found solid ground somewhere beneath the creek, bouncing us up before the entire trunk landed in the water. My shoulder slammed against something hard, but the pain barely registered. Our tangle of limbs intertwined, and I pushed up, trying to shake her off as her arms found their way around my middle. My lungs struggled against her added weight. I kicked away from what I assumed was the bottom of the creek, adrenaline fueling a last desperate attempt to propel us to the surface.

My head came up first, and I sucked in a glorious breath before she popped up beside me, still clinging to my shirt, gasping just the same. We struggled to keep our heads above water as the creek carried us away from our broken tree, downriver. We dipped and surfaced every few seconds, making it impossible to find anything to grab onto.

This was it. This was how I would die.

And then, miraculously, the dark arm of a new tree appeared ahead of us. I reached out to take hold, desperately hoping it wouldn't give. I found a solid part and latched onto the bark with a death grip, sending us both whipping to the side.

We hung suspended in the river. I was frozen in disbelief, trying to calm my fear so I could move. Her weight tugged at me, demanding a new journey with the current. It was one I wasn't willing to risk.

"Get over," I spluttered through the waves, looking up toward the tree. "Grab on!" My chest was so tight, I barely forced the words out.

"Don't let go," she yelled as she clawed up my neck. There was more pain, dulled by adrenaline, as I drew blood beneath my nails from my tight grip on the splintering bark. Her feet found my shoulders, pushing me down, underwater.

Once her weight shifted to the wood I held onto, I clenched my jaw and tried pulling myself up, but my tired muscles took three tries to get my waist up and over the tree. By that time, the woman I'd rescued was nearly to the other side. After several deep breaths and a relieved look at the sky, I followed.

6

ELI

LAND NEVER FELT SO GOOD. I collapsed backward on the grass, not bothering to peel my backpack off as I released a grateful breath. God damn, we were lucky to be alive. Closing my eyes, I focused on my slowing heart, aware of my fading adrenaline. Pain appeared like spots in my vision — an aching shoulder, possibly a bruised jaw, and my hands...

I opened my eyes as I brought my palms to meet my face — shredded to hell, bloodied from my grip on the bark. I let them drop on either side of me, limp and useless, like the rest of my body. My core burned, muscles shook with tremors, every inch of me soaked and heavy.

I turned my head to take in the woman I'd almost met my demise for. The petite girl sat in a dirt patch a few feet away, knees pulled into her chest, rocking back and forth as she trembled with silent sobs. Drenched curls clung to her tan skin like strange veins, curving upward at the edges. She wore a simple pair of jeans and a purple t-shirt, both dark from the creek, and when she lifted her face to the sky, I could see a large, bleeding gash across her cheek. The blood from her wound mixed with residual water and tears traveled toward her chin.

"Hey," I said, my voice unsteady. I cleared my throat. "Hey," I repeated, louder.

As if on cue, she dipped her head between her legs and grasped her knees in desperation, loud cries finally matching the way her body shuddered with sobs. I groaned, rolling away, irritated by her flood of emotion.

"Lady," I said, summoning enough strength to sit up. A sharp pain shot through my shoulder. "Hey, you!" I yelled with my best air of authority over the sound of her wails. The change was instant, as if I'd slapped her. She straightened and turned, eyes wide, nose running, and lips trembling.

"Hey," I said, softer this time. "You okay?"

She opened her mouth, inhaled, then released a shuddering breath. She took one more, blowing up through her bottom lip toward her nose, before she looked at me and started laughing. Her chuckle turned into full on hilarity as she brought a hand to her chest to try to stop. The sudden change in demeanor caught me by surprise and, despite my best intentions, a smile spread across my face — partial disbelief, partial relief.

"I'll take that as a yes."

"I'm. Sorry," she breathed between laughs, calming herself back to neutral. "I'm sorry." Her face crinkled and for a moment, I thought she might cry again. "I'm so sorry."

You should be.

The thought seemed cruel to voice, so instead, I shook

my head. "We're okay," I said, a strange sense of relief settling over me.

She nodded, hugging her knees to her chest. "We're okay," she repeated.

We sat in silence for a few moments before I asked, "You hurt?"

The woman looked down at both sides of her body, then brought her eyes back to meet mine. "I don't think so."

There was something peculiar about her. She seemed almost childlike in the way she glanced at me and back at the creek, as though she hadn't realized how close she'd been to death. Had she even known how much danger she'd been in? How much danger she'd put *me* in?

"You've got a cut," I said, pointing to my own cheek.

She pressed her fingers gently to her wound, wincing as she made contact. And then it came to me. The woman lacked any supplies or weaponry on her person. Even her clothes seemed ill-equipped for survival. She was too well-fed, too oblivious, somehow too *naïve*...

I froze. Like the cottontail, I worried I'd sensed danger too late. I'd left my rifle back by the traps. My heart thudded as I scanned my surroundings. Was it possible someone more dangerous lurked between the trees? Had I fallen for the age-old bait and switch?

I shrugged my soggy backpack off, pulling it between my legs, keeping my eyes on the woman as I unzipped the top pouch. The pack had once been waterproof, but there was a chance the fall into the creek had waterlogged my weapon.

The black 9mm sat inches from my fingers, which I let rest on the fabric of the bag. My suspicion convinced me one wrong move would land a bullet between my eyes from a sniper in the distance.

"Where are we?" she croaked, wiping some of the moisture away from her face with the tips of her fingers. "I was stationed up in the Z-zone on scavenging duty. I need to…" She paused, swallowing hard. "I left my horse," she said, shaking her head, her gaze distant. "I'll need to get back to her — need to explain…" She trailed off, looking back at me for an answer.

"The Z-zone," I repeated, stealing a glance at my fingers, which edged closer to the handgun's grip. "Where's that?"

Confusion flickered across her face and she raised her head, straightened her back, gaze fixed upon mine like an oblivious doe before the kill shot. She tilted her head as my fingers slipped over the textured grip.

"The Z-zone," she stressed, perhaps thinking I hadn't heard her right. "Scavenging zone," she continued. "Well, surely you know where my grandfather's ranch is?"

"Your grandfather?"

"JC Family Ranch?"

I looked at her blankly.

"The *John Coutts* Family Ranch?"

I grabbed the gun, switched off the safety, and scrambled across the forest floor before she'd even finished her inflection, situating myself behind her, arm around her chest, gun aimed at her temple. She screamed, trying to get to her feet, but I kept her trapped in a tight grip, muscles straining against her fight. I breathed heavily in her ear, looking out at the trees surrounding us.

"Where are they?" I hissed.

"W-w-who?" she cried, writhing as her fingernails scratched my forearm.

"Whoever you're with!" Hysteria filled my voice. I couldn't help it. "What the hell were you doing in that creek?" I pushed the barrel up against her still-wet hair, pressing it into the side of her head. "Trying to find us, hm? Couldn't leave us alone?"

"P-p-please!"

"WHERE ARE THEY?"

"I'm alone! I swear! Oh, please, Jesus, please!" The girl went limp with sobs, becoming dead weight in my arms. I tightened my grip across her body, keeping my gaze fixed on the other side of the rushing creek, where the tree foliage blocked the sun from shining. Any flash of an unnatural green and I'd...

Kill her?

I glanced down. The woman had collapsed to her side, arms and legs limp, shoulders shaking as she cried. The gun aimed at her head seemed foreign, like it wasn't my arm holding it. My stomach rolled, but still, I waited, holding her, challenging the person — if there was a person — waiting in the shadows.

But minutes passed and her cries slowed, and nobody came to her rescue. My adrenaline faded, revealing the flaws in my assumption. Placing her in the creek was suicide. What if it had swept her away? What if I hadn't seen her? What were the chances I would've even helped her in the first place? I could've drowned as easily as her. It would've been a lousy trap for a community as insidious as the Coutts.

Decades before all the electricity had gone out and most of the population had been wiped from existence, the Coutts Family had single-handedly transformed whatever the United States had once been. Under the command of their third-generation leader, Peter Coutts, the massive cult had grown substantially. Peter and his cronies had their hands in every big business imaginable, but his ownership of the pharmaceutical industry in the wake of multiple pandemics ultimately gave him unfathomable financial power. Looking to challenge the industry's unfair price gouging, The Coutts Organization recruited some of biopharma's most brilliant minds and proprietary secrets. He claimed his resources were free to all, as long as they respected the rules. *His* rules. And those rules came with chains.

Despite the strict requirements Peter expected from each of his followers, the draw was massive, driven by desperation. We'd run out of resources. Plagues, storms, and poverty had decimated us. Our government had collapsed, supply chains had dried up, and medical care was a laughable luxury not even the wealthy could afford. And as the only leader in the world with the means to provide his community with the things we all desperately needed, people flocked to him in droves.

If you ignored the claims of sexual abuse, financial fraud, and extensive corruption, Peter Coutts might've been a true Prophet. He held an exorbitant amount of power. He ruled an empire. He created a utopia in the midst of a crumbling world. But really, he was a wicked puppet master, pulling the strings. He withheld life-saving medicines and necessary resources, allowing inexplicable suffering to happen to those who refused to follow him, all in the name of God. So if you didn't join him, you were left with one choice — survive on your own. You can guess where most people went. And what happened to those who didn't.

Then H5N1 hit. Somehow, some of us unlucky bastards survived over a decade of pandemics — COVID, SARS, and Zika, only to be met with an airborne nuke that swept the planet without mercy. The consequences of a warming world. And somehow, as if that hadn't been enough, the Coutts family sought us out even after most of us died. They'd come to our town, knocked down our doors, done the unthinkable...

"Please," came a feeble voice, breaking my trance. The woman in my grip shook violently, craning her neck upwards, trying to look at me. "Please don't do this. I swear to you, I'm alone. Please. Please. Please."

Sudden revulsion swept over me as I came out of my adrenaline haze. With my senses heightened, I recognized the arm and hand holding the gun as my own and, even worse, my trembling finger against the trigger. I had shoved my weapon so forcefully against the woman's head her skin had turned raw from the sharp barrel edge.

I pulled it away, letting my grip around her slacken, sliding my thumb over the safety. Bile rose in my throat. A single move, one flinch of the finger, and the body in my arms would've ceased to exist. The full weight of what I'd almost done settled in my chest and, disgusted, I shoved the small woman away from me.

She stumbled on uncertain footing and landed on all fours in the dirt, a cloud of debris rising around her. She coughed, turning where she lay, and raised a quivering arm over her head to shield the sun from her eyes. My shadow towered over her, a thin, tall version of myself, spreading across the browning grass.

"Please don't!" she pleaded, her voice small.

I still held the gun in my hands, though I didn't aim it at her. It seemed almost cruel to point the weapon at her pathetic form, curled up on the ground. She reminded me of the animals we hunted. But at least they had an instinct to sense danger, contributing to the thrill of the hunt. It was a challenge I'd always justified with a certain fairness. But this? This was anything but fair.

"I'm sorry," I croaked, letting my arms fall to my sides.

The young woman's mouth gaped at me, trying to find words, but failing. I turned, looking at the gun, shifting it from hand to hand as I walked, settling on a flat rock overlooking the creek. I wanted to vomit. The rushing water drowned out everything else around me as I considered an unfamiliar part of myself.

My attack had been instinctual, like something inside me had snapped. I'd barely been aware of my body or arms, the deliberate movements of my hands. Could I have—?

No. I was no killer. Not of the unarmed. Those horrors were for the Coutts to execute.

I squeezed my eyes closed, hands resting upon the weapon. It felt hot, like the object had known what I'd been about to do, but was disappointed I'd stopped short of the act itself. It was a foolish thought, a fear that weaved its way in and I pushed it away, tending to the other thing calling for my attention as I watched the sun sink lower in the sky, its gold glow blending into the blue beyond.

Dusk was within reach. Thanks to our spill in the creek, I was miles from where I'd started. Urgency replaced my fading fear.

Shit.

I stood, eyeing the girl who still lay curled on the ground, her curls smeared with dirt and small twigs, the gash on her cheek a bright red blemish on her brown skin. Her dark eyes followed me as I approached, but she made no move to shield herself, making her appear even smaller.

"You're a Coutts then?" I spat at her, narrowing my gaze.

She nodded.

"Then go back to where you came from."

I turned, finding my still-soaked backpack and slung it over my shoulder, before setting off in the direction of the sun. It would be dark in under an hour and I needed to find a familiar landmark if I wanted to make it back to camp alive.

"Wait! Don't go."

I stopped dead in my tracks. The woman's voice shook, dripping with panic, disturbing the certainty I'd had in leaving. I returned my gaze to her. Fresh tears made lines through the dirt coating her cheeks. She had no supplies and no weapon. Out here, in the dark, something would eat her alive before morning.

Remorse flooded through me at the thought of her running blind from a predator, and my nausea returned. Was leaving her out here as good as shooting her dead? I nearly laughed at myself for having gone through the trouble of saving her in the first place.

You didn't know she was a Coutts.

But that was the thing. I had never even *seen* a Coutts woman outside their borders, despite living beside the commune my entire life. Someone had allowed her to be out here, to fall into the creek, to be swept away to her death. Had no one warned her of the dangers?

"I can't help you," I answered, my voice empty.

"Please," she continued, getting to her knees, somehow emboldened by my response. "I've no idea how to get back. Please! Please don't leave me out here." The woman pressed her hands together and looked up at me, features frozen in terror. Desperation dripped from her. To ask someone who'd just had a gun pointed at your head for help. Well, stranger things had happened, I was sure.

Leave, Eli.

But I couldn't. I might as well shoot her dead. In fact, it might've been kinder. But just as I knew I couldn't leave her in the creek, I knew I couldn't leave her lying in the dirt as night approached. This world had squeezed away some of my humanity, but not all of it. I looked at the sun, marking its descent. Time was running out. In one swift movement, I pulled the gun into my hands and pointed it at her.

"Get up," I said, and she scrambled to her feet.

There was only one option in front of me, and I wasn't sure I liked it.

7

MAURA

SOMEHOW, I got to my feet. Our surroundings were hazy, but I only had eyes for my captor — or savior? It was hard to decide. One minute he was pulling me out of the creek, the next, holding a gun to my head.

He was taller than Andrew, a towering form with broad shoulders and dark features. An unruly beard covered the bottom half of his face below a flat nose, sunburnt at the tip. His green eyes glowered in the sun, thick brows furrowed in conflict. But what spoke truths was his white shirt, still opaque from the water. Beneath, I could just make out a black tattoo snaking its way around his upper arm, peeking out over his collar.

Coutts men were clean-shaven. This man looked like he'd been out here for months. And tattoos were considered sacrilegious. Abigail had said so, telling us stories of newcomers getting them painfully removed from their bodies. But then — who was he? I scoured my mind for an explanation. He was a living, breathing soul. No sickness plagued him. Those things conflicted one another. Not a

Coutts man, yet not a sick Outsider. Not just healthy, but thriving. I willed God to send me an answer that made sense.

His hands remained gripped tight around the gun, still pointed at me. I should've been frightened. But a stronger need deafened the threat. I needed to understand. So much depended on his answer.

"Are you—"

"Can you walk?"

"—from the Coutts commune?"

Our overlapping questions broke the silence, and he tilted his head at me as if considering something a little gross. I pressed my lips together. He glanced down at himself, arms still outstretched, then back up at me.

"No," he said, seemingly bewildered. "I'm definitely *not* from the Coutts commune."

"So who are you? What are you doing out here?" The words tumbled from my mouth before I could stop them.

His expression hardened, and he shook his head slow. "I know you all think you own everything, but like it or not, this is not Coutts territory—"

"I mean, *how* are you here?" I asked, frowning at his misunderstanding. "Did you repent?"

He raised his brows. "You mean, did I buy into all the crap you Coutts have been spouting off for decades?"

"It's not—"

"I'm not part of your cult, if that's what you're asking. Never have been, never wanna be," he said. "Now, if you want to die, you're welcome to stay out here and hope God saves you. But I would *highly* suggest you come with me before nightfall." He glanced toward the setting sun, the sky shifting between brilliant shades of orange, blue, and pink.

"It's not a—"

The man waved the gun at me. "I'm not interested." His definitive tone sliced through me and obedience kept my questions at bay. He didn't live in the commune and had no interest in repentance. But that meant a very impossible thing.

Countless times we'd been told how the end happened. A massive sickness wiped out every person on Earth outside of our devout commune. We were the only survivors. God chose us. Spared us for a greater purpose. Father had ensured our safety and as long as we followed him and his divine teachings, we would be welcomed into the Kingdom of Heaven. The Outsiders — those who had defied Father, had defied God. And God punished them for it. Father told us. He preached it every day since.

Could the almighty Prophet be unaware there was an Outsider left alive? Had his omniscience failed him? The possibility prompted a dull ache in my temple.

"You coming, or what?"

"Back to the commune?"

The man's eyes widened, and he threw his head back and laughed — a loud, booming note spread through the trees, rattling my core.

"Are you insane?"

"But my horse..." My stomach dropped as I imagined Sweetheart trotting through my scavenging zone looking for me. "She'll be waiting for me. And my family..." I trailed off, stomach turning at the thought of Abigail and Joanna hearing the news of my disappearance. And Andrew. My face flushed in shame. After all he'd done for me, the grace he'd shown in my inability to conceive, the patience he had for my meager scavenging returns, this was how I repaid him!

"I have to go back," I said, defiant.

"Go, then." The man shrugged. "But the dark out here ain't like that commune of yours. Once it's dark, it's dark."

I turned to look at the creek, remembering the window. If I found the structure, I could make my way back to Sweetheart. But thinking about explaining my disobedience ate away at me. There would be no tolerance for mistakes. Andrew made it quite clear that morning, he expected me to return with something of substance by the afternoon. Trying to reason with him about the window seemed laughable. The idea of returning, not only empty-handed, but late, dirty, and bleeding, was enough to give me pause.

"Then where are you going?"

"*That* is none of your business," he answered, rolling his shoulders before considering me for a moment. "Listen," he said with a sigh. "I'd love for you to go right back from where you came, but seeing as you have no weapon and no supplies, I'd be offering you up on a platter for any predator crossing your path — and that's not just animals. You understand?"

"Not just animals? You mean…there's *more* people out here?"

The man released one hand from the gun and pressed it to his forehead, eyes wide in disbelief. "You really don't know?"

"Know what?"

"Yes," he said impatiently, "there's more people out here, sticking around to leech off whatever resources they can scrounge up from what you Coutts throw away. People who'd like nothing more than to take you as bounty, and they'd do worse things to you than not tell you where their camp was."

I considered reminding him he'd just held a gun to my head, but he spoke before I could. "Enough questions, lady."

"Maura," I offered.

"What?"

"Maura," I said again. "I'm not lady. I'm Maura."

"Fine, Maura." He turned toward the sun and back again. "I need to get moving. You coming?"

I sifted through my options. Returning was a journey I was certainly not confident taking in the dark. Perhaps I could stay here and wait out the night, but if what the man said was true, I was not prepared to take on a predator. In the commune, our Hunters and high fences kept the animals at bay. This was why they had enforced our borders. But now I was way outside the safe limits of our commune.

"Well?"

I paused, shifting my weight from foot to foot before he gave an exasperated grunt and turned his back on me. He walked away from the creek and, with a deep breath and a quick prayer to God, I followed.

Though he still held the gun in his hand, he kept it pointed at the ground and I allowed the tension to ease from my limbs, sore from the bumps and bruises I'd accumulated in the creek. My lower back ached as we climbed at a slight incline. Rocks, branches, and mossy mounds laid out before us like scattered toys, the tree cover growing thicker the farther we went.

Every so often I caught the man glancing back at me, eyes narrowed in suspicion. And at times, even through the shadows, his features looked conflicted. Although the warm summer air had begun to dry my clothes, I felt exposed as we walked on. The scenery, while not much different from my scavenging area, was still unfamiliar, and I wrapped my arms around myself, wishing I hadn't lost my canvas bag in the creek.

I pushed away the regret that surfaced every few minutes — convincing myself I'd made the wrong choice, that I should've turned around and tried to get back. Now, I was at the mercy of this man who had tried to kill me and whose existence challenged something I knew to be true.

Well, what I *thought* I knew to be true. There had to be an explanation for this man's presence. Until I saw another living being, I refused to trust his words.

But doubt hovered. I recognized it from when I'd questioned Father's decision to gift Jeremiah partial ownership of the JC Family Ranch; heaviness in the pit of my stomach, same as when I'd left my family. Same as the day I'd married Andrew.

The forest floor leveled. Fading sunlight gave us a clear sight through a wide expanse of thinning trees. We hurried past pine needles and broken trunks until we reached the edge of the tree line. Below where we stood, a wide, paved road stretched across the landscape until it disappeared into more trees in both directions. Across the way stood a small cluster of structures.

I had only heard of these places in stories. In the privacy of our shared bedroom, Morgan had done her best to describe what the Outside looked like, but I had always imagined homes like the ones in the commune, with siding and windows, shutters and shingles. Even from this distance, I saw the difference. These patchwork houses seemed to be made from any kind of material — brick, wood, metal, and tarp.

"Is that—?"

I started forward, but the man held out his arm to stop me from going any further.

"I don't trust you," he said, pocketing his weapon. He relieved himself of his backpack, unzipped a pouch, and plunged his hand inside.

"I'm sorry," I answered, uncertain of the correct response.

He frowned at me before pulling out a dirty, black cloth. "It's a pretty straightforward walk from here," he said, ignoring my apology as he dropped the bag and stretched the fabric out with both hands. "Should be fine, even with the blindfold."

"What?"

"I'm going to blindfold you," he repeated.

"No!" I recoiled.

The man's shoulders sagged. "Well, it's either that, or you can sleep here." He glanced behind me and I followed his gaze. Vast darkness settled over the ground we'd covered and I swallowed hard, looking for some sign he was bluffing.

"Your choice," he prompted, holding up the black fabric, not an inch of humor on his face. I hesitated. Following this man was one thing, but following him blind?

As if on cue, an animal called in the distance — a low

growl, the call of a bird, the snap of twigs. I jumped into the air toward him, my heart pounding.

"Fine," I whispered, clasping my hands behind my back.

The man nodded at me. I braced myself for impact, expecting him to handle my blindfolding as he had our initial encounter. But his hands were gentle as he worked the fabric over my face, folding it so it rested across my nose. He tugged at my hair, tying the makeshift blindfold in a clumsy knot so darkness engulfed my vision.

"My name's Eli." His voice was gruff and a little strained. The surrounding noises were amplified in the darkness and I heard him pull the backpack on again before he squeezed my shoulder, guiding me into the unknown.

———

WITHOUT THE ABILITY TO SEE, my heightened senses stretched beyond their normal capacities. I tried to imagine where my feet were stepping, but remained aware of how reliant I was of the grip on my shoulder. We'd left the forest a while back, just after Eli had slipped the blindfold over my eyes. The terrain had shifted from soft dirt to solid asphalt, back to grass. He'd guided me over a metal guardrail, down a steep, rocky decline, and back to flat, grassy ground once more.

Despite the absence of light, I sensed night had fallen. The bullfrogs and insects rounded out a loud symphony, eager to claim their evening terrain. A cool breeze drifted across our path, emphasizing the dampness in my clothes. My calves ached, sending shooting pains into my lower back and hips. Eli's long strides forced me to walk quicker than usual, making my gait awkward and hurried. Exhaustion had snuck into my bones. I needed to lie down — I didn't care where — for a few moments of rest. But I didn't dare speak without being spoken to, especially to a man with a weapon.

When I was almost certain I couldn't take another step, Eli turned me left. "Almost there," he said, his voice low.

Though I expected relief, my chest tightened. I'd been so focused on following Eli's guidance, I hadn't thought of what might come next.

"Where are we going?" I heard the desperation in my voice and I hated how small it made me feel.

"Come on," was all he said, pulling me along.

I followed, but with each treacherous step forward, I worried he might push me away and leave me out in the dark to fend for myself. Perhaps it was an adequate punishment for my sins. And what then? Out here, I no longer had the security of my status or the arm of my powerful husband to lean on. I didn't have Father's wisdom to seek. I didn't have Morgan's bravery or Abigail's sternness or Joanna's abrasiveness. I was a coddled child, just like they'd said. Weak and afraid of my shadow, following a complete stranger in a blindfold.

The terrain changed again. We left the grass for something flatter — dirt or pavement, I couldn't tell. Eli tightened his grip, and we turned twice more before stopping. I opened my mouth to ask why we'd paused before two loud clicks echoed in the night air.

I knew that sound. One evening, when I was still at Mother's house, a bear wandered into the commune.

Father had gotten some of his men to eliminate the danger, and they stormed out into the dark, cocking their guns — a rapid fire *click, click*.

My brain registered, and I turned toward the noise. The voice that came next was one I did not recognize.

"Put your fucking hands up."

8

ELI

TIME SLOWED as the silver barrel of a shotgun came into view, pointed at Maura beside me. Thick dreadlocks, a single diamond earring, and a towering, dark, muscular body followed, inching forward in the pale moonlight. My brother through adoption, studied us from behind his weapon, his breathing heavy and even. Even in the waning dusk, I saw the merciless contempt his eyes held for the stranger on our property. He wouldn't hesitate to blow her into the street if I didn't explain myself. Sid was a marksman, and he never missed.

I had expected this on my journey back to camp, mulling over the right way to justify my decision. *I found a Coutts in the river and didn't want to let her die.* A pathetic excuse. We had an ugly history with the Coutts and though I'd felt justified in my decision, that didn't mean everyone would agree. Certainly not Sid.

"Stop," I hissed, taking a step toward him with an outstretched hand.

"Eli?" His voice wavered, but he made no move to lower his weapon.

"Yeah?"

"You asshole. Scared the shit out of me."

"Sorry, I—"

"Care to explain who the hell this is?"

"Let's get inside the fence."

"*Eli*," Sid growled, readjusting his grip on the shotgun. "She's *blindfolded*."

His grasp relaxed, but he didn't point the gun away.

"Come on," I urged, throwing a quick glance at our dark surroundings, my grip still on Maura's trembling shoulder.

We approached a tall, mismatched wood fence connected to the side of Mom's old trailer, the rotted blue siding slipping from its exposed frame. Sid kept his back to our childhood home, weapon aimed at Maura, who took small, clumsy steps forward, despite my guidance.

The usually locked fence gate hung open, thrown wide by Sid, who'd likely run from his roof perch down to the front lawn in a matter of seconds when he saw us approaching. He entered the backyard first, taking careful steps, the shotgun steady in his hands. I pushed Maura forward, situating her beside the gate, before locking it behind us.

"I'm waiting," Sid said as I turned, glancing at the girl. Her knees had betrayed her, and she sat on the ground, crying beneath her blindfold. The fabric over her eyes suddenly felt cruel, but it had been a precaution I'd needed to take. I looked back at Sid.

"I don't think you need the friggin' gun on her," I said,

looking at the dark house. A set of wooden stairs led to the flimsy back kitchen door, its window covered with cardboard like the rest. If anyone else had been awake, I would've seen the flicker of a candle between the cracks, but there was none. Good. I didn't need an audience for this.

"I'm gonna ask you again—"

"Okay!" I said, rounding on my brother, even though my frustration was misplaced. If Sid had returned home with a stranger, I'd probably react the same way.

"I was out by the creek, checking all the traps you set yesterday and I heard someone," I paused, gesturing toward the woman, "screaming. She was *alone*."

"You sure?"

"I waited," I answered. "Had her in a hold, gun to her head. No one came."

Sid gave a small nod, tilting his head from side to side as if considering whether to lower the gun.

"She's a Coutts."

My brother raised his gaze to mine, eyes widening, then narrowing, lips pressed into a thin line. In seconds, the very nature of him darkened as his jaw clenched, nostrils flared, vein throbbing in his temple. Anger radiated from him like heat, and he tightened his hold, stepping forward in a hurried gait. For a second I worried he'd shoot the woman at point blank range, but he reached for the black fabric, ripping it from her face so her head and hair pulled at an awkward angle.

She gave a surprised gasp, whimpering as she fell back against the fence. Sid threw the fabric aside, raising the gun in his hands and guided the barrel beneath her chin, lifting her face in a delicate yet violent dance. Her jaw trembled against the steel, eyes flicking down, then back up every few seconds.

Sid grimaced, his eyes wild and dark as he pulled the weapon back an inch, keeping the barrel level with her face. Maura's cries turned to heavy, desperate gasps. Her eyes bulged from their sockets as she pressed herself up against the fencing.

"Sid." I stepped forward to grab his shoulder. The tendons beneath his skin stretched so taut, I was sure they would snap.

"Don't," he growled, his upper lip quivering as his gaze flickered to me, then back to the girl. "You dumb little fuck. Are you insane?"

"No," I said, itching to defend myself. "She almost *drowned*—"

"She's a Coutts!" He'd lost control of his voice and it echoed through the air, bouncing off the nearby empty houses. "A *Coutts*!"

"I know, I—"

"Why the hell would you do this?" he hissed in an anguished whisper. "*How* could you do this?"

"I didn't know she was a Coutts when I pulled her out of the creek!"

"But you figured it out eventually, didn't you? Then what? You brought her back here? Invited her home for a cup of tea? What the *hell* is wrong with you?"

"I couldn't leave her out there," I said, glancing back at Maura, who shivered so violently the fence behind her rattled. "No weapons, no food. We were miles from the Coutts commune by then. She would've died."

"Better than bringing her back here!" he yelled.

"Jesus, Sid."

"Don't you act like it's me!" he snarled. "Bringing the enemy straight into camp? After what they did to Mom? To Neil? We've got a kid here, Eli."

"Exactly." I shook my head, trying to will him into understanding his own absurdity. "We have a *kid* here. And what're you gonna tell her when she wakes up to brain matter all over the fence?"

"That I protected her."

"From *what* exactly?" I said, trying to pull reason back into our conversation. I gestured toward Maura. "She's not exactly dangerous, is she?"

"Hoo boy," Sid said with a vicious laugh. "You and I have mighty different understandings of what makes someone dangerous."

I took a deep breath, making a conscious effort not to roll my eyes. "I just mean she's not coming in here guns blazing, trying to infiltrate our camp or get information back to her people. She was lost, and I helped her. It's as simple as that."

"Nothing about this is *simple*, Eli, you little—"

"*What* on earth is going on out here?" The back door hinges squeaked as Holli joined us in the night air, tying her robe around herself in a neat knot. Her short, graying hair stood up around her crown wildly, suggesting we'd woken her. The middle-aged woman gave us both an exasperated look that rivaled Mom's, before she realized Sid was pointing his gun at a weeping woman. Even I had to admit, it didn't look good.

"What!" She waved her hands at the shotgun as she flew down the wooden steps and into the grass. She was more than a foot shorter than my brother, but the mere presence of her made up the height difference. "Sid!" she scolded.

"Holli, step back," Sid warned, shooting her a glance. "She's a Coutts."

"She's a—" Holli's hand flew to her heart, and she blinked, chin tucked inward, before finding her words again. "A *Coutts*?" She turned to me.

"Hol, please," I started.

"Don't!" Sid shouted.

"Shut up!" Holli seethed. She pointed at the house. "If you wake that little girl up, I'll have your head. She doesn't need to be involved in whatever this is." She rounded on me again. "A *Coutts*? What's a Coutts doing in our backyard?"

"Yeah, Eli. Why don't you tell her?"

After scowling at Sid, I told Holli about my afternoon in the creek and the justification for not shooting Maura dead in the woods. Holli listened with her arms crossed. Unlike my brother, Holli was level-headed and calm, but I saw the discomfort crossing her face as she considered the position I'd put us in.

"I wasn't going to let her die out there," I finished, finding my justification weak. The more I recounted the decision I'd made, the more I realized I hadn't thought it through. I'd acted on impulse and now not only had I put myself in danger, but my entire crew. A knot of regret appeared in my stomach.

Holli sighed, uncrossed her arms, and placed her hands on her hips before leaning back to look at the sky. She seemed neither pleased nor angry, almost indifferent, watching the stars above us.

"What do we do?" I whispered, trying to hide how desperate I was for an answer.

Holli looked at Sid, at the gun, at Maura, then back at me. "I think we let her stay tonight," she said. "She can sleep out here." She cast a glance toward the far end of what was once Mom's backyard. The long yard sloped downward, where the remnants of a tree fort remained beside our makeshift chicken coop, outhouse, and an old plastic lounge chair.

"What—?" Sid interrupted, but Holli held up her hand.

"Sid can keep watch from the roof on his overnight shift. We'll reassess in the morning."

"And if someone comes looking for her?" Sid cast us a sideways glance.

Holli raised her eyebrows. "That's why we have you on watch."

Her tone was final. After a moment's hesitation, Sid let his grip go slack before shouldering his gun.

Still huddled against the fence, Maura gave a soft whimper before dissolving into tears again. I glanced at her quickly, but discomfort forced me to turn away. Though I knew I'd only done what I thought was right, I felt responsible for her pain.

Holli approached Maura, offering her a hand to get to her feet. The girl reluctantly took it, barely able to stand on shaking legs.

"Sid, get back on watch," she said, pointing to the roof with her free hand. "You," she said, turning to me. "Go get her a blanket. Maybe something to eat."

Sid and I nodded while Holli guided the young woman down to the end of the yard. I hated my relief, but it felt good to pass the responsibility off to someone else. As I approached the back door, Sid stepped in front of my path.

"You shouldn't have brought her here," he snarled.

"Yeah," I said. "I get it. I screwed up."

He scoffed, then turned toward a metal ladder leaned up against the roof on the other side of the back door. With the gun over his shoulder, he climbed it effortlessly, disappearing over the ridge.

I glanced back at the dark shapes huddled together in the distant yard, shame blooming in my stomach as I questioned every decision I'd made in the past few hours. How could someone so small and meek have caused me such a colossal screw up? I wanted to hate her. I couldn't help it.

Did she know what her people had done to us?

9

MAURA

I COULDN'T BREATHE. My heart beat in my ears like a drum, muffling the surrounding sounds of nature, reminding me where my disobedience had led me with every thud. I was in trouble. The things I was so certain of no longer made sense. All I could focus on was the memory of the tall man's wild eyes, hatred seeping from his glare as he'd threatened me with his gun.

They'd called the woman beside me Holli. She matched me in height and couldn't have been much older than Sister Abigail. Gray strands weaved through browns and fading reds in her wavy hair, framing her pale, heart-shaped face. She had the kinds of wrinkles that told you she once smiled often and when she spoke, a few missing teeth were visible.

She pulled a sun-bleached lounger toward a small structure. Someone had stripped most of the wood from its sides, leaving only the four beams holding the roof intact. She situated the long chair beneath it, wiping away dirt from its blue, plastic cushion. It rocked, lopsided, on the uneven ground.

"Well," she said, straightening, "it's a bit damp. But it'll do for tonight."

She looked back at me, but I had no reaction to give. I was grateful to be alive, to be safe from the creek and the guns and from — horribly enough, Andrew, Joanna, and Abigail's judgment. But I couldn't calm the terror growing in my chest. There were Outsiders. Alive and armed. Deciding on my behalf. Speaking ill of my family name. Giving me a place to sleep.

A shadow in the distance appeared, hurrying forward, arm outstretched. Eli handed Holli a blanket, a small cup, and a pull-tab can. He took one look at me and scurried back off to the house again without another word.

"Come, now," Holli said, gathering the things in her hands and gesturing toward the lawn chair. "Seems you've had a long journey today. Some rest'll do you good. There's an outhouse—" She pointed at a dark outline of a distant structure, "there, beside the chicken coop."

Her kindness made me pause, and I watched as she folded the blanket around the cushion, creating a makeshift bed. There was comfort in her order, something to obey, something to keep me grounded. My body ached for rest, so even if I'd wanted to defy her, I wasn't sure I'd be able to.

When she was done, she looked up at me, green eyes soft and sad, trailing over my features. "I'll fix that cut up for you first thing in the morning," she said very matter-of-factly, pointing at my cheek.

I brought my hand to my face — I'd forgotten.

"I—" I stared at her, mouth hanging open with unsaid words, and shook my head.

"Get some rest," she said, handing me the food and water before she turned to leave.

"Thank you," I said, and she paused, chin at her shoulder to give me a nod, before walking on.

Ducking beneath the small roof, I sat on the lounger. It sagged with my added weight, the cushion shifting against the plastic, its leg tilting as I tried to balance myself on it. Parched and famished, I drank the cup of water without a breath in between, then pulled away the can's metal top, inhaling mouthful after mouthful of kidney beans.

After discarding the can, with my boots still tied, I dragged my legs up and curled into a ball, pulling the blanket over myself even though the night was warm. It acted as a comfort, a barrier, an act of normalcy, though I knew, as I inspected the rotting wood above me, that this was anything but normal.

Despite my exhaustion, my mind refused to settle into sleep, hindered by the events of the day and what my family might be thinking and doing now. Would it be Abigail or Joanna sharing Andrew's bed tonight? Was Father planning a rescue mission? Had they found Sweetheart roaming near the creek? Did Morgan and Mother know? Were they frightened, or worse, being punished for my wrongdoing?

I winced at the thought, working hard to push down the cries I longed to release. Clouds drifted across the moon, casting shadows in the unfamiliar yard, darkening the edges of everything. It crept into the small enclosure, seeping into my vision, enveloping my sore and heavy body. I shifted my head, too comfortable to care, too tired to know anything else, comforted at last, in a bed of my own.

———

SWEET, warm breath lingered on my face, tickling me from a hazy slumber. Praying for a few more moments of sleep, I nuzzled my head against the bed, met with plastic woven mesh instead of fresh cotton. I wiggled my nose, trying to find a comfortable spot. My cheek brushed against my arm, then a spot of sudden pain shocked me awake.

My eyes flew open, and I saw a small blonde-haired child kneeled beside me, no older than seven. She inspected my face with brutal curiosity, honey-brown eyes wide and startled as they met my own. Still wobbly from sleep, I tried sitting up and as I did, saw a flicker of panic cross her features. I wanted to reassure her, to let her know I brought no harm with me.

But the lounger had other plans and as I reached out for the child, it rocked to the side, the legs buckling beneath the shift in weight, sending me toppling to the ground. I landed in a tangle of blankets, dirt, and humiliation and as I looked up to see what the little girl might think about this embarrassing turn of events, I saw only her dirty heels as she sprinted back to the house, wailing.

"Holli!" I heard her cry, the metal door slamming shut behind her.

My chest hollow, I scooped up the blanket and my remaining pride and leveled the lounger to sit.

Misty clouds covered the sun, making it a gray, distant orb. The cool breeze was a welcome companion to the drying sweat on my back from my slumber. In the daylight, the backyard didn't seem so dark and dangerous, but lush and full of life. A large garden took up most of the area from the broken structure I sat beneath, all the way to the far edge of the house. Vines, vegetables, fruits, flowers, and herbs bloomed from every inch of space, from pots and makeshift garden beds, across trellis arches made from plastic bottles, and up the sides of the fence.

To my right stood a chicken coop, beside a structure made of mismatched wood, a small moon carved into the door — the outhouse Holli had pointed out yesterday. A plastic wading pool covered some of the ground beside it, stuffed full of outdoor toys, dolls, and a pair of rain boots.

The back door banged open again, only this time it was Holli who emerged, a filled basket in her arms. She scurried down the stairs and crossed the lawn, depositing a large bag near the coop before marching toward me.

"Good morning," she said, peering into my dark enclosure. Holli wore a loose brown tunic and knee-high rain boots, her hair pulled back by a thick headband. "Come with me," she said, waving me along with her elbow.

I shrugged off the blanket and stood, following her out into the cloudy day. She walked along the length of the garden to the back stairs, then stopped, pointing at them with her head.

"Sit," she said.

I lowered myself to the top step, squinting up at her. She placed the basket down on the ground beside us, pulling out a baggie with bandages and a small dish filled with what looked like chewed up spinach. I scrunched my nose at the sight of it — was this medicine? Did she want me to eat it?

"*This* is yarrow poultice," Holli said, answering the question I hadn't asked. "An amazing herbal remedy that grows like a weed — acts as an antiseptic and anti-inflammatory. It'll soothe and heal that wound for you."

I wasn't convinced. Back home, wound care required Andrew's approval. If it was medically necessary, we'd go see the doctor who'd give us an antibiotic and a proper dressing. Not some squished up flowers.

Holli reached for my face, but I flinched at her touch and looked at my knees. "I'm fine," I mumbled, placing my hand against my cheek, ignoring the sharp sting.

"Honey," Holli said. "Just let me have a look."

"What if...I get an infection from that?" I pointed at the dish, repulsed by the idea of putting it on my face.

Her smile spread before she let her shoulders drop. "I take it you're used to more...*conventional* medicine?"

I met her eyes. "Usually we go to the doctor for things like this."

"Well..." Holli seemed to think for a moment. "I was a doctor. Before."

I tilted my head. "You were?"

She nodded. "I was what they called an herbalist."

"What's that?"

"It's someone who uses plants for healing," she said. "After identifying illness or ailments, I'd recommend herbal supplements for my patients to use, usually things they could find in their own yards. This—" She held up the dish a little higher, "—was just one of those."

I squinted at the green concoction, wondering what it smelled like.

"Why wouldn't your patients just visit a *regular* doctor?" I regretted the question as soon as I'd asked it.

Though she tried to hide it, Holli's face darkened, her smile fading as she looked down.

"Well, there weren't many doctors available out here and sometimes people couldn't afford it. With herbalism, people could grow their own medicine outside for themselves without much trouble. Yarrow, for example, is a perennial, so you can plant it once and it'll come back year after year."

My eyes widened. To think! If what Holli said was true, I could grow an entire garden of this stuff. Perhaps Andrew would even let me plant it on the plot of land promised to me.

I let my hand drop.

With a faint smile, she went to work, cleaning my cheek with a small, wet cloth. Then she scooped the yarrow out of the dish, spreading it over my wound. It soothed on contact, with a pleasant, earthy aroma.

"Now..." Holli stepped back, eyeing her work as she tucked the dish back in her basket before reaching for the bandages. She pressed one to my cheek, where it stuck to the poultice. "That's that."

I reached my fingers up to touch the place she'd mended. For the first time since I'd fallen into the creek, my heart felt light. I looked back up at Holli, inspecting her lined face, the tired bags beneath her eyes.

"I'm sorry if I scared your daughter," I mumbled.

Her smile reappeared. "Oh, Mia's not mine. Wish she was. She's a special little girl."

"You're not her...oh! I'm sorry—" My stomach lurched. I knew the horrible feeling of being asked when I would conceive, why there was no baby in my belly, and being lost for an answer.

Holli waved her hand at me. "S'okay. Her mother passed before the worst of it happened. Her father, well…" She eyed me. "That's a story for another day. But me? No kids. The world always seemed too ugly for it."

Instinct guided me to argue and persuade. To remind her a woman should leave the decision in God's hands. The Prophet had proclaimed we were to multiply, especially with the state of the world. But as she shifted her weight, bending to scoop up her basket, I remembered where I was and who I was with.

"Well, while you're here," she said with a grunt, holding the basket beneath her arm. "You can help me with the hens."

And without a look back, she started toward the chicken coop. Bewildered and slightly conflicted, I stood to follow.

10

ELI

AN ACHE in my shoulder yanked me from a sleep so deep it felt only minutes long. I rolled to the side of Mom's mattress, wrapped beneath her faded floral comforter, bleary eyes finding my watch on the built-in bedside table. These days we relied on the sun to dictate our sleeping schedule, but I found comfort in my old watch — an eighteenth birthday gift from Mom.

10:28 a.m.

I wrinkled my nose, easing myself into a sitting position, a dull ache between my eyes. Sid hadn't woken me. Normally, he would've shaken me awake to monitor things before he went out to check our traps we had scattered near the creek and in the forest, but this morning he hadn't.

The part of me that despised conflict suggested he'd let me sleep in because he'd known I'd needed it, but I was sure his reasoning was far less kind. The weight of his anger still sat on my shoulders. I rubbed my face, trying to rid myself of the guilt I'd hoped to sleep off.

I dressed before leaving the comfortable silence of the bedroom and entered the carpeted belly of our home. Things we'd collected over the past year cluttered the once spacious area. Jars, baggies, baskets, dried flowers, herbs, non-perishable foods, and jugs of filtered water filled the kitchen counters. Gardening tools, aprons, twine, and small plastic pots sat piled by the back door. Blankets, spare clothes, books, and Mia's dolls lay scattered across the living room floor beside the ratty old couch and torn leather recliner. Stacked cardboard boxes lay against the front door, beside a mess of supplies — tape, medical supplies, spare jugs and glass containers.

The things we no longer needed, like the VCR Mom spent two months saving up for, or the bulky television that only sometimes worked when the Coutts weren't interfering with the cable, were now piled up in front of the house, where we threw any trash we accumulated, which wasn't much since we reused everything we could.

Sunlight poured across the space as the back door swung wide. Mia scampered in, pink-faced, with Holli behind her, arms full with a large basket. The little girl ran off down the hall toward one of the back bedrooms, her chubby hands full of flowers.

"Morning," Holli said, letting the door close behind her. "I've got yarrow for your hands." She placed the basket down on the floor, then handed me the supplies.

"Thanks," I said, taking a seat on the recliner and going to work on my still raw palms.

Holli joined me in the living room with a huff, wiping her brow with the back of her hand, before draping her arms over her legs and looking at me. I felt her eyes as I wrapped my wounds.

"What?" I asked, elongating the middle of the word.

"Are we gonna talk?"

I tucked the edges of the bandage in and looked up. "Yes," I said, a little shorter than intended. She raised her brows expectantly. "I mean, what do you want me to say? I couldn't leave her there, you know?"

Holli nodded. "I know."

"Do you think I should have?" Uncertainty tugged at the very fibers of my being. Sid being upset was one thing, but Holli was a different story.

"No," she answered with a definitive shake of her head. "I'm glad you didn't." She looked up at me. "Then you wouldn't be you. You'd never be that cruel, Eli. That would've followed you for the rest of your life."

She wasn't wrong.

"But I can understand why Sid is upset."

There it was.

"So you think I did the wrong thing?"

She leaned forward. "It's not that simple. I'm saying both of you have the right to your own reactions. Sid is angry because he feels she jeopardizes our safety, which —" She tilted her head from side to side, "—he's not wrong about, by the way."

"I know that," I said, growing restless.

"But you had no other choice," she soothed. "If she was just a woman out there on her own, she'd be absolutely harmless," Holli said. "But as a part of that community, she has the potential to be dangerous for us."

I hated how right Holli was.

"You did the right thing," she reminded me. "But we need to be prepared for the fallout."

The fallout terrified me. I'd given it some thought

before I'd been able to drift off to sleep the previous night. It might mean an ambush or that we'd have to give up the place we'd called home for almost a year now. I glanced around at the filled room, wondering how we'd fare if we needed to start over.

"So, what do you think we should do?" I asked, desperate for a reasonable answer.

"I really don't know," Holli said, glancing at the kitchen's back door. "Sending her back might secure a most certain death for her. I can't imagine the Coutts take kindly to one of their own accidentally stumbling outside their borders. But bringing her with us might secure the same fate for us."

"All those people up there and you really think they'd come after one person?"

Holli raised her eyebrows. "You know what they've done out here. I'm sure they raised the alarm the minute she didn't return home. The whole thing works up there *because* they don't let people like her leave. Can you imagine what would happen if she saw their violence in action? Bringing that kind of information back to her people would ruin the facade Peter built. That's a disaster the Coutts do not want. It would destroy everything."

"So you're saying we're screwed."

She paused, then smiled. "I'm saying we need to be smart. Right now, she's in more danger than we are. So, if we're going to help her, we have to decide where to draw the line."

"You think we could use her?"

"Perhaps." Holli ran her fingers across her chin. "She might know something that could help us. We can ask her a few questions about her day-to-day life," she suggested.

"Maybe see if she recognizes Neil's photo. Get some clarity on what those armored men are up to and if they're likely to attack again."

She and I knew if the Coutts came after us, we had little chance of surviving. But we'd come this far. We'd stayed alive this long. So for now, hope was still alive. "I almost left her," I admitted, looking at the floor. "But then I'd realized I'd never even seen a Coutts woman outside of that commune. Only ones going in. It felt wrong to leave."

Holli nodded, and we sat in silence for a moment.

"Do you think she has any idea what her leaders have done to us?" I asked.

Holli sighed, as though my naiveté frustrated her. "Did it seem like it to you?"

I shook my head.

"She said John Coutts was her grandfather," I shared. "Which means—"

"She's Coutts blood." Holli's eyes widened before she forced a breath out. "Well, it makes sense."

"What makes sense?"

"Her behavior." Holli began to fiddle with her cuticles. "She's absolutely bewildered by us and the way we live, which makes sense if she was born into that community. So, no, I don't think she knows the actual truth about anything Peter Coutts has ever done outside of what he wants them to believe."

"And what about the others? The ones that joined under his threats? The ones that know better?"

"Well, I'd imagine they're kept separate from people like Maura. When Peter started The Coutts Organization, he did a good job separating it from The Coutts Family.

Claimed to be a big believer in separation of business and religion." She rolled her eyes.

I gave a strained laugh. "That worked well." After Peter Coutts closed his borders and ceased all trade agreements, there was no longer a distinction between the pharmaceutical company he'd created and the religious organization he'd inherited ownership of, establishing what was now the Coutts commune.

"You're telling me," she answered. "You have to remember, most people suffered long-term effects from the pandemics. A lot of them are *still* heavily reliant on the Coutts's medical care. Not to mention people with diabetes or cancer." She shook her head.

"But they can't all be sick," I argued.

She shrugged. "I can't speak for them, but I'd imagine once you become reliant on the power plants, water treatment centers, hospitals…" She listed them off on her fingers, "…it'd be hard to leave. The ones that wanted to leave, probably did, and are surviving the same as us, or resting, same as your Mom."

"You know," I said, "she seemed almost *surprised* that I was alive when I first met her. Like she didn't totally believe that I wasn't part of the commune. That's strange, isn't it?"

Holli rubbed her hand over her mouth. "Not particularly, no."

I cocked my eyebrow, waiting for her to continue.

"Think about it," she said, her eyes dazed, "what would be more convincing to people than to say your cause and your people were the only ones to survive the worst pandemic in the history of man? That would've bolstered his message and kept obedience amidst the chaos. And I suspect that's exactly what Peter did."

Though the temperature hadn't changed, goosebumps erupted across my skin.

"Right, but wouldn't they have still seen death?" I argued. "How'd he explain the sickness to his followers?"

"Sin," Holli said with a shrug. "You ever read the Bible?"

I laughed. "Do I look like someone who's ever read the Bible?"

Holli smiled. "It's a brutal book. Sinners are punished horribly — stoning, murder, slavery. I'm sure the Coutts are no strangers to death being a punishment for sin. But the concept of sin is subjective. I mean, Peter probably condemns his followers for sinful thoughts. Nobody could prove it, but who'd argue with him? The most powerful man in the world? A self-proclaimed prophet? It's the perfect excuse. Though I don't think they'd have needed to use it for long."

"Meaning?

"Meaning, my suspicion is they have some kind of treatment or cure up there we don't know about. From what we've seen, their population is booming, not dwindling. And they've kept those secrets before. Why not do it again, now?"

"I feel like that defeats the purpose, though," I countered.

"Of?"

"Recruiting people to their cause. A treatment would've probably gotten a lot of people to go willingly. Rather than do what they tried to do after the flu hit."

Holli scoffed. "Oh, come off it Eli. You know better

than anyone that it wouldn't have. Can you imagine someone like Sid ever going willingly?" She laughed. "They would've always needed to threaten us with weapons and death. Always."

I sighed. She was right. No matter what the Coutts offered, Mom had always refused to listen to anything they had to say, and as Sid and I got older, we agreed. Mom wanted to be *free*. Mom wanted to make her own choices, no matter how hard life had gotten. And we continued to pursue that legacy. Loyalty to Peter Coutts made me sick to my stomach.

"Anyway, the rest of us holdouts are probably more trouble to Peter than we're worth," Holli continued. "I think that's why they've left us alone this long. Why waste the resources just for us to wreak havoc? It's easier to just let nature finish us off or, if we get in the way, threaten us with violence, until—poof," she made a little explosion with her hands, "there's none of us left."

"Now that's cheerful."

"You know I aim to please."

The world rumbled as Holli finished her thought; a deep, cracking sound that cut through the walls. Mia shrieked, her bare feet making soft thuds as she ran down the hall and straight into Holli's arms.

"Ton-der!" she cried, her brown eyes wide as she chewed on her thumb for comfort.

Holli cradled her, clutching her to her chest, before looking back up at me. I got to my feet, looking beneath one of the cardboard-covered windows. Though most of the pale blue sky looked harmless, a large, gray cloud had formed in the distance, its black edges spreading outward, like ink in water. A flash of lightning caught my eye and I let the cardboard drop, glancing over my shoulder at Holli.

"Sid should be back within the hour?" I asked Holli, trying not to let my panic get the best of me. The shifting climate had not only unearthed Pandora's Box of pandemics, but brought severe storms into our once tame weather patterns. Thunderstorms often turned into monsoons, dangerous lightning storms, or hail the size of melons. Sid was more than capable of finding shelter during a storm, but we were safer together.

"He should," she confirmed, rocking Mia. "What about her?" she mouthed, sticking her thumb over her shoulder toward the back door.

Yet another hurdle I hadn't expected. Inviting a Coutts into our home was an invitation for trouble. Keeping her out back, under the cover of the dilapidated treehouse, ensured they wouldn't blame us for her absence — perhaps she had crawled back there and nobody had noticed. I knew better than most how unfair the Coutts were, but the small nuance might mean life or death if they ambushed us.

If they found her dead body on our property, however...

I sighed in defeat before going outside. Damp air hung heavy in the atmosphere, a coolness settling over the still-warm ground. I glimpsed Maura near one of the garden beds, hunched over as she inspected a sage bush between her fingers. A low rumble of thunder rolled once more, and she straightened, shoulders tight, nose in the air as she scanned her surroundings.

Her eyes widened as she noticed my approach and she stood to her full height, grasping her hands together behind her back. It gave her the look of a disobedient child who was trying to convince their parent they were following the rules. I frowned at her.

"There's a storm coming," I said, stopping a few feet away. "You should come inside."

"Inside?"

I pressed my lips together. "Yes," I said. "Inside the house." I pointed the trailer. "You can't be out here. It's too dangerous. C'mon." I waved her along, hating the foreboding feeling I got as I thought of Maura and Sid in the same 1,000 square feet.

11

MAURA

The stairs creaked beneath our weight as I followed Eli through the back door of the house. It took a minute for my eyes to adjust to the dark inside. Cardboard blocked the light from any visible window. Various items lay strewn about, chipped paint and peeling wallpaper lining the interior. The dated furniture looked as sturdy as the lawn chair I'd slept on. It was the polar opposite of Andrew's home.

I paused as the door closed, wishing I could disappear into the wall. Holli and Mia sat side by side on the couch, their gazes fixed on me for a moment before Holli distracted the young girl with a book she held in her hands. Thunder rumbled once more, muffled by the walls around us. I scanned my surroundings for the tall, dark man, but he was nowhere to be found.

Eli turned toward me, arms crossed, expression indifferent. "I, uh—" He scratched at his beard. "I thought we might talk."

Talk? I tensed. Did he want me to leave? Was he going

to send me out there after the storm? How would I find my way back? Voicing those questions aloud seemed too daunting a task, so I pushed them away, swallowing them whole, as I nodded my head.

"Good." His awkward tone made him sound like he wasn't sure what to make of me. And the feeling was mutual. "We can go down here."

I followed him away from the living area, down a dark hallway, past two closed doors, to an open one at the end, entering a small bedroom. The mattress took up most of the space and it smelled damp and stale, with a faint edge of sweat. Eli pulled up a floral comforter so that it covered the mattress and sat near the headboard.

As I closed the door and turned to him, the room spun. Being in a bedroom with a man had been something I'd been terrified of ever since I learned about the prospect of being married. And while Andrew had been patient at my inability to conceive, he had expected, like all Coutts men, that I would fulfill my wifely duties on our wedding night. The trouble was, I didn't know what to expect. Sister Abigail had described our wedding nights as a divine ritual, something between husband and wife, blessed by God. At nine, I'd imagined sharing a meal or a drink with my future husband. They did not give us details about what actually awaited us.

Hours after we'd said our vows, it happened. It was bloody, messy, and painful. The act itself seemed ugly and primal — not some glorious ceremony that made me a woman. Those thoughts had been sinful, but I failed to see the holiness in what we'd done.

As I entered adulthood, Abigail warned us of man's evils outside our sacred walls — the lust of men, their greed and insatiable appetites. Was that what this was? Did Eli expect me to lie still while he satisfied his desires? Sweat formed on my neck as he studied me.

"Maura," he began, and I braced myself with a breath. "What were you doing out in that creek?"

I turned my head, uncertain if I'd heard him right. "What?"

"Why were you in the creek?" he asked. "You must've been at the border of the Coutts commune to even fall in."

I nearly laughed in relief. "I'm a Scavenger," I shared. "It's my responsibility to travel out to specified zones in the commune and scavenge for any items our families can use." I closed my eyes. I didn't want to think of Sweetheart out by the creek, waiting faithfully. I didn't want to think of Morgan, or Mother, or of the worry my absence would've caused. The disappointment and humiliation this would bring to our family made my stomach churn. I wanted to explode.

And so I did. Endless words spilled from my mouth like water from a broken dam. I told Eli about Andrew, of the other wives, of the children and how I had none of my own, but wished I did. I told him I was a direct descendant of Father, the Prophet, of how I was expected to do better, to *be* better, about my daily scavenging trips, the meager resources I continued to bring home, my shame at the inability to provide. I told him about the glass, shimmering in the distance, filled with promises. I told him of my foolish plan to cross the river, just to *see*.

"I thought maybe there was something out there." Tears stung the corners of my eyes. "Medicine, or supplies — something I could bring home for my family. I wanted to do something right." I released a shuddering breath. "I wanted to prove I deserve a place in my family."

The words that rolled from my tongue filled me with regret and shame, the marks of a true sinner. I winced, angry at myself for not stopping my rolling boulder of emotion, terrified to be seen for what I truly was — an imposter of the very community I was supposed to be devoted to.

"Would they be looking for you?"

I glanced up, caught off-guard at the question. "Who?"

He cocked his head. "Your family. Wouldn't they...be looking for you by now?"

I looked at my hands, using my pointer finger to trace the freckles on my knuckles. When Morgan ran off, I had begged Mother to ask Father to send men out after her. The Outside was so dangerous, so unfamiliar. She wouldn't survive out there. Where would she go? How would she eat? Pray? Sleep? But Father refused. It wasn't until just before the great plague that he sent his men to search for her. He wanted her home. He brought her back to safety.

"I—"

Silence hung like honey between us.

Eli looked away as I caught his gaze. I knew that look. It was the same one I got from Abigail, Joanna, and even Andrew. He pitied me.

"You seemed surprised when we first met," Eli continued, not meeting my eyes. "Like you expected I was part of your...commune."

I inhaled through my nose and held my breath. Could it be possible Father knew they were out here? How could he have missed them?

"It's just…" My face grew hot. "They told us…"

Another roll of thunder came, stopping the words before they formed. They were there, on the very tip of my tongue, but I couldn't speak them. The wind howled outside the bedroom window, growing louder by the minute as my mind raced. I heard Father's voice in my mind, how adamantly he had stressed we were the only ones left. We were the righteous ones, saved by God. He had protected us from infection.

I looked up at Eli. He leaned against the bed, thumbs hooked behind his head, watching me. Calm sat within his green eyes. Judging me. Seeing me. Dissecting my every move.

"They told us there was no one," I said, my voice sounding foreign. "They told us we were the only survivors of the great plague. That God had saved us. That the only survivors were…"

"People in the Coutts commune." Eli leaned forward. "So you've all been operating under the assumption that nobody existed out here?" The question was rhetorical, but I nodded regardless. He scoffed, his eyes going wide, then slowly wiped his hand across his mouth.

"They searched the outskirts of our commune high and low for months," I reasoned. "Across states, even north and south, outside the U.S. borders. They confirmed there were no survivors."

"Well…" Eli held his hands out. "Looks like there are."

My pulse quickened. Everything was all wrong. I should have woken up in Andrew's bed this morning, sidled down to the kitchen to begin breakfast before Abigail came bustling through the front door with her gaggle of kids. I should have gone to church, then to the stables, then down to my zone with Sweetheart. I shouldn't be here, talking to a man who wasn't supposed to exist.

"And have you noticed more people in your commune since everything fell apart out here?" Eli continued, waving his hand at the last word. "New faces you couldn't explain?"

I bit my lip, working hard to process his questions. "It's a large place," I answered. "We had an influx of followers arrive when things started to get bad, some from other communes around the world and Outsiders looking to change their ways."

His eyes searched my face for more, before he reached for something on the table beside the bed. He handed me a brass frame.

"Have you ever seen this man?" he asked.

I studied the photo. The man had a gentle face, eyes crinkled up at the edges from his smile. His scruff of a beard hid his chin, and his shaggy brown hair fell over a pair of golden-brown eyes. He held a much younger Mia in his arms and I recognized the resemblance instantly. But I couldn't place him.

"No," I said, looking back up at Eli. "I'm sorry." And then, after a moment's hesitation, I asked, "Why?"

Eli looked surprised by the question. "He's missing," he answered, taking the frame back. "We think he may have…may be in your commune."

"Is he Mia's father?" I whispered.

Eli nodded.

"Like I said, the commune's a large place. It's possible he could be there. Our borders extend hundreds of miles, out toward the ocean and south into the cities. I'm only supposed to interact with the people who live on Coutts Peak."

People of high status. People unlike me.

"Okay," Eli replied, sounding disappointed. "How about your family?" he asked, rubbing his fingers across his beard. "What does your husband do?"

"Well…" I shifted in my chair, surprised at how uncomfortable the question made me. "Andrew's a Hunter in the commune."

"A Hunter?" Eli interrupted, his face darkening. "What's that?"

"They hunt for meat," I answered, my heart picking up its pace. "They assess threats, expand our borders, and distribute goods to their communities. They protect us. Andrew leads the group of Hunters for Coutts Peak, and there are other leaders, like him, who work in other areas, like the cities, or near the oceans."

"Don't you all have massive farms? Food production systems? You still need people to go beyond the borders for game?"

I swallowed. "We do," I said, "but I guess there's a need for more meat?"

"You guess?"

"I don't ask questions. I keep to myself, do the Lord's work, and go about my day, and that's that. The men ration."

"Okay." Eli wrung his hands together. "What time of day does your husband usually go out?" he asked.

I pursed my lips. "He leaves a little after me, so late morning. He returns around dinner time." Sometimes Andrew *did* go missing at night, leaving his side of the bed cool to the touch. Secretly, I relished those moments.

Alone, at last, without the constant weight of expectation choking me to sleep. Those nights made things a little more bearable.

"How about at night?"

I paused. Something nagged me, telling me I shouldn't reveal that information all at once for the sake of Andrew's safety. "I'm not sure," I answered.

"You don't know when your husband goes out?"

The shame of being misinformed choked me. "Maybe only under special circumstances?" I felt foolish again, like a child. "Just when Father needs him."

"And what would he would need him for in the middle of the night?"

"I—" I shook my head.

"Do these Hunters of yours…do they drive big, black trucks?"

I looked up at him, eyes widening. "Yes," I whispered. "Why?"

"Just wanted to confirm," he said, glancing at his bandaged hands. Why would he care? I searched his face again, looking for any sign he might understand something I didn't. Was he looking for clues to go after Andrew? A way to sneak into the commune? Confirmation that I was who I said I was?

Perhaps he was a miscreant, like Father had said. Perhaps he'd tricked me. Perhaps I'd made a deal with the devil.

"Like I said," I continued. "I'm just a Scavenger."

"You're a Coutts," Eli answered, looking up to catch my eyes. "You're the daughter of Peter Coutts. You are much more than just a Scavenger."

I should've been proud by his declaration, but shame

flared within me. His harsh tone made *Coutts* seem like the worst thing imaginable.

"I'm sorry I can't help you more," I answered.

Eli's gaze softened. "It's not your fault."

There it was again. It wasn't my fault they left me out. It wasn't my fault I didn't have the answer, or how to accomplish something simple. Not little old Maura. It's not her fault she's stupid and inept and not praying hard enough. Someone jump in to help her, because Maura can't do it alone.

"What about your day-to-day?" he asked, his voice harder to hear now as the storm outside intensified. "Has anything significant changed in the past year?"

I considered his question. "Well, for one, I would've never become a Scavenger. Before, women weren't given laborious tasks. But we'd been called to a higher purpose. And our community is bigger, of course, as the borders expand."

When the pandemics first began, followers flocked to us, but we also had many Outsiders who saw the light and joined our cause. With plague after plague, there was no denying God's wrath anymore. Those people wanted to be healthy — physically and spiritually. Joining us was the only way how.

"And with all of those people," Eli interrupted. "You haven't seen mass death? People haven't gotten sick? How is it," he said, leaning forward now, "that the whole world out here got sick and died, but somehow, in that neat little circle of privilege you have, you didn't lose significant amounts of people? Even with all of your resources, it should've decimated your population."

Heat rose from my belly into my chest and up through

my throat, flushing my face. "We didn't lose people because we are God's most devout servants," I spat. "The people out here died for their sins! They died because of what they'd done to the world. We kept ourselves safe through the glory of God."

Eli sat straight-backed, an edge of a smile playing on the corner of his lips. Suddenly, all I wanted was to smack him. Father had been right all along.

"Okay," he said.

"I know you don't believe me!" I cried. "I know you must think we're all foolish up there, believing things that aren't real. But God saved us for a reason. He knows who is righteous and who isn't. He knows who his loyal followers are. We've been told what you thought of us, what you must still think! Well!" I said, looking around at the bedroom, "look how far it's gotten you!" My heart pounded as I finished and already, I regretted my reaction.

Eli sighed. "I'd say you're the one doing the judging here," he answered. "Seems like you've got us all figured out already when, in fact, you don't know us at all. People in glass houses... oh, never mind."

Even through the wind's roar, the slam of the back door was unmistakable. Eli stood, beelining for the door behind me. I jumped out of the way as he grasped for the handle, pulling it wide. Down the hallway, drenched with rainwater, stood Sid.

12

ELI

"You alright?" I hurried down the hall. Soft drizzle had turned to hard rain in the last few moments, pounding against the roof like pellets.

Sid tightened his jaw, his eyes fixed on the girl who stood behind me. "Yeah," he said. I froze as I watched him shrug off the hunting rifle I'd left abandoned the day I'd rescued Maura from the creek. He propped it against the wall beside the door. "What now? We're having private meetings with people from the Coutts commune?"

I frowned. "Had a few questions, is all."

Sid scoffed, turning to shed his gear, dripping water as he went. The cottontail I'd left out by the creek was now secured to his belt among two small squirrels, their limp heads bouncing as he reached the kitchen island. He deposited them in the sink.

"So, what, now she's going to sleep in Mom's bedroom? Have you got any shame?" he hissed. "We've just decided to abandon reason?" He directed the last bit over my shoulder at Holli.

"Sid—"

"No! It wasn't bad enough that you brought her back here, Eli, but now you're protecting her?"

"She's not an animal," Holli interjected from the couch. "Leaving her out there would be cruel. You know what storms can do."

Sid didn't dare challenge Holli. She'd lost her husband during a severe storm while they were working to improve their prepping skills. Holli's other half dedicated his life to survival, his fear driving him to conduct several preparation drills for when the lights cut out for good. He never lived to see the real thing, but his knowledge passed along to Holli was what had kept us going this long. I would always be grateful to him, and I knew Sid felt the same.

With a grunt, Sid left the kitchen, his back turned to us as he disappeared down the opposite hallway toward the other two bedrooms in the trailer. I looked at Holli, who offered nothing but a stony expression. I flashed her a bitter smile.

"You should talk to him," she suggested, tilting her head toward the hall. I paused, listening to the rain and the howl of the wind, before following my brother.

The door to our old shared bedroom remained ajar, and I cautiously pushed it open with my shoulder, sticking my head inside. The wood-paneled room still featured faded posters and magazine cut-outs. Tucked in the corner next to a small dresser was a wire-framed bunk bed. Sid sat on a metal folding chair beneath the far window, his fingers sliding against the dark edges of a half-smoked blunt — Holli had reluctantly let him use space in the backyard for a cannabis plant.

I paused at the door, watching him light it and take a drag, letting the smoke filter out through his nose and mouth. He closed his eyes to savor it, ignoring my presence.

"We need to talk," I said, entering the room fully.

Sid opened his eyes just to roll them at me. I took a deep breath, trying to steady my anger as I closed the door behind me. The smoke created a dim haze that filtered through the room, the smell earthy and sharp. "Look, I know you don't want to talk about this, but we have to." Sid leaned back in the chair. "I talked to her today about her family."

Sid scoffed. "Yeah? And how'd that go? Had a nice little chat, I imagine." His words dripped in sarcasm, tainted by anger. I knew I frustrated him. Bringing Maura back to this house wasn't my finest moment. But he hadn't been there. He wasn't out there by the creek with us. He didn't hear her scream.

"Don't be an ass."

"Like you?" He cocked a brow.

I clenched my fists. "She's the daughter of Peter Coutts, Sid. I mean *direct* descendant."

That got his attention. Sid sat forward, placing his elbows on his knees before looking up at me.

"So, what did you find out then?"

"Well, her husband is something she called a *Hunter*."

"A Hunter," he repeated, taking another drag.

I nodded as I crossed the room and sat on the lower bunk. "She said he goes out to hunt for food, assesses threats, expands borders, and distributes goods. We know they have farms up there with plenty of damn animals, and the only threats I know of are the Coutts themselves.

So they *must* be expanding their borders. My guess is they're moving farther south. Otherwise we'd have seen them out this way."

We'd been waiting to see if the Coutts would make any expansion efforts north. If they had, moving northwest had always been our plan, which we hadn't needed to enact yet. Moving south made sense. The Coutts would have more resources and warmer months for growing. The compacted land up north made it difficult for crops to survive and the winter months tended to impact the growing season. It was just one more thing the Coutts took away from us. But we were survivors. Moving north was trickier, sure. But not impossible.

Sid stood, holding the smoking blunt up to his eyes, watching as the fire burned out halfway before tucking it in an ashtray on the dresser.

"I also showed her Neil's photo, but she didn't recognize him."

Sid closed his eyes and inhaled, his grip tight on the dresser. "You sure that was smart?"

"What?"

He shook his head. "Eli, c'mon. Don't be so fucking naïve."

I narrowed my eyes. Anger settled in my chest and I crossed my arms, as if to hide it. "I'm not being naïve."

"You are," he said, pulling a dry shirt from one of the drawers. "You can't tell me you trust a word that comes out of that woman's mouth."

"Why not?" I asked. Sid paused, giving me an exasperated sigh. His face had hardened over the past few years. The mischievous twinkle that used to bring life to his dark brown eyes had faded. Along the way, he'd added a thin, raised scar to the side of his nose. His thick eyebrows furrowed as he silently challenged me from where he stood. Sid and I fought more often than I would have liked, but I knew it was because, deep down, we loved each other.

"Because she's a brainwashed, God-obsessed lunatic, Eli. Come on. She probably *has* seen Neil and now she's gonna go back and tell her people that we were looking for him and probably kill him too. She could be here to spy on us for all we know." He pulled his drenched shirt away from his body, letting it fall to the ground beside him with a squish, before pulling the dry one over his head.

"She's not."

"How can you be so sure?"

"I told you," I said, exasperated. "I waited. I had a friggin' gun to her head and nobody came. She was as good as dead in the middle of the creek. You really think she went through all that to come *spy* on us? It doesn't make sense."

"Then why didn't she turn around and go back to her own people?" Sid retorted.

"I told you! She had no weapons, no food, nothing to even suggest she's got the skills to make it miles back to that place. She'd have been dead before morning."

Sid seemed to ponder this. "All I know is I don't believe a goddamn thing she says. I can't believe you do, after everything we've been through." He shook his head.

My heart beat in my throat. "We'd be stupid not to."

Sid returned to his chair. "Would we be?" he asked, before sitting. His eyes narrowed in on me. "Would Mom think we were?"

"Yes," I answered with finality. "Sid. You know Mom

would have done the same thing if she found Maura in the creek."

Sid laughed. "Mom's gone because of the very people that girl supports. You don't know what she'd want because she's *dead*."

I shook my head and looked at the ceiling, every muscle tense. "Maura didn't kill Mom," I reminded him. "Maura didn't create that community, she didn't ask to be part of it, she doesn't *know* anything else."

"I do not care."

"Sid!" I cried.

"You're being an idiot," he snarled. "And you're betraying Mom's memory."

"What?" My voice cracked. "Are you serious? The only one betraying Mom's memory here is *you*. Mom wouldn't want us to be hateful. She'd want us to help. You know that. I know you do."

Sid rolled his eyes.

"So, what do you want me to do?" I pushed.

"I don't *know*, Eli," Sid seethed. "We let her stay, they come after us. We let her go with any chance of getting back to that commune alive, we have to move. She knows where we are now, and even if you don't think she could, there's always the possibility she leads her people right to us. They've come after us before, and I bet they'd do it again. She's a liability now. You, of all people, should understand that."

I opened my mouth to respond, but stopped. Realization hovered over me. Sid was right, and I hated him for it. Whether or not I liked it, this would change everything about how we'd been living. And it was my fault.

"Sending her back on her own is a death sentence," I breathed. "We'd have blood on our hands."

"Whose blood do you want on your hands?" Sid retorted. "Hers? Or ours?"

"Neither."

"Well, that's tough fucking luck," he said.

I drew a steady breath. I wanted to lash out, but I knew, in the depths of my soul, the only person who deserved my anger was me.

"I can't send her back."

Sid glared at me.

"We can use her," I tried to reason. "She could be valuable. Maybe she could even become our ally. Protect us from those Hunters." But even as I tried to spin it, I heard how ridiculous it all sounded.

"You know what those people are," Sid said. "They're going to hunt us down, no matter what she says about us."

THE STORM LASTED ALMOST three days without reprieve. Nights grew cold and windy, mornings bleak and drenched. The backyard turned to a mud pit, sludge collecting at the far end of the yard so the lounger Maura had once slept on sunk halfway into the ground. Our garden benefited from the moisture at first, but soon Holli began bringing some pots inside, situating them in the old bathtub, on top of the toilet, in the sink, and down the hallway, until you could barely move without needing to step over or around a potted plant.

Thunder rolled over us in waves, disrupting our sleep, sending Mia into crying fits every so often. Without the ability to catch more game, we relied on our preserves and drenched garden vegetables. On the upside, our barrels overflowed with water — something we never took for granted. Month-long droughts could sometimes follow intense storms.

Sid and I kept each other at arm's length, muttering greetings, but not much else as the days passed. Maura's constant presence made things at our camp awkward, so we only spoke when necessary. The girl lingered in shadows, sitting alone, ducking into empty rooms and disappearing as soon as someone joined her. I noticed she watched us a lot — our interactions with each other, how we prepared our food, even showing interest in our game of Go Fish, one of Mia's favorites.

Maura never asked for anything. She took the food we offered, but only a single helping. In the mornings, when she woke, she folded her blanket in a tidy square, leaving it beside the small pillow we'd scrounged up from somewhere. She washed her dishes, wiped her feet, and even chewed with her mouth closed. If she hadn't been a Coutts, I'd have labeled her a polite house guest.

But once the storm was over, I had a decision to make. Every day with Maura in our camp became more dangerous. We did not know if the Hunters would venture out in this weather to search, but I had a hunch a little rain wouldn't stop them from finding someone they wanted.

Then, finally, on the eve of the third night, the wind ceased, and the thunder rolled away, and I woke to silence in the pitch-black darkness only midnight brought.

I ventured out of Mom's old bedroom into the main area of the house, careful to watch each step as I skirted the plants. Maura had taken residence in the living room and I glimpsed her small figure huddled up on the couch, her chest rising and falling gently as she slumbered. Considering her made my cheeks flush. How had I ever thought someone so meek and small was such a danger? She was a naïve, scared girl who wasn't even confident her family would come searching for her. The thought made me horribly sad.

A soft glow emerged from the other end of the hall and I looked up, breath catching in my throat, until I saw Holli's distinct outline. She noticed me, nodding in my direction as she approached. Holli carried her lantern past the kitchen, opening the back door, waving me out to the garden.

Damp, cool air washed over us and I inhaled, more awake than I'd been all day. Holli sat on the back steps and I joined her as she placed the lantern between us. I glanced at her. Deep purple circles made her kind eyes seem sunken. Though the plague had ravaged us for a few months, it had faded away as our population decreased. However, there was still always the chance of getting sick, and not just from what had killed all those people. It was Holli I worried about most. She was healthy and strong, but age caught up with all of us.

"How are you feeling?" I asked.

"Oh honey," she said, waving me off. "I'm just fine. Don't you worry yourself over me." She coughed into her elbow.

I nudged her with my shoulder. "I'll always worry."

"That's kind of you." She raised her chin to look at the sky.

Silence hung between us, the pressing matter begging to be freed. I dropped my head, eyes traveling over the rain-soaked wood we sat on. Moss grew from the edges of the nails, barely holding the structure together.

"What am I gonna do with the girl?" It came as a whisper, as if I wasn't sure I wanted Holli to hear the question in its entirety. Not being able to decide felt shameful, like I was waiting for someone else to tell me what to do. Holli tilted her head to look at me.

"She can't go out there alone. She's totally clueless."

"Unfortunately," she agreed.

"But sending her back—" I huffed in annoyance, shaking my head at my indecisiveness. "I don't know."

"I don't think there's a simple answer here, Eli," Holli said. Her voice was gentle, not accusatory.

Silence came again, before I said, "I want to tell her what happened out here."

Holli gave me a stern look. "Why?"

"Because she should know. She thinks her people are these kind, devout, holy people, when they're really just a bunch of monsters."

I looked at Holli, expecting her to give me a nod of agreement. Instead, she pursed her lips. "Telling her may not go the way you're expecting it to." I could tell she was choosing her words carefully. "She's not going to reason like you and me, Eli. She's from a different world."

"So you think I should lie to her?"

Holli sighed. "No. You can say whatever you want to say to her. I just want you to understand that her response may not be what you think it's going to be. She may be too blind to see the truth, even if you throw it in her face."

"Well, I can try," I said, clinging to my determination.

"You can try," Holli agreed. "And then—?"

She studied me as I pressed my still bandaged hands

into my face. "I have to take her back," I whispered through my fingers.

Holli sighed. "It's not ideal and I hate to say it, but I think it's our best option. But you'd have to do it quickly, and without being seen. You can't march right into the commune and deliver her to Peter."

"No," I said. "But I could definitely get her close."

Holli shifted her weight on the step. "You'll be risking your own safety crossing that creek," she stressed. "So you'd be wise to think that through before you decide."

"What choice do I have?"

Her silence answered the question.

"I can't throw her out without making sure she made it back safely. I don't think I could live with myself. I made a mess and now I have to clean it up. I can't get more blood on my hands after Mom." My voice cracked, and I allowed myself to curl inward as emotion found me. I hated failure. I hated feeling responsible for something I had such little control over. If I believed in God, I might've called this divine intervention. But after all I'd fought through, God was nothing more than a fairytale.

I hadn't cried in some time. Not since after Mom had died, in fact. Our environment didn't allow for it. Death didn't scare me. Not really. I figured it was inevitable at this point. It was disappointing others that got me. I cared about the family we'd built. I was responsible for them. Sid and I were the protectors of our camp. Of Holli. Of little Mia. And, by a cruel twist of fate, Maura.

Shame of my irresponsibility flared within me and I sat with it for a moment until Holli placed her hands on my shoulders. She caressed me for a few minutes, bringing my head to her chest, where I rested and cried, allowing myself a sliver of peace.

"We'll support you with whatever you choose," she whispered, as I moved to wipe my tears. "Know that. You are loved, and you are needed. But if you're going to guide her back, you need to make a choice. Tomorrow."

I nodded, the full gravity of the situation settling on my chest like a rock. All our lives were about to change. Again.

13

MAURA

"GET UP."

The voice was low, yet too deep to be Andrew's. I woke, rubbing my cheek back against the flimsy pillow as my brain took inventory of my surroundings. A soft glow danced beside me. A flicker.

A flame.

I sat up with a gasp, sudden realization washing over me. I was far from home, away from safety, in a place unfamiliar to me. The cold of the darkness made me shiver, and I reached for the blanket at my feet.

There was a heavy *plop*, followed by footsteps. Eli appeared, his narrow face strange and shadowed. He glanced at the material he'd placed beside me, and I followed his gaze to a camouflage jacket.

"Here," he breathed. "Put this on."

"Okay," I mumbled, reaching for it. Coming out of sleep was intimate, something I learned early on when sharing a bed with Andrew. From yawning to stretching, it felt intrusive to watch a near stranger start their day.

And although Eli turned to give me a moment of privacy, I still felt exposed. I pulled my arms through the oversized jacket and fumbled with my tired fingers to zip it up.

"Get your shoes on," he told me, turning toward the door. "Meet me outside."

"Why?" I asked, fear bubbling up in my throat.

"We're walking," he said.

The tension in my shoulders remained. Maybe he was taking me out back to shoot me. Maybe he was walking me back to the creek to push me in, where I would tumble and roll until I drowned, my body left for the Hunters to find. But maybe… just maybe, it was breakfast.

Lord above, I hoped it was breakfast.

DAYLIGHT WAITED at the edge of our line of vision, casting a dim blue glow as it crept over the tops of the trees in the distance. Moisture clung to our surroundings from the rain, making the air smell earthy and fresh. Eli stood outside the fence, hands clasped to his hips, facing the road. He wore a similar jacket, one far more faded and creased than my own. A backpack slung over his shoulder weighed his left side down.

Stillness settled over the empty collection of homes surrounding the trailer, now clear in the hazy sun. About a dozen structures, some raised on cinderblocks, some sitting on the sunken ground, some more established with brick, wood, and metal roofing, dotted the area between. Each small structure had its own characteristics — stickers covered one front door, another had a painted mural of a sunset over the ocean, and another had hung hand-written warnings that the homeowners, whoever they were, would *Shoot On Sight*. Broken furniture, electronics, and uncollected trash bags of varying colors were crammed together on many of the lawns, with dead, overgrown grass packing the spaces between.

I closed the gate behind me with a click. Eli's head tilted as I approached, but he didn't shift his gaze from the landscape. Just beyond the trees, I could make out the distant purple peaks of our mountains, shadowed by dark clouds that would melt away with the last of dawn.

I'd never witnessed the mountains from this angle and it was strange to see how distant the majestic summits looked from below. I had always thought our peaks towered over the Outside, a constant reminder of our imminent Judgment Day. But from here they were a simple, yet beautiful backdrop to the tree-filled land surrounding us.

"It's strange seeing the mountains this way," I commented. Sleep tinted my voice as it carried away. Eli remained silent, square jaw locked in place.

"Sometimes it's like nothing's changed," he whispered, turning his head toward me. I met his eyes. They were different this time, without the cloudiness of chaos and fear. In the delicate light his features softened, something not even his beard could hide. "All of this," he tilted his chin forward. "It's all the same as it was. Not like the other places. Nature always grew here."

"Just as God intended," I said.

Eli shifted, hoisting the backpack higher on his shoulder. "Here." He reached into his pocket, producing a wrinkled granola bar that he threw to me. "Breakfast."

I caught it between my hands and unwrapped it.

"Let's go," he said, beginning to walk. After taking a bite of the bar, I followed.

The sun rose ahead of us, washing away the cool air night left behind. Clouds drifted across our path, casting shadows over the packed dirt road we walked. The homes ended, the path leading out to the main paved road. Eli followed it left and I followed. Looming pine trees and tall grass lined either side, most of it yellow with spots of green. Weeds sprouted through cracks in the neglected pavement, making it look cobblestoned.

I wasn't sure what I'd expected of the Outside. Father had described it as a place of sin, so I'd imagined fire and brimstone, snakes in the grass, and the Mark of the Beast on every corner. But these small assortments of homes did not make me fearful. If anything, my heart ached for the people who had once lived here in an empty wasteland. Even in the emptiness, their poverty was obvious, and a wicked thought crossed my mind. Why had we not helped them?

Father's voice quickly reminded me of the answer: They had not wanted our help. They had not accepted the Prophet as their Savior and so God had punished them for their sins. But as we walked around a curve of the main road, we passed another collection of tired-looking homes. I saw the remnants of a makeshift playground, scattered with broken plastic sand toys and a tire swing with a thick, frayed rope, and couldn't help but wonder.

We walked on. A familiar ache crept up into my calves and just as I thought about asking Eli how much further we had to go, he turned left down a new road, more overgrown than the one we were leaving behind. Trees lined this road too and through the foliage, I heard the faint rush of the creek somewhere unseen.

The trees thinned and we entered what I could only describe as a small town, though the word itself was generous. There were five brick structures with similar signs hung over their doors — United States Post Office, Tim's Grocery and Hardware, Calhoun's Auto Repair and Car Exchange, Relcrown Credit Union, and a thrift shop. Glass from their shattered windows and doors littered the street, reflecting like diamonds in the sunlight.

Our footsteps echoed off the brick buildings as we walked. I squinted, gazing into the cloudy windows, eager to get a glimpse of what life might've been like on the Outside before. But the town was over before it began, and the realization left me with a miserable pit in my belly. Our towns were filled with resources and luxuries I was sure the people who lived here had never seen.

I shook the thought away and hurried ahead. "Where are we going?" I asked, fed up with our silence.

Eli's steps didn't falter. "I have to take you back," he said. "It's too dangerous for you to be here."

My heart sank, though I was not surprised. I had known my welcome would be short and at some point, I'd need to return to my rightful place.

"But first I want to show you something," he repeated, with a glance over his shoulder. "Now that you're down off that mountain, you should know what happened."

"What *happened*?" I asked, hurrying my pace to keep up. "Yep."

"I know what happened," I retorted with an edge of frustration. I wasn't ignorant. Father had shared information with us. "I know how it killed and how many it killed. I know—"

"I don't care what you *think* you know," Eli said. "I want you to see our side. *My* side. So you know what you're returning to."

I raised my eyebrows and looked down at the pavement. I'd annoyed him. Better to stay quiet until we got to where we were going. I'd learned the importance of holding my tongue at a young age, but sometimes my curiosity got the best of me. It was a flaw I'd had since childhood. One Mother had tried to correct countless times. And here I was, of age, still questioning. Still wondering. Still not satisfied.

A wide building with a half-circle driveway came into view. Stairs led to faded double doors, words carved into crumbling stone over the entrance: *Relcrown School*. For a moment, it looked like Eli was heading into the building, but he turned before the driveway, leading us through more trees toward the back of the building. There, we approached a chain-link fence and Eli let his hand trail along it until he stopped, finding a break he must've known was there.

With just enough room to wiggle through, we emerged on the other side of the fence together into a large patch of dirt I recognized vaguely as a baseball field. Women were not allowed to play or attend sporting events in our commune, but I still understood. My brother, Mark, had been invited to play a few times before I'd left Mother's home for good.

Eli paused, looking out at the field, and I watched him, puzzled by the interruption. And then I saw it. Beyond the dirt, at least fifty makeshift crosses dotted the grass field, some areas more freshly disturbed than others. Eli walked across the dirt, pausing before the graves. I followed.

"We're here," he said through gritted teeth.

I looked up at him. "A graveyard?" I asked.

He looked down at me. The fire behind his eyes blazed, yet sadness reigned across his features. This place meant something to him. Something that devastated him.

"Yes," he said. "We used this field because of the fence — so animals couldn't get a hold of the bodies. But these people...they didn't all die in the plague. Some of them were victims of an attack afterward."

"After?" I repeated, looking back at the grass. I brought a hand to my mouth, horror settling in my chest.

Eli looked at the graveyard. "Your people killed them," he said without hesitation. "Your people murdered them."

His words drove a knife through my middle, slicing through me with cold fury. I turned them over in my mind. *Your people.* He meant the Coutts.

"My people?" I almost laughed. "No. You're mistaken."

Eli looked toward the heavens and sighed. "I wish I was. But I know exactly what your people do when they leave that mountain of yours." He lowered his chin. "They've lied to you."

Doubt spilled from my chest. I wanted to tell him he was foolish or he'd gotten the God-fearing Coutts mixed up with someone else. Someone else's atrocities. Someone else's mistakes. But his gaze stopped me dead in my tracks. Urgency fueled him. He wanted to tell me his story, and he wanted me to listen.

I ran my fingers through my hair, trying to ease my lightheadedness and revulsion at his claim. He was wrong, but I also couldn't ignore the fact that I was indebted to him for his mercy these past few days, so I said, "Okay. Tell me, then. I'll listen. I owe you that."

His face softened at my words and he nodded, taking a seat on the ground. With weak knees and a heavy heart, I sank into the grass beside him.

14

ELI

WE'D BEEN MARCHING toward humanity's demise for some time now. There was no big bang, no sudden thing that stomped us out. Instead, we came to a rolling stop that, for many, was almost a relief.

Things started out simple enough. In 2020, a virus found its way to our shore. The Coutts Organization rose to the challenge, creating a vaccine so effective Peter negotiated a deal with the United Nations, allowing him complete governing power over his land, without interference from outside authority. Desperate to appease their people and to stop millions more from dying, the powers that be agreed, and released the vaccine.

It worked, but it was only the beginning of the onslaught of viruses. Every few years, some new contagion appeared. With nothing else to negotiate, the governments had no choice but to let Peter keep his life-saving vaccines and medications for those who joined him, and in the wake of each pandemic, that number grew.

Unfortunately, for us on the Outside, that meant an exodus of essential workers like medical providers, farmers, engineers, scientists, and supply chain employees. The scientists who had not yet followed Peter tried and failed to create vaccines. The shortage meant manufacturers were unable to produce basic pharmaceuticals fast enough and when they finally met demand, there was no one to ship them out. Hospital beds filled up and pharmacies shuttered their doors. Doctors and nurses burned out or got sick and died themselves.

One day the supermarket might be full, followed by weeks of empty shelves. Stores ran out of things like baby formula while remaining stocked full of cheap clothing and cosmetics. Police stations closed with no sheriffs or cops to enforce the law, allowing crime to run rampant throughout remaining cities and neighborhoods. Courts became congested with trials without judges to fill seats. Some schools remained open, with parents or volunteers teaching the children still attending, but soon those closed, too. Even people with great financial wealth were at the mercy of the Coutts. Paper meant nothing if you couldn't buy anything with it.

People on the Outside, like Mom, adapted. She grew food, collected water, learned how to trade her sewing and cooking skills for things she couldn't acquire, like a basketball or an old VCR for me and Sid. Truth be told, we wouldn't have known how poor and under resourced we were, had the Coutts not consistently broadcast their wealth across the television networks and social media platforms they owned. And then, in 2031, citing dwindling resources, Peter closed his borders for good.

The end of those trade agreements caused a sudden

influx of people in our area outside the borders of the Coutts commune. Some argued it was dangerous, but Mom argued it was necessary. Teams of scavengers began sifting through the Coutts' trash, finding food and damaged resources we put to good use. Those were the things that started showing up on our shelves. The Coutts's waste kept us alive.

The severing of ties between the Coutts Organization and the U.S. government put what remained of our country into a tailspin. The army had more bombs, guns, and tanks than we knew what to do with, but what good were they if we attacked the people who might save our lives? It took only two more years for the U.S. government to collapse, dissolving into nothing more than a spectacle that fizzled out once the media stopped covering their bickering.

And then, in spring of 2035 — a little over one year ago, H5N1 arrived.

April showers brought May flowers, but not enough to cover up the smell that came with high heat and dead bodies in the street. With fewer people alive than dead, the rancid odor of decay carried across the globe for months after the worst had settled. It lingered, even now. Like any foul scent, you could forget it, if you tried hard enough.

We were no strangers to lack of medical care during a crisis, but even with experience, this sickness was worse than the last. Towns instructed us to go west if we were sick. They had no resources to offer and the vague idea of more hospitals, doctors, and supplies appealed to many. Whether there was actually anyone out there that could help them was another question entirely.

The town of Relcrown was quiet and reserved. Most of us didn't trust anyone out west to protect us. We had learned how to survive and weren't about to ask for help now. In the end, most people died politely in their homes.

Sometimes, when I thought about it too deeply, I got frustrated nobody *did* anything. I think we all thought someone would come and save us. They call that the bystander effect. The social psychological theory tells us individuals are less likely to help a victim in need when others are present. Mutual denial. It wasn't our responsibility, but *surely* someone would figure it out.

Humanity's ego wiped us away for good.

Mom and I kept to ourselves during those dark days. We missed months of the world burning by remaining self-sustainable, even after the grocery closed and the mayor died. Every other week, we watched another neighbor pack up their car and make the trek west. They had no other choice.

We worried about Sid often. When things had gotten bad, he'd promised to find his way to us, but the idea itself felt impossible. California might as well have been another world entirely. Mom had advised him to stay. West was where they'd promised things were better, anyway. Still, I think Mom hoped one day he'd come walking through the door. We toyed with the idea of leaving ourselves, but Mom said it was too risky. The devil we knew versus the devil we didn't.

It wasn't all bad. Mom was the perfect companion. At thirty years my senior, she could fend for herself and I never once worried about her keeping up. She never made me feel less than her son, even though I wasn't Sid. We still found moments of joy to share; things that kept us going. After we lost power, we passed the time by playing board games, taking long afternoon naps, and finding new ways to cook food. I fished in the creek and began hunting squirrels, rabbits, and the occasional deer. Mom grew her garden and tended to the chickens. We laughed for hours when our first attempt at washing laundry ended up with stiff pants and underwear.

Our small town had its share of survivors — people who, like us, had avoided the sickness, and learned to fend for themselves. Every so often, Mom would wave me over to the window with a low hiss. *There's someone outside, Eli!* Together we'd watch them like hawks, inspecting their every move, wondering if they were getting on better or worse than we were. But interacting was a much trickier decision. We weren't ready for that yet. For us, the end was quiet.

Until it wasn't.

It was an unseasonably warm fall day and Mom and I had combed through some empty houses near town, looking for new knitting needles and any unclaimed food. Noises previously ignored were amplified in the nature buzz of our new world. Breezes rustled leaves free from their branches, crickets hummed, frogs gave throaty croaks between woodpecker beats against hard bark. That's why when the engines came closer, everyone left in town came out to see what it was.

Together, we collected on the main road, walking down our dilapidated streets and the homes we knew still held the dead. We watched the fleet approach from the tree-lined roads, jaws slack, eyes wide, mesmerized.

"Maybe it's the military," someone said.

"No way," another responded. "They'd have tanks."

"Maybe it's supplies," a different neighbor whispered. We all murmured our agreement. Later, I would reminisce on how unbelievably narrow-minded this was, but when you see a glimmer of hope in the middle of despair, you'll do little to contradict it.

The trucks roared down the only major road connecting all of us, turning into our small little town, their tires screeching as they stopped in front of the school. We approached their vans with caution. I remember my momentary gratitude for thinking the National Guard had come to rescue us. But as they all exited their cars, fear replaced my relief. Something was wrong. They were unmarked, dressed in sophisticated green armored suits and thick helmets obscuring all identifying features. And even more chilling, each held an AK-47.

"Line up!" one of the armed men barked. Most of the civilians listened, collecting outside the post office. Mom and I stayed where we were.

"Who are you?" I asked.

"We're saviors!" his deep voice shouted, motioning to the line forming. "Now *line up!*"

This was not a request, but an order. Mom nudged me from behind. Without a gun, defiance would've been foolish. Being unarmed was a mistake I would never make again. We formed a straight line that stretched across the single street. Lined up, we got a good look at who had survived. Fifteen souls in total.

The man who barked the orders stepped up, aligning the tips of his boots with the toes of my sneakers. Sewn into his breast pocket was a thick number 11. He stood a few inches above me and did not remove his helmet as he spoke. In his hands, he held a wooden clipboard.

"Age?" he asked.

"Why do you want to know?"

"Age?" he asked again, voice tinted with annoyance.

"What, you're not gonna buy me dinner first?" I asked.

The man reacted instantly, his fist connecting with the left side of my jaw. Pain seared across my face, through each tooth, up into my skull. My eyes watered as my head snapped back, an immediate reaction to the surprise of the force. I caught the jolt in my throat with a gasp, before catching my balance and righting myself again.

I refocused on the man's helmet, my ears ringing with pain. Even with his facial features concealed, his stature seemed too calm.

"What the fuck?" My adrenaline surged. I considered grabbing his gun and beating him to the ground with the back of it, but my rational brain grounded me in the present. They all had guns and, given how easily the man had used violence, I assumed they wouldn't hesitate to use them. Letting my anger get the best of me wasn't an option. Gingerly, I brought my fingers to my burning face.

"Age?"

"Nineteen."

He nodded and wrote something on his clipboard. "Do you have any symptoms of disease?"

"Do I look like I do?" I asked between my teeth, holding my arms out. He stiffened, and I straightened, frustrated by my fear of him. "No," I said. "I don't."

The man reached into his pocket and pulled out a device that looked like a security metal detector. He waved it in front of my face, waited for it to beep, then pocketed it without another word.

I looked to my left. Mom spoke to another armored individual, head high and eyes defiant. But from the corner of her eye, I saw her shoot me a worried glance. The heat on the left side of my face grew. I would have a bruise there later.

"Get over here," the man before me said, taking hold of my arm. I tensed, resisting the movement away from Mom, but he tightened his grip in response, making sure I knew I had no choice but to follow him.

He dragged me from line and put me on the right side of the black trucks opposite the main road. In the distance, I saw something I didn't think I'd ever see again. A school bus made its way into town, large and yellow, looking wildly out of place.

"What the hell is this? What'd they check us for? Why are they separating us?" a fearful younger woman beside me asked.

I shook my head. "No idea." Distracted, I watched an armed man grab Mom by the arm and yank her in the other direction. I jolted in protest, but another man pushed me back in line. My gaze followed Mom, a pit of dread growing in my belly.

15

ELI

HEAT WASHED over my back in slow waves. There was no reprieve from the late September sun; the leaves had begun their migration from green to yellows and reds, brightening the landscape with colors only Mother Earth could dream up. The black trucks and yellow school bus blocked my view from Mom.

Her absence left me antsy. I tried sifting through my cloudy thoughts to find words to get us out of this. A trade, perhaps? A promise to make good on later? But anything we had to give, I knew, was of no interest to these men. The warm sting of the armed man's punch dispelled any confidence I'd had left.

I eyed the five others standing next to me; two young teens, a woman who had worked as one of our grocery store cashiers, and a man named Neil and his young daughter. We looked like wild animals. Our bodies had all thinned, weakened by months of irregular food supply and little outdoor exercise.

The teenagers clung to each other — siblings, I

assumed, from their similar fair features. The girl's shoulder protruded forward awkwardly, likely the result of an incorrectly healed broken bone. Her brother's long nose peeled from a sunburn a few days old. I presumed the other woman was a few years older than I was, but whatever her substance of choice had been did a number on her pockmarked covered face, her lips perpetually puckered.

I knew Neil and his daughter in passing. He'd lost his wife to cancer a year after the little girl was born. His receding hairline made him appear older than he was, his overgrown beard contradicting his boyish features. His daughter looked around five years old, with golden brown eyes and blonde hair tied back in neat braids.

I rocked back and forth on my heels, clenching and unclenching my fingers, straining my calves to gain height to see Mom, but it was useless.

Number 11 came around the side of one of the trucks and faced us. At his presence, the other men straightened and my anger surged. I imagined him as a righteous asshole on a power trip who needed a good punch to the face himself.

"Alright, listen up!" he barked. "You've been *chosen*. By the grace of God, you will return to the Coutts commune. We will provide you refuge and resources, but *only if* you abide by the Prophets's law. He is gracious and looks to invite you to His Kingdom. It's time to leave the devilish ways of your previous life down here at the base of the mountains to take your place as the sons and daughters of God."

"What the hell are you talking about?" the female teenager snarled, brows knitted together in anger. "You're the reason we're in this mess in the first place! Fuck the Coutts!"

The man cocked his head, a sign he was done putting up with our shit. Time froze. Number 11 nodded, and another armed guard appeared in front of the young woman. Confidence melted from her posture and she stepped back into line, eyes still fierce, but no longer willing to fight.

"Where are you taking the others?"

The man in charge didn't bother acknowledging me, instead signaling something to his men. In seconds, the armed guards circled us, guns drawn in tight grips. Number 11 knocked on the school bus door and it opened. He waved us forward with a gloved hand.

None of us moved. I waited for someone to say something. To question it. Number 11 gave a nod, and suddenly, something touched the base of my spine. A slender cylinder crept its way up my back, cold to the touch through my thin t-shirt.

A gun.

I froze. My skin prickled. To my knowledge, the Coutts had never been an outwardly violent group. True, they had their sins to answer for, but gun violence had never been one. What were they doing out here, rounding us all up like this?

Afraid to make any sudden movements, I sucked in a breath, eyes shifting to my left. All rationale left my body when I saw Neil gripping his small daughter for dear life, a gun at his back, too. Breath caught in my throat as I tried to make sense of what I was seeing, of the brutal nature in which they'd entered our town, months after the worst had happened, and threatened us with weapons. These were the revered Coutts men of God?

The woman beside me began to cry. The brother at the end of the row threw his arms around his sister, yelling something incomprehensible in his desperate attempt to protect her. My vision tunneled at the sight of us, lined up for what felt like an execution. We were unarmed and worse, we'd marched out here willingly, serving ourselves up for an ambush.

"Get on the bus," the man behind me growled.

This time, there was no hesitation. We moved in a singular line toward the open door. Shadows of feet shuffled along beneath the bus and I tried picking out Mom's worn Nikes even though there was no way to distinguish one from the rest.

First in line, I approached the door, meeting a different individual who clutched zip ties in their hand. "Wrists together," he instructed me. I did as I was told, gun still at my back, helpless as they secured my hands together.

The plastic dug into my wrists as they shoved me toward the stairs, forcing me to climb. Eager to see the other side of the road from the windows, I climbed aboard, searching for Mom. But my heart sank as I took in the view. The street was empty.

Dread consumed me as zip-tie man barked at us to hurry and sit down and I moved, my hands grasped together, down the aisle. The interior smelled stale and sour. I wondered what might have happened to the kids who had once taken this vehicle to school. Alive? Dead?

"What is this?" my neighbor Neil asked as he settled into a seat diagonal from me. His wrists were bound, but his daughters weren't. She climbed up on his lap and placed her head on his chest. Neil's eyes brimmed with tears.

I shook my head. "I don't know," I whispered. "More Coutts bull."

"Seems out of character for them, no?"

I nodded my agreement.

The siblings were last on the bus, the girl leaning against the seats for support as her brother urged her forward. Her eyes rolled, nostrils flaring as she gasped for each breath. Together, they clambered into the seat ahead of me.

"It's gonna be okay," the brother whispered. "Shelter, clean water, food! Maybe they'll even take a look at your shoulder." His tone wavered and even through my fright, it was clear he didn't believe his own words.

Most of the men who remained on the streets piled back into the black vans. Number 11 climbed aboard our bus, gun slung over his shoulder. And then, with a rumble, the engine started. Anxiety flooded me at the thought of leaving Mom behind. I hoped she'd figure a way to get out of this. We'd meet back at the house, come up with another plan. If we had to leave, then we would. We'd figure it out. Together, we could figure anything out.

Distinct shots sliced through my thoughts from somewhere in the distance — three in quick succession, a pause, then four more. A primal scream followed, so guttural I felt the terror in my own bones. I turned toward the sound, heart thrashing in my ears as I got to my feet, catching my balance with bound wrists on the seat in front of me.

"What the hell was that?" I cried, alarm radiating through each word. "What's going on?"

I looked down the middle of the bus, met with fearful glances, tear-filled eyes. Neil's little girl had begun to cry.

"Sit down!" the man in front screamed, picking up his gun. He brandished it so the barrel faced us, threatening to rip us to shreds. The pock-faced woman shrieked, and I melted backward, succumbing to the seat behind my knees. Distant gunfire came again, but this time, no screams followed.

I couldn't breathe. The solid seat seemed to shift beneath me, the walls closing in. Tears stung my eyes, and I tried to force them back. I watched my knuckles turn white as I gripped the seat, turning my face to the inside of my elbow to muffle my sobs that came like an unrelenting storm.

Mom.

The bus began to move and together we all rattled in our seats, along for the ride to wherever the hell we were going. The Coutts commune? A mass grave? My head spun. Was this a dream? My brain refused to register the reality of my current situation. I wanted to kick myself for being so naïve. We should have been prepared.

We pulled away from the main road, back onto the windy route leading toward other towns like ours. My mind wandered as we drove. Our focus had been on basic survival necessities. Food, water, and sleep when we could get it. We weren't prepared to fight. The Coutts must have known that before they came.

This was an ambush.

Muffled sobs echoed throughout the bus as we continued to drive and after a while, it was hard to tell how long we'd been traveling. Hours? Minutes? It didn't matter. The sound of gunshots wouldn't leave my mind. I imagined the worst — Mom's mangled body shot dead with bullet holes.

Neil caught my attention with a wave. I swallowed, wiping my tears on my shoulder before tilting my head against my hand so it looked like I was resting against the seat.

"I think we're gonna stop soon," he mouthed

I followed his gaze out the window. The trees had thinned, the occasional house or farm stand whipping by.

I turned back to Neil, shaking my head. "So?"

"The emergency door." He pointed to the red handle. Was he suggesting what I thought he was? "When we slow," he mouthed. "Pulling into the next town."

I considered the suggestion. Even if I could get the door open, it'd mean jumping from a moving vehicle which had the potential to be both dangerous and painful. I looked up the center aisle at the armored man with his gun, bouncing along the road with the rest of us. Neil was right. We couldn't stay on this bus. Whether we were headed to our deaths or the Coutts mountains, it didn't really matter. Broken bones and scraped knees were better than the other two options. It wasn't the best plan, but it was something. It would be tricky to get the handle open with the zip ties, but not impossible. But could we do it without getting shot first? I closed my eyes, swallowing bile.

Neil's eyes were wide when I met them next. I saw his determination in the way he looked down at his daughter with adoration. The way he soothed her with his bound hands, the way he gently kissed the wisps of hair framing her forehead. It was no secret what the Coutts did with young girls. The gruesome details of their perversions were there — somewhere, hidden in the horrible stories that snuck their way out from the corners of the commune. We just didn't talk about it. Sometimes, when you know justice won't be served, it becomes easier to pretend certain horrors don't exist.

The armed man and the driver began guffawing like they were at a bachelor party, cracking open some beers instead of kidnapping a bunch of innocent people ravaged by a plague. My seething hatred fueled me for what came next.

The bus slowed as we approached the turn for the town over, the driver easing us to the right. It was now or never. I stood, rushing to the back door, gripping the red handle awkwardly with my tied hands before pushing it up to release the door. It swung open, the wind taking it wide, revealing my terrifying potential for freedom. An endless buzzing filled the bus, filling my ears, and distorting my senses.

Disoriented, I watched the pavement whiz past like static. Though we'd slowed, the ground sped by too fast, but what other choice did I have? Any more hesitation and Neil and his little girl wouldn't make it. I held my breath and jumped, curling myself into the fetal position, hands positioned over my face.

I bounced like a rag doll across the road. Pain choked the air from my lungs and I was certain I felt a rib pop as the uneven pavement tore into my skin and rattled my bones. I tasted blood and the ratty remains of my bottom lip I'd accidentally chewed through. For those brief moments, I was sure I'd die which was certainly a better fate than becoming a Coutts minion. But despite my morbid thought, my body came to a stop.

There was no time to assess the damage. I could still hear the bus buzzing.

Too close.

I struggled to get to my feet, gasping down any air I could, hugging my tattered arms to my chest. To this day, I'll never understand how I managed. The human will to live is beyond our understanding.

Too preoccupied with my survival, I didn't pause to see how close the bus was, to see if Neil had made it off. I took off, sprinting down the empty road, across the yellow lines, over a guardrail, and down a steep incline.

Bullets whizzed overhead, some catching the metal in the guardrail, others flying through the leaves. There was no earth to catch me, and so I fell, tattered skin ripping against the sharp edges of the rocky hill I'd stumbled down. I found my footing a few feet down.

I knew I needed to hurry. The bus still buzzed in the distance, but I slowed, pulling the zip tie around my wrists tighter with my teeth. Keeping my arms steady and wrists straight, I brought my arms up and down across my abdomen, breaking the plastic with sheer force.

And then, I ran.

16

ELI

MY BOOTS HIT the ground like thunder, every stride pounding in my ears beside my hammering heart. I darted through overgrowth, branches scraping my forearms and face, overgrown weeds clawing at my ankles. Thick tree cover shielded me from sunlight, but I still felt exposed at all angles. I tried hard not to think about the guns those men held in their hands, the speed at which the bullets left the chamber, and what they might do to my body. What they might've done to Mom.

Sweat poured from my forehead, impeding my vision, rolling down my nose and onto my lips where I tasted my salty fear. After some time, my head began to throb from exertion and I slowed my pace. My throat was on fire, my chest tight as my lungs struggled to keep up. For the first time since I'd left the bus, I paused, resting my back on a peeling tree trunk as I sucked down a few deep breaths.

Against my better judgment, I looked over my shoulder at the ground I'd covered. Spots of sun made lone, yellow rays that bounced across green overgrowth, making small insects visible in the light. The world was still, yet my ears rang with static from the buzzing bus alarm and the bullets that had whizzed over my head. I closed my eyes, trying to rid my vision of stars and shake the noise away.

Shouting voices came from the distance, calling out in deep, hurried tones. I tried to make out the words they spoke to one another. An uncontrollable ache had settled in my limbs and once my adrenaline faded, I would be in agony. The tree at my back was a relief; I was so tired, so eager to lie down, to rest my aching body — perhaps here would be fine...

My eyes shot open, palms flat against the tree.

No. Run!

I turned, willing my legs to pick up speed, but rest had slowed my momentum and even with fear as my fuel sprinting seemed impossible. I heard them more clearly now as they got closer to where I stumbled forward.

In the distance, a large overturned tree with its roots in the air showed where the ground had come apart from the floods at the start of summer. I ran toward it, ducking beneath uneven, muddy earth, a rock at my back, the roots hanging a foot over my head, shielding me from view.

I tried to calm my breath and avoid the dry cough tickling my throat, straining to listen. The voices came closer; too close for me to allow myself to breathe freely. They spoke in raised, angry tones, but their words sounded foreign, muddled by the low hum that wouldn't seem to leave my ears. For a moment, I wondered if I was still rooted in reality at all.

Time slipped past me, unreachable and endless. The

voices faded, still bouncing around the area until quieting completely. It began to drizzle, a lazy type of rain that pitter-pattered off the earth, dripping down the ends of the tree's roots. I watched as it collected in dark puddles, making the dirt so damp it seeped into my clothes. But I refused to move. Not until I was safe. Not until I knew I wouldn't meet the armed guards again.

Night came and my legs gave out, leaving me half sitting, half laying in dead leaves and dirt. I felt useless and battered. Helpless. I slept for winks at a time until the dark was so black I could barely see my hands. Moving in the dark had its advantages. If they'd left someone on watch, they'd have a hard time seeing me now. The thought brought me to my feet.

I climbed out from beneath the tree roots, the forest a cluster of dark shadows. The muggy night washed over me with thick heat, vulnerability heightening my senses, making the forest seem alive. Sounds startled me as I began to walk, convinced every crack of a dry branch was some imminent danger.

And then there was something else — a soft sound. A bird, I thought at first. I followed it, intrigued, even though my journey took me uphill, and even though I was retracing the steps I'd already taken to get here. And as I came closer, I realized it was no song at all, but a cry. A desperate, gut-wrenching cry that no grown person could make.

I ran. The cry grew louder, more frantic. Placing the location was tricky. The sound bounced across the forest, and I along with it. Eventually, I'd followed it far enough, tracing disturbed land straight to a massive tree.

"Who's there?" I whispered into the night.

The crying ceased, sucked in by a breath at the sound of my voice. The distinct sound of fear.

"It's alright," I said, keeping my tone low. "I'm not going to hurt you."

Movement came from the depths of the dark middle of the tree, one brown eye, and then another. A short upturned nose, freckles, and tattered pigtail braids. The small child grasped the sides of the opening and pulled herself through, stumbling out before me. I gasped, my legs weak.

Neil's little girl.

"Hi," I tried, my voice shaking. "Do you remember me? I'm Eli."

She stood still, eyes focused on the ground.

"What's your name again?" I asked.

"M-m-mia," she cried, succumbing to her tears once more, letting out a howl that permeated every inch of me.

"Where's...da-daddy?"

"I...don't know," I answered, shaking my head. Where had he gone? "Did he leave you here?"

She just stared at me, her lip trembling. There was no chance he'd left her here this long, but I glanced around at the dark forest anyway even though I knew it was empty. I'd have seen Neil as I was following Mia's cries. Perhaps he was injured or lost, but the idea of yelling his name terrified me. It was safer to run, safer to return to town, to keep Mia safe. If Neil had managed to escape, he would return home to see if Mia had done the same.

I returned my helpless gaze to the little girl. "Mia," I said, "Are you hurt?"

She shook her head, bringing her thumb to her mouth.

"I had a accident," she said, glancing down at her shorts, tears leaking from her eyes.

"It's okay," I said, shaking my head. She started forward, arms outstretched, and I kneeled, scooping her up, cradling her small body to my chest. She stunk of urine and fear and her arms, legs, and cheeks were scraped up, same as mine. She and Neil must have jumped from the bus after I had.

At least Mia had escaped, and I'd found her. I stood, soothing her until she calmed, urgency taunting me as each second slid by. We needed to find home. With Mia to protect, I was certain of two things: I needed to return to town. And I needed a gun.

Although we moved slowly, the night was a blur. Mia and I did our best to navigate the forest, to find familiar landmarks, to continue the journey back to our homes. My shoulder screamed in pain with the added weight of the little girl, but I pushed through, stopping every once in a while when my vision swam. My skin was torn in inconvenient places — elbows, knees, and the back of my head. But we were *alive*.

I tried not to ask her too many questions. I promised I would protect her. That once we figured things out, we would do everything we could to find her father.

I knew nothing about small children, but understood she needed reassurance. As the hours pressed on, I put Mia on my back. Her weight was a minor detail as we marched onward, and she grew more comfortable and sleepy. She pointed out the things she thought were pretty. The way the stars between the trees twinkled. The squishy green moss between the crevices of the boulders. Strange mushrooms and lush flowers. And when she put her tired head against the top of my uninjured shoulder to sleep, I continued on, following the terrain's guidance as it led me forward.

Get to town, I kept thinking. *Just get back home.*

As the sun crept up through the darkness, we found the tree line and, just beyond, the wide mouth of the creek rushing through a valley. Unmistakable with its grand rapids and massive boulders, I knew it was the creek that ran behind our small town. I nearly cried from relief. I stumbled to the edge of the water, waking Mia. Together, we washed dirt from our hands. I cleaned our wounds. We drank and rested for a while. I drifted in and out of sleep until I was ready to move again. We followed the creek until the trees thinned.

As the world brightened, I saw the fence surrounding the baseball field behind the school, shining in the distance like a weird, familiar beacon. I'd hesitated, worried about every critical step forward, so aware of being unarmed, and terrified the armed men still lingered, despite how far we'd traveled. I studied the details from the day before. Why had they come? What had they wanted from us? Why didn't they just leave us alone?

As we walked, I clung to any inch of hope I could scrape up, though gunshots still rang loud in my ears. *Maybe*, I told myself. *Maybe she'd escaped*. We headed toward the baseball field and I absorbed every detail, scrutinizing each broken branch. Some part of me longed to call out her name, but I was terrified to make any sound at all.

I ached all over, my limbs trembling from exhaustion, dehydration, and hunger. Mia hadn't fared much better. We were dirty and delirious, but our adrenaline kept us going. Pausing only to look over my shoulders, I kept one fist tight and one firmly around Mia's hand.

We reached the fence. The back wire gate hung wide open. Inside the diamond were five long masses, covered with mismatched sheets, and a woman with wild hair, a shovel and a blue face mask, digging a large hole between other graves. Her presence paralyzed me and I watched her like a deer caught in the headlights of a speeding car. Mia's hand tightened around my own.

The distant woman stopped, looked over her shoulder, and put a hand on the gun at her hip.

"You armed?" she asked in a muffled voice, her eyes traveling from my own to the small child beside me.

"No." I could hardly speak. My focus remained on the five sheets. I knew what they were. I would have been stupid not to. The woman had done a careful job of tucking the bodies in beneath individual sheets. Peacefully and respectfully, like they had a right to. To this day, I'm not sure I thanked Holli for moving Mom for me. I think I would have lost my mind if I'd seen what they'd done to her.

"Well, come on," she said, waving us over. "Let me take a look at you both."

"The people," I said, pointing to the sheet-covered bodies. "My Mom," was all that came out, before I hung my head trying to hide my tears.

The woman dropped her shovel and sighed. "Oh dear."

I was a little boy again, shoulders hunched, chin to my chest, weeping. My grief erupted, the pain encompassing my entire being. My mother, in all her resilience, her strength, her beauty, had succumbed to something as ugly as a gun. They'd taken away her life, without thought or care of what she'd meant to the world. To me. Holli would tell me later that Mom was past child-bearing age, so it was likely the Coutts determined they had no use for her. Women were good for one thing, and one thing only. They'd thrown her away like a used toy.

Holli helped me find her, third in from the left. She only let me look at her face, though the dried blood across the sheets was hard to ignore. She looked peaceful, like she was sleeping — a visual I still replayed in my head. I lay beside her weeping and sweating, until the flies collected, willing myself to never forget all the small things that made Mom, mom.

The older woman brought us to her small house, a single bedroom place where I was left to grieve and sleep, and Holli was able to wash Mia up and venture back to Neil's home to collect some familiar things. Later that night, Holli explained her knowledge of the Coutts, of how she suspected they were collecting people from surrounding areas and bringing them back to their commune.

She and her husband had been survivalists for years until a test run went wrong. Widowed, Holli returned to her home, becoming somewhat of a recluse, obsessed with stockpiling resources for when the end came. When the armed Coutts men had arrived in town, she hadn't moved from her home.

"I don't want anything they've got," she told me, as we sat across from each other, talking on the floor of her living room that night.

"I just wish we hadn't been so eager for help."

"It's not your fault," she said with a sad smile, trying to

catch my eye. I refused to meet her gaze, uncomfortable she'd somehow known I'd been carrying so much guilt.

I swallowed and looked down at my feet. "She would have been so pissed they killed her like that," I said. "Unfair advantage. She couldn't even fight back." Tears prickled my swollen eyes once more. "It's not fucking fair."

Holli shook her head. "I know it's not. We'll lay her to rest. Give her a proper burial," she said, catching my eye. "You can go visit her now. Any time you want."

She meant her words to comfort, but nothing would ever close the hole in my heart. No matter what I did, I'd never be able to clean up that loss. I would never forget those gunshots, the casual demeanor of the armed men, or the worried glance Mom shot me when they'd lined us up. But later I was grateful for that grave. Holli had given me a place to visit Mom, to finish the things I'd never gotten to say.

The next day, Holli and I finished digging the graves and loaded the bodies in. Mia lay in the shade, doodling across pages of notebook paper Holli's late husband had tucked into his filing cabinet. When we were done, covered in dirt and sweat, we came back to Mom's and slept a full day. The day after, we started moving over Holli's supplies to Mom's house. Neither of us wanted to be alone.

It was the last time we'd seen those armed men. Holli and I made plans for what to do and where to go if they ever returned. But she theorized the Coutts wouldn't go out of their way to look for people. Not yet, anyway.

Each night I hoped for Neil's return, wishing Holli or I would see his shadow walking toward us one evening, grateful tears spilling from his eyes. But as days turned into weeks, I stopped hoping. I kept expecting more people to show up, others who maybe had escaped somehow — but after a few weeks had gone by, it was clear there was nobody left but us.

———

Two weeks after Mom died, Sid arrived.

To be honest, I was uncertain if my brother would show at all. Mom had been less than thrilled with his move to California several years prior. Unlike the midwest where we'd been instructed to flee, we'd heard the West Coast had become a wasteland. Wildfires had decimated most of the coast and resources were so scarce I'd heard of people dying as they waited for rations. The people who survived out there were hardcore rebels who thrived in chaos and had no problem murdering someone in cold blood for a new t-shirt. Sid had shared his half-baked plan of a fishing boat and a gun trade when he'd left, but we'd never heard much about what he was doing out there since.

Mom acted like she didn't care, but there were times I caught her sadness disguised as pride when she spoke of him as though he were a memory. She feared for his life, panicking when we managed to tune into one of the Coutts' news stations announcing some recent disaster out west — *a sure sign God was punishing their depravity*, the anchors would say.

But Sid arrived no worse for wear, cruising into town on a black sports bike so casually it was like the bird flu hadn't affected him at all. The sound of an engine spooked

Holli and me, unable to see the driver from the inside the house. We'd convinced Mia to stay in her room with headphones connected to a battery-powered cassette tape player.

But the minute I saw the bike round the corner on our street, I loosened the grip on the handgun Holli had handed me.

"That," I said, securing the safety, "is my god damn brother."

Holli's shoulders sagged as she looked at me. "I thought your brother lived in California?"

"He did," I answered. "I guess he decided to finally come home."

Sid parked the bike out in front of the house, placed his hands on his hips, looked at the sky, and breathed in. It was so unmistakably him. Sid could find a moment of solitude in the middle of a war zone. His rich sepia skin shone in the late autumn sun as he turned to warm both sides of his face. He'd grown a bit of unkempt facial hair, I assumed because of his travel. Sid was obsessive about his grooming habits, something that stayed with him to this very day.

Sid pushed the palm of his hand against his square jaw to crack his neck before I left the safety of our backyard to greet him. He was sweaty and smelly, but none of it mattered. Any grudge I'd held against him for leaving us disintegrated.

"Eli," he said in his deep, raspy voice, holding his arms out for me. We clapped each other on the back hard, a greeting we'd concocted as young teenagers — who knocked the wind out of the other one first? But before I even got a word out, emotion choked me.

Sid grasped my shoulders and held me at arm's length, trying to make sense of my grief-stricken features. "What is it?" he asked.

"Mom," I croaked.

"Mom?" Sid's voice faltered too, as he looked at the house and then back at me. "What? Is she sick?"

I shook my head.

"Eli," he said, his fingernails curling into my shoulders. "What?"

I glanced around at the empty neighborhood, heart pounding in my chest. "We should get inside," I whispered, trying to keep my voice steady.

"What is it, Eli?" Sid asked again, ignoring my request. "What is it?" His voice rose now, hysterical and on alert. "God damn it, Eli. You tell me what it is right now!"

And in that moment, I knew he knew what was coming, but wasn't ready to hear it. He didn't want to believe he'd driven all this way just to find out Mom was dead. That he had missed her by two weeks. That he hadn't been here to protect her.

"I'm sorry." My tears dripped from my chin and onto the pavement. "I'm so fucking sorry, man."

"Is she?" Sid pushed me backward and stepped back toward the road, his hands all over his face like he wasn't sure what to do with them. "Oh my god, oh my god." He dropped to his knees, palms in the grass, forehead to the dirt, and sobbed.

"Sid!" I cried, sliding to my knees beside him. I tried meeting him where he was, to comfort him — the only surviving member of my family.

"No, no, no," he whined, pounding his fists into the

ground as he wept, shuddering with his grief too big for anyone to hold.

Later, once we'd both calmed, we sat in the front yard, watching the sun as it moved across the sky. We walked together to the baseball diamond, and I showed him where we'd laid Mom to rest. After about an hour, Holli joined us with Mia, and Sid met the rest of our small crew.

But by the time we'd returned to the house, Sid was a changed man. He stayed quiet and sullen, locked in the bedroom for long periods of time. Mia's presence softened him occasionally, but he carried an edge on him that never let up. He had wanted to move, to get away from this place and the memory of Mom. But the hope of Neil returning to Mia had kept him quiet. And eventually, every so often, I'd see him walking toward the baseball diamond before he went to hunt.

17

MAURA

THE SUN SHONE high in the sky by the time Eli finished his story. And it was just that, wasn't it? A story. Since my arrival, I'd known my presence was a problem, simply for my surname. But for a moment, I'd had faith Eli wouldn't try to hold it against me. After all, he saved me from the creek. He invited me back to his camp, knowing who I was. But his blasphemous lies about my family I would not tolerate.

Heat rose in my cheeks as he looked toward the marked graves. To use the death of your own mother in such an obvious lie was wretched and unforgivable. And yet, the details of his story swirled through my mind. For the man to pick up a small child in the middle of nowhere and take her in as if she was his own wasn't what a sinner would do. It contradicted the fact that he still believed something untrue.

"Eli," I said, choosing my words with care, "I am really very sorry about your mother. But it wasn't my people that did this. It couldn't have been." I thought of Father and Andrew, the two most important people in my life. Certainly, Father could be ruthless, especially with miscreants, but to innocent people? The idea was laughable. "We aren't violent."

"But they have weapons?" he pressed.

"Well, yes, of course," I answered. "For hunting."

"They need automatic weapons for hunting?"

"I don't know anything about guns."

"Are you sure they're hunting animals?" Eli asked, his tone more critical with each inflection. "You wouldn't really, would you? Because I've seen them take people with my own eyes."

"They hunt for food," I answered, though his question rattled me. There were evenings Andrew came home with a small kill, or even empty-handed, but I'd always just assumed he'd given his conquests to others more in need. But the more I thought about it, the more I couldn't quite line up the edges Eli had revealed. Still, there was no *possible* way Father would condone killing innocent people the way Eli had described, even if he had known they existed. Killing was wrong. A mortal sin. I'd known that for as long as I could remember.

"Okay," Eli said, pressing his fingers against his forehead, "let me ask you this. Where did that group come from, then? Your men must have seen them at some point, hm? If they came down from that mountain?" He pointed toward Coutts Peak, its tip just visible above the trees. "Or do you just think I made that up for fun?"

I narrowed my eyes at him. "I don't think you made it up," I whispered.

"Then?" He shook his head, waiting for my answer. "Where'd they come from?"

"I wouldn't know," I said, "I told you. I keep to myself. I do my duties serving God and the Prophet, and that's all. I don't know—"

"You *do* know!" Eli's face reddened, and he got to his knees, his figure towering over mine. "They killed my friends! My neighbors! My mother! And you're just going to sit here and tell me you *don't know*?"

I wrung my hands together and met his gaze, my eyes studying his dark, dilated pupils.

"I *don't*!" I stressed, my chest heavy. "I just know Father would never condone killing. It goes against everything we believe in — everything he believes in!"

Eli sighed, sitting back on his heels. "Maura," he said, "did you ever think maybe your Father is lying to you?"

"No," I said, though that question nagged at me too. This wouldn't be the first time I'd had the same blasphemous thought. "Why would he?"

His face softened. "To keep you in line? Get you to behave? If he lied to you knowing we were out here—"

"But I don't know if he did!" I cried. "I don't know what he knows and—" I squeezed my eyes shut, "—I'm not *supposed to know*!"

"Maura." His voice was gentle now, more understanding.

"We live a structured and dutiful life to serve the Lord God and Father. The Prophet doesn't tell us everything. Women like me in the community have their parts to play. It would be unnecessary to burden us with every detail. So maybe he's hidden some things." Even that admission felt strange to say aloud. "But there are always reasons for his secrets."

I opened my eyes. Eli looked unconvinced.

"What you're suggesting is impossible," I whispered.

"Please," Eli said in a small voice. He sat back down, pulled his knees to his chest, and hugged them. "Consider that I'm telling you the truth, okay? I have no reason to lie to you. I've helped you. I've let you into our camp, shared my darkest days with you. I need to know you won't betray me."

"Betray you?" I asked. "Why would I—?"

"I mean, after I take you back," he said, placing his chin on his knees. "I need you to understand that we're in danger from your people. If you go back and tell them where we are…" He gave a heavy sigh. "Please, Maura."

Discovering people on the Outside was extraordinary. We had heard so many different times in so many different ways that the rest of the planet was empty. The last great plague swept away anyone who had sins to atone for. Everyone except the glorious Coutts commune. We had refused to embrace sin. We had been devout, knowing the Almighty God would come to bring us to his kingdom in the darkest of days. I squirmed, unwilling to admit I'd thought about that very thing — going to Father and telling him of the people I'd met out here. He had to know. He was the only one who could make things right again.

"Okay. If that's what you want, then I'll agree to it." I owed him that. And I would keep my promise of not revealing where they lived, even if I didn't believe his fears.

The tension in Eli's body slid away, and he sighed, laying his forehead against his knees, before looking back up at me sideways. "Thank you," he said. "I—"

A sharp bang plowed through whatever he'd meant to say.

In seconds, Eli flattened himself to the earth and covered his head with his hands. I shot straight up into the air, wide eyes darting from side to side, taking in our surroundings. My vision tunneled. I froze.

"Is that a—?"

"Get down!" Eli hissed, tugging the bottom of my large jacket. I collapsed to my knees, his arm around my back forcing me low to the ground. I pressed my face into the grass, inhaling earth, heart hammering as I turned to look at him. Crumbles of dirt lay between the whiskers of his beard. From here I saw dots of freckles and sun spots across his flat nose, his nostrils flaring as he breathed.

"It's them! The armed men!" I hissed.

"Shh!" he whispered, the tips of his fingers pressed against my lips. I wanted to ask him what we should do, where we should go, and if we were going to die, but couldn't form the words.

Eli lifted his head and looked around. I followed his gaze, trying to understand our options. Situated behind the brick school, the baseball field hid us from town, but I had no idea where the sound had come from.

"We need to move," he said, lifting himself from the ground as if in slow motion. He paused, eyes drifting toward the side of the building where there was nothing but an empty road.

"Follow me." Eli came to a low squat, using small steps to approach the gate we'd entered through. I mimicked his movements and together, we squeezed through. "C'mon," he said, grabbing my arm. "We need to get to cover."

We moved between the trees in a crouched run. I tried to keep my breath steady and stay in line with Eli, but the rocky terrain slowed my pace. We skirted a large tree, ducking behind a rock formation before a shrill scream echoed toward the heavens — pained, fearful, and desperate. No good came from that sound. It stopped me in my tracks.

An urgent hand tugged on my bicep. "Come on," he hissed. "Hurry!"

I blinked, meeting Eli's eyes, bright with fear. We hurried forward, dodging tree trunks and rocks, turning right, then left, leading us somewhere. With urgency driving me, I didn't stop to question where we were going.

He slowed, ducking between low bushes surrounding a large rock. I squatted beside him, thankful for something at our backs. We both rested against the solid surface, the air thick with our fear, both trying to steady our breathing. Eli dropped his knapsack to the forest floor, then flipped out the sides of his jacket, removing a small, black handgun from a holster on his hip.

I looked away. When I'd been afraid, Mother reminded me to breathe. To find something to focus on. To know God will always be there. I looked skyward. Trees waved in the wind, distorting the thick foliage, but I could still see the blue beyond. The sky's consistency kept me level, even when fear chewed away at me. God's most beautiful masterpiece.

I cried out to the Lord in my great trouble,
and He answered me.
I called to you from the land of the dead,
and Lord, you heard me!

"It's them," he confirmed. I looked back at him. He was standing now, his abdomen against the rock, squinting into the distance, the gun gripped in his right hand.

Not my Hunters, I told myself, squeezing my eyes closed, frozen in fear. *Not my people*. I hated my doubt. It went against everything Father, Mother, and Abigail had taught me, everything I'd studied and practiced. And yet, there was something very wrong about this. Eli's story seemed plausible, and I struggled to understand why.

I sucked in a breath and waited in silence for him to say something else. His body tensed each time he turned just a fraction of an inch. I became conscious of my own limbs, my breath as it came in and out, my fear still present but fading at the edges. I shrugged myself out of the heavy coat Eli had given me a few hours prior, my skin clammy with sweat.

"What about Mia? And the others?" I asked..

"They'll be okay. We've planned for this. They know what to do." He sounded confident. I hoped to God he was right. I placed my chin on my shoulder and looked up at him. He met my gaze.

"What about us?" I whispered.

"I'm a good shot. But if I tell you to run, you run that way." He pointed away from the town. Perhaps it was foolish, but I trusted him to protect me. Not God. Not Andrew. Not even Father. This man I barely knew.

Eli looked back over the rock. Using my hands against the flat surface, I straightened, turning so my head came just above the top at full height. It took a minute to understand what I was looking at. We had a good vantage point at the five buildings and paved road that made up the small town. A large, black truck idled, blocking the way to the main road.

But the thing that caught my attention was the group standing on the road. The green suits hanging in the hallway of Andrew's home suited three of the armed men. They surrounded three people kneeling on the ground.

I swallowed a gasp, blinking rapidly, trying to erase the image from my mind. Perhaps the suits had been stolen. Copied, even. Father had mentioned many communities like ours had once existed, but none had been so devout as ours. Perhaps this was another attempt?

Without realizing it, I'd shifted to stand in the brush, completely exposed. I felt a tug at my shoulder and I looked to my side. Eli studied me.

"You okay?"

I wasn't. Not even in the slightest. "I need to get closer," I told him in a forced voice, and before he reacted, I made my move, sprinting out from behind the rock, through the thinning trees where I paused at the back of two buildings.

"Maura!" Eli hissed, but I didn't turn. Dizzy from adrenaline, I darted forward until I could peer around the brick structure. Those suits. I recognized those suits.

Carefully, I came around the building where an old dumpster sat toward the front. I got low beside it, peering down the road, my heart beating in my throat. I was so close, I could make out the seams on their clothing, the handiwork of each weapon. And even though they faced away from me with their attention fixed on the people in front of them, it felt all too familiar.

Through the pounding of my ears came strained

voices. Someone was shouting. Someone else was crying. I had forgotten Eli behind me.

Then I heard it. His voice was so obvious, I almost cried out.

"Where the *hell* is she?"

I'd know that voice anywhere.

Anywhere.

It was Andrew.

I WASN'T sure how long I sat there, back up against the dumpster, watching my yellow bile gleam in the sun. There was a dead body nearby, killed by Andrew's hand. They had taken off in the truck with two prisoners. And they had been looking for *me*.

Horrible guilt settled on my shoulders. Had I been responsible for this innocent man's death? Had Andrew needed to kill in order to find me? Those things made little sense to me, but I grasped at them, trying to hold on to a reality that was falling out of my grip.

"Maura?"

A shadow blinked out the sun. Eli. A welcome, familiar face. He hovered over me, looking worried. I lost my words, but cried again, pointing around the dumpster toward the man Andrew had killed.

Killed. Oh, God. Dear God, God my Savior, please forgive me. Please forgive Andrew. Please.

Eli knelt next to me, his timid hand finding my shoulder. "Come on," he said, tugging at my shirt. "We need to get out of here. We can come back for him. Later."

I tried to find rationality in the depths of my brain, but

it was hidden beneath the layers of emotion consuming me. Eli took my hands and helped me stand.

The journey back to the group was slow and painful. It couldn't have been longer than a half mile, but it felt like days. I cried the whole way, an act that kept my face swollen through the next morning. There were too many things to work through, too many realizations and revelations slamming into me like bullets. I played those moments over in a loop, unable to get away from the purposeless death, the removal of the other people, the screams and pleas that fell on Andrew's deaf ears.

Eli kept his hand on my shoulder as we traveled together. I realized later, had someone from the Coutts Family seen us, the gesture would have been sinful. They taught us from a young age that men outside of family could not touch women. But then again, we were also taught not to murder people in cold blood.

I sensed the panic as we came into the trailer, the scurry of feet, the whispered discussions. But it all felt so far away. I dragged myself back to the living room couch, brimming with emotions I hadn't allowed myself to feel outside the comfort of my shared bedroom with Morgan. Forbidden feelings. Doubt. Anger. Hate.

Marrying Andrew had been downright terrifying. Joining a plural household with wives who'd grown to despise me had destroyed my confidence, uprooted jealous feelings I had to keep suppressed, and taken me away from the only home I'd ever known. It was against the Prophet's scripture to hate, to have feelings of doubt, to question the head of the household.

But now?

I had no choice. The dam I'd tried so hard to keep

closed had opened. Questions flew through my head without order, without reason, allowing me no time to slow down and remember the teachings of the Prophet. I could barely recall my name or what I was doing here. I stared at my hands, almost uncertain if they were mine. My husband was a liar. *A murderer*. He had betrayed the very teachings that built and structured our lives.

As I sat in the living room, I stared straight ahead at a dusty framed photo of Eli, Sid, and their mother.

I wondered if Andrew had been the one who killed her.

18

ELI

"WE NEED TO MOVE. Get up to the old office buildings. We can crash for the night and keep moving." Sid leaned his body against the wall next to the back kitchen door.

"We should wait until dark," I suggested.

"So, you want to sit here and wait for them to knock on the door?" Sid crossed his arms.

"Of course not. I just want to be smart about it, is all," I answered. I'd lugged Maura the entire way home, every nerve of my being on edge, fearful the Hunters would ambush us. My adrenaline waned, exhaustion hovering in my peripheral. "They didn't follow us. They don't know we're here. If we leave now, there's too much of a chance they'll see us. Plus, even with the three of us, we can't possibly pack up everything we'd need to take in the next hour. We can't leave all of this behind."

He picked his head up from the wall and narrowed his eyes at me. "Yes we can, Eli. Jesus. We can find fresh supplies. It doesn't matter when we leave, they could see us either way. Let's *go*."

I drummed my fingers against the kitchen island. "Just give me a minute to think."

"Like you did when you picked her up?"

"Sid, I swear—"

"They can make it up and down that mountain in as little as two hours. Even if they go back and drop those people off, they could be back before *you* decide it's safe to move," Sid challenged. "You're being stupid and letting your emotions cloud your judgment. You want to live? We need to move. Fast. Before they're on our doorstep."

Before it's too late.

I inhaled, closing my eyes as I clenched my fingers into fists. How could Sid be okay with leaving all of this behind? The home Mom worked so hard to provide for us, the garden Holli worked so hard to cultivate, and the only home I'd ever known. But those thoughts brought the truth to light — Sid was right. I *was* attached to this place, the memories that lived within these walls, both before and after the worst had hit us. The idea of leaving Mom's body at the baseball diamond made my stomach turn. What if we never came back?

Through a crack in the door at the end of the hall, I watched Holli scoop Mia up and lay her back on the bed. I glanced back at Sid. "Fine." I pushed myself back from the island.

Sid lifted himself off the wall, following me. "You know why they're here, right?" he asked.

"Don't start," I warned.

"The longer she's with us, the more of a target we're painting on our backs."

"I *tried*," I said. "We were on our way back. What'd you want me to do? Leave her out there again?" I forced a laugh. "No. Let me guess. You probably wish we'd gotten shot out there," I spat. "I suppose then you wouldn't have to worry about this, right? It'd have made your life a whole helluva lot easier."

"Fuck you."

"Go pack up the guns and ammo," I growled.

"Now I'm supposed to take orders from *you*?"

"What, you want to keep fighting?" I yelled. "I thought you said we needed to move."

Sid closed the space between us, staring down his nose at me, his nostrils flaring. I tensed, straightening, waiting for him to make the first move and the truth, I would've welcomed it. Anything to distract me from the nightmare circumstances we found ourselves in. He flinched, bringing his fist up to my chin without touching me, his eyes narrowed in on the spot he wished to hit. I looked up at him, *daring* him, but he closed his eyes and let his arm fall to his side. With a huff, I turned away from him before I said something I regretted and didn't turn back around until the hallway door slammed.

I ran my hands over my face, bringing my fingertips together at my nose. Between my fingers I watched Maura sitting in the living room, the same glazed over expression washed across her features. My intention had not been to traumatize her today. But there was a part of me that felt triumphant she'd seen her people for what they were. Guilty satisfaction. It made me feel like a piece of shit.

With a heaviness in my chest, I approached the couch. "Maura?" She held her distant gaze. "Hey, listen. I'm sorry you had to see them do that. But…"

"I know the man who killed him," she declared.

"You do?" I tried to hide my curiosity. "Who was it?"

She stifled a sob, choking it down with an inhale. "Andrew," she said. "My...h-h-husband." She cupped her head in her hands and wailed, rocking back and forth where she sat. It was no longer easy to surprise me with much, but a chill settled over me as I processed her answer. Although I knew Maura's husband was a Hunter, it was still a horrible revelation. The slight satisfaction I'd felt earlier melted, replaced with undeniable pity. I was familiar with grief and its all-consuming nature, how it would eat away at any semblance of happiness you might, somehow, be able to cling onto — and I suspected Maura had very little. Betrayal was one of the worst kinds of grief.

"Your husband?"

She nodded, continuing to weep.

"I'm so sorry," I said, knowing it wouldn't help at all. "But Maura, you need to listen to me." She looked up, her breath coming in short, small bursts as she tried to contain her cries. "Sid's right — we need to leave before they come back. If they hadn't found those people, they might've found us. I'm pretty sure they went back toward your commune, but I can't be sure. They could come back in no time. And they will." I grimaced. "For you."

"I thought you wanted to take me back?" Her eyes shone with fresh tears.

"I—"

"Eli, I don't know if I can go b-b-back."

I unraveled her words with a heavy heart, struggling with my empathy. I wanted to be indifferent to her plight and prioritize the safety of my group, but that would mean leaving Maura behind. And what kind of man did that make me? I'd be no better than the Coutts.

I nodded, worried what Sid's fury might look like if we dragged Maura along forever. He might leave. Worse, he might try to kill her himself. There was no way around the fact that at some point, she needed to go back. But I couldn't worry about that right now.

"I understand," I heard myself say. "You can...come with us."

Her shoulders sagged with visible relief and she tucked her chin to her chest, fresh tears rolling down her swollen cheeks.

"Thank you," she whispered, glancing back up at me. "I can't thank you enough."

"It's nothing," I lied. I raised my gaze as Holli wandered into the kitchen from the back bedroom, her hands on her hips.

"Hol," I said, standing from the couch. "We've gotta move."

She sighed, hanging her head. "Figured as much," she said, eyeing the jars and preserves she'd gathered over the past few months.

"Can I help?" Maura asked.

I glanced at Holli, worried she might question why Maura assumed she was coming with us. But there was nothing in her expression to make me think she disapproved of my decision. "Mia," she said, nodding toward the bedroom. "Help her pack her things."

Maura nodded before standing, wobbling on unsteady legs. I threw out an arm to catch her, and she gripped me with her fingernails.

"You okay?" The question felt stupid as soon as it left my mouth.

She tilted her head to look up at me. "No," she answered, and I found myself surprised by her honesty.

"That's fair," I answered. "I don't think most of us are."

I CREAKED open the door to my old bedroom. Sid stood over our small collection of guns, laid out on the lower bunk — two hunting rifles, one revolver, and one pistol. My handgun remained in my hip holster. Boxes of bullets sat beside the weapons, a few of the cardboard lids open, revealing our meager ammo. Concerning, but not the priority right now.

"Hey," I said.

He didn't look up.

I sighed. "I'm sorry. I shouldn't have said you wished me dead. But we have to take Maura with us," I said. At this, he looked up, his jaw tightening. "She can't stay here. If they find her—"

"They find her!" he shouted. "She's who they're looking for!"

"She's shaken. That man out there wasn't just some Hunter. It was her husband."

Sid's lips curled into a vicious smile. "Good."

"It's not," I said. "It's horrible."

"Yeah, well, horrible things happen to horrible people. It's called karma."

"Sid."

He shrugged. "I'm calling it like I see it."

"No," I said, crossing my arms. "You're being an asshole. She's not involved in all the shit that's gone on, so stop. Your hatred is solving nothing."

"She's a grown ass woman. And you're trying to tell me she's got no idea what the people she worships are doing around her? That she doesn't *agree* with the crap they've pulled over the years?" He pulled a brown duffel bag from the dresser. "And now you're just dragging her along with us like none of that even matters?"

"She doesn't *know* anything else," I said through my teeth. "How many times do I need to go over this with you?"

"You know what they did to people like me?" Sid stopped in his tracks, eyes wide, staring me down. His hateful glare unsettled me. "You know what those monsters did to the people in my community? All under the false pretenses of their *religion*? They made it okay to hurt people because of who they loved. They made it *okay*." His voice cracked.

"Sid, I—"

He shook his head. "You don't *get it*, Eli, and you never will. That's why I left here in the first place. I shouldn't have come back." He turned away. "You'll never understand what that feels like."

"I'm sorry. I wasn't thinking," I admitted, tense frustration working its way into my shoulders. "I was trying to help someone in need. Just like Mom taught us we should."

He gave a strained laugh. "Mom's dead. Remember?"

"As if you've ever let me forget," I said under my breath. "I know you're angry. But it's *not* Maura's fault.

And Mom would want you to give her a chance. She'd give her a chance."

"Well, we have no way of knowing, do we?" Sid said. "It doesn't matter, anyway. I see where your loyalties lie. We all do."

"What the hell is that supposed to mean?"

"That you should've thought more before you brought her back here!" he shouted, turning his body so he faced me. I took a step back at his presence. "Now we're not just losing our camp, but we're uprooting Mia. Haven't you considered—"

"Don't!" I growled. "Don't bring up Neil."

"Well, that's why we've been sitting out here for so goddamn long, ain't it?" he spat back, eyes narrowed and full of hate. He pointed his finger toward the hallway. "To wait for Neil? To find him for Mia? And you want to help a *Coutts* family member over your own?" His upper lip curled as he looked me up and down. "For what?"

"For a *person*," I said. "Maura's a person, just like you and me! You think what I did out there was easy? You think I could have left her out there to die? Jesus Christ Sid, I'm not like—"

"Like what?" he sneered.

I closed my mouth. Sid had done unspeakable things to make it back here alive. I knew it even though he'd never said it outright.

"Like nothing," I answered. "Forget it, I didn't mean—"

"Sure," Sid said, hanging onto the last syllable. "Just like you didn't mean for her to follow you, just like you didn't mean for those Hunters to find us, and just like you didn't mean for us all to leave our camp. I got it now, Eli."

He turned his back, leaving me in the muddy water of doubt. I couldn't remember the last time Sid had ever been this angry with me. Could my mistake change our relationship forever? The possibility hurt so much worse than leaving our camp behind.

19

MAURA

I LET my hand trail across the flimsy wooden wainscoting. The hall seemed longer than it was, dark without windows, the corners cluttered with overflowing laundry baskets. It had been hours — hadn't it? And I still couldn't shake the hum reverberating between my ears. I tried hard to shut it out, but that distinct pop of the gun kept returning. The memory made me flinch each time I thought of it, so close, yet somehow unreachable.

Did Andrew return home after he shot that man? Did he unlace his muddy boots and walk into the kitchen, kissing his wives, patting his children on the head as if he hadn't taken a life hours before? And what of the other two he'd ordered them to take? The children, begging for their own father's life? The memory of their cries made my stomach ache, and I paused, hand against the wall, inhaling long breaths.

I'd only questioned my Prophet a few times in my life. The first time had been quite a scandal among us young girls still in purpose training as we whispered during our free time. A woman in the commune had gotten pregnant — a true blessing from God! But, according to the girls telling the story, the baby hadn't grown in the right place and the woman sought medical care without her husband's permission.

I was still young, but even then I'd been taught inter-ference in God's creation was blasphemy. The Lord made no mistakes. Weeks later, another rumor spread. Both the mother and baby died as the Lord saw fit. The woman had deceived her husband. But even in my juvenility, I failed to see how her actions had been wrong, but her husbands hadn't. Father boasted about what gifts the Lord bestowed upon him so he could share his medical knowledge with the righteous, so why didn't he save them?

The second time was not a rumor. During my gradua-tion year of purpose training, I witnessed a marriage between the daughter of a farmer who lived low on Coutts Peak. A wicked Outsider had killed her father and her young, widowed mother was in line to be married, and so the daughter was too. Despite Abigail's insistence it was what the Lord ordered, a marriage between a thir-teen-year-old and a man in his fifties with six wives never sat quite right with me. But then again, neither had the third time I'd questioned my Prophet, which was when he'd arranged my marriage to Andrew.

But even if I didn't quite understand the reasoning behind Father's decisions, I could always chalk it up to God somehow. I explained these things away and passed them off as something above my level of comprehension. Yet there was something this time that snapped within me, like a bubble bursting from pressure, and all of those things I'd questioned — those things I'd tied up tight in a bow felt like they were unraveling again.

I approached the door at the end of the hall, lingering in the doorframe. It was a small room with brown carpet that might've been fluffy and soft once but had since been matted down by decades of feet upon it. A white trundle bed was pushed up into the corner, colorful drawings covering the wall beside it. Mia lay on her back, her feet dangling off the edge of the bed. She looked up as I entered, her brown eyes less fearful than the first time we'd met.

"Hi Maura." She said my name with an emphasis at the end before breaking into a grin.

"Hi," I said with a little wave. "I'm here to help you pack up your things."

"For what?"

"Well..." I dug the toe of my shoe into the floor. "We have to leave here. From this house." Despite my best efforts, I couldn't help but look away. Meeting her gaze felt shameful, like she saw through me and understood this was my fault.

"To be safe?" Her little voice asked so casually, I almost wasn't sure I heard her correctly. I looked up.

"Yes," I said. "To be safe."

She nodded as if this were a very normal thing. "Holli said we might have to." She hopped up off the bed and walked to her closet. Pulling aside a bi-folding door, she reached inside, then handed me a small backpack. "I'll pack this one. Holli said only the important stuff."

I was charmed by her no-nonsense approach. This group had been here a full year, for about as long as I'd been married to Andrew. I missed Mother's home, but I'd made my peace with the unfamiliar house. And yet, the thought of picking up and leaving, even with my minimal belongings, would be upsetting.

"This is my dad," Mia told me, handing me the same brass frame Eli had shown me a few days prior. I scanned it again — Neil's gentle grin prompted, no doubt, by the way Mia laughed in his arms.

And now that man was missing. Eli blamed his absence on the Hunters, and after what I'd witnessed out in broad daylight, I think I believed him. If Andrew and his men were capable of killing an innocent man, then they were certainly capable of orphaning a child. I forced a smile at the photo, pinprick tears threatening the corner of my eyes.

"Your dad looks like a very nice man," I said, taking a spare t-shirt from her bed to wrap it for the backpack.

"He is," she said, returning to dig in the closet. "Here's my favorite pajamas," she said, holding up a mismatched pair of Christmas sleepwear. She handed it to me and I folded it for the bag.

One by one, Mia packed her most prized possessions. A few of her favorite outfits. A stuffed bear named Mindy. A handcrafted wooden heart that slid open to reveal a photo of her beautiful, red-haired mother. Two head-bands, five ponytail elastics, her toothbrush and tooth-paste, three books, and a man's long-sleeved t-shirt. It was all that would fit.

We left the room. Eli sat on the living room couch, packing a bag of medical supplies. Holli bustled around the kitchen, glasses and jars clanging against each other every so often as she collected her remedies.

"I need a pen," Mia announced as she placed her backpack by the back door.

"In the kitchen, love," Holli called. "What do you need it for?"

Mia smiled. "I'm writing daddy a note to tell him we're leaving," she said.

A stark silence followed her statement. Holli froze in her tracks, two jars wobbling in her grip. Eli pushed his lips together, gauze and band-aids forgotten, and looked over his shoulder at Mia.

As she took inventory of the room, Mia's smile vanished. She tensed, fists clenching and arms coming up to hug her middle, like she hoped to disappear within herself.

"Oh Mia," Eli breathed, getting to his feet. "We...can't leave your dad a note right now."

"Yes, we can," she said, moving to step around him. "I need a pen."

"Mia." Eli reached out to catch her small frame as she tried to pass. "Mia," he said again, clutching her to his chest. "I'm so sorry, but we can't."

"Please?" she said, struggling against his strength. "We have to tell him where we're going," she said, her voice quivering with panic. "He...he won't be able to find me if we don't."

Holli came around the side of the island and got to her knees in front of the little girl. Mia calmed, her eyes meeting Holli's.

"Mia," Holli soothed, "We're in trouble. We need to leave, to hide, for a little while. Okay? Let's write daddy a note, but we won't tell him *where* we're going. We'll just tell him we love him very much."

Mia slumped in defeat, her quest for the pen forgotten. Instead, she succumbed to a shuddering cry, pained and confused; a cry of longing. Holli reached out for her, wrapping the girl and Eli up into a hug. She hushed her; a meager attempt at comfort that couldn't even patch up the agony Mia must have felt.

The emptiness and guilt from Andrew's act intensified, and I backed up, bumping against the living room wall, stepping over a pile of blankets. I wished I could disappear. Father told us these people should be monsters. They should be killing each other in the name of greed. They should be careless, hateful, and filled with sin. But as I watched the three of them, I knew, despite my teachings, it couldn't be further from the truth. These people were kind. There was love in their hearts. They wanted safety. They wanted to live. Mia wanted to find her father. The father my people might've taken.

I felt sick.

The men who were supposed to be the Servants of the Lord were murdering innocent folk. The people who were supposed to be plagued by the Devil, it seemed, were not. My soul was soaked in fear and grief. As long as I lived, I would never get the image of Andrew out of my head, nor would I forget his cruelty and indifference. I could never trust him. Panic built in my chest at the thought of returning home. How could I ever learn to love a monster?

20

ELI

OUR NEIGHBOR, Marco, had driven home a used Dodge RAM a few weeks before the worst of the bird flu hit. He'd boasted about the size of the truck bed to everyone who would listen. Six weeks later, Mom and I found Marco, bloated and belly up nearby the rainwater reservoir we'd been collecting our water from. The keys to his truck were still in his pocket.

Mom had cried the whole way home, wondering whether or not to knock on his front door to tell his family. He'd had a wife and a daughter too, but we hadn't seen them in weeks. I offered to go and later came home, crying myself, sweaty and dirt-covered, after burying them in their backyard.

We sifted through their house for anything of use. It felt morbid and cruel as we sterilized the food and tools they would never put to use. After Mom died and Holli joined us, she'd suggested the idea of a getaway vehicle, and Marco's truck had been the first thing to cross my mind. We kept it maintained, changing its oil, and driving it every so often up and down our little dirt street.

As the sun lowered behind Coutts Peak, I turned the key in the ignition, bringing the truck to life with a roar. It rumbled beneath my feet as though it were trying to show off its power.

Maura scurried out from the gate with Mia in her arms, their packs bouncing in sync. She reached for the rear passenger side door and helped Mia up, before climbing in herself. The pair smelled of sweat, sticky sweet in the afternoon heat.

"Sid and Holli are doing a last sweep," she said, closing the door behind her.

I nodded, glancing at them in the rearview mirror. Maura busied herself with buckling Mia into the middle seat. It felt almost normal, as if the girl from the Coutts commune had been part of our group all along. But the illusion shattered as I caught sight of Mom's old trailer. My heart still ached at the memory of her.

I'd made my way in and out of the crumbling state system by the time I was seven, and over the next two years, I lost both parents to addiction. While the loss had been profound, there was nothing from those relationships to salvage, even at that young age. I loved my parents blindly, but I didn't really know them.

And then, at nine years old, after spending two months in a crowded group home for orphaned children, Mom reached out to my social worker to inquire about my situation. Sid and I had been friends since preschool and, even though she was a single mother herself, she wanted to do something. My last foster placement was in the

Simmons' home, and I was adopted into their little family a year later.

This place had always been home to me. Before the flu, before Mom's death, before Holli, Mia, and Maura. This place meant safety. I'd grown here, I had learned and been reprimanded. I'd skinned my knees, had my first kiss, and gotten into my first fight on this property. There were marks on the walls I knew well, stains on the carpets and floors that clutched me in their memories. The backyard, now covered with crops and an outhouse, had once been a place of exploration, a quiet refuge for a few lanky kids to figure life out. Sid and I had adventured back there, created stories and imaginary sights. We'd talked about girls, drank our first beer, and smoked our first joints beneath the sliver of the moon, unbothered by the horrors unfolding in the world.

It was more than a house, more than a property, and more than a piece of land. It was my home. A good home. One that protected me as best it could. I found love in that home. I found a family.

The high gate swung open. Tote bags filled Holli's arms, all of which I assumed contained seeds and flowers and herbal remedies. Sid followed, two rifles slung over his shoulder, the brown duffel clutched in his hands. His eyes darted to either side of the property before he pulled the gate closed behind them. The pair entered the truck — Sid climbing into the passenger seat, and Holli into the backseat.

"Good?" I asked, eyeing my brother. Tension hung thick in the air between us.

"Yep," he answered, looking out the window. "Let's go."

With a heavy sigh, I began to drive.

"SLOWLY," Sid said.

Half his body hung out the side window as he guided the truck around a collapsed part of the road with his flashlight. Years of relentless storms and no maintenance work led to failing infrastructure across the country, and in the year since H5N1 hit, things only worsened.

Night had fallen about an hour ago. We'd made it a good thirty miles before we'd lost the sun, and without knowing where the Hunters were, headlights were out of the question.

"Good." He wiggled his fingers to encourage me forward. "Keep coming."

Even with the truck's power, the tires sunk in the muddy grass, tilting us sideways. I pressed my toe against the gas pedal, inching us around the treacherous drop. The darkness made it impossible to see how far down we might fall if the ground gave way beneath us. I'd made a conscious decision not to look at my passengers.

Sid's shoulders relaxed, and he pulled himself back into the vehicle, giving me a nod of finality. I let out a breath, allowing my gaze to travel over the three people in our backseat. Mia slept in Holli's lap, her blonde hair over her face, moving up and down with every breath she took. The older woman pressed her head up against the window, tired eyes inspecting the road. Maura leaned back in her seat, curly hair framing her face. Her dark lashes lay against her round cheeks, but even though her eyes were closed, I could tell she wasn't sleeping.

"Shouldn't be much further," Sid offered, shifting in his seat.

I nodded. After the turmoil of the past few days, my body and brain were more exhausted than they'd been in quite some time, and the overwhelming darkness was not helping my fatigue.

With the Coutts commune mountains to our right, the mountainous terrain declined, making way to the flatter land we approached. Our destination sat dead ahead — the last remnants of corporate America in our area. Rows of old office and apartment buildings, empty since the start of the millennia, sat nestled up against a rocky, tree-filled backdrop.

Only a few miles beyond sat the Coutts' landfills, incinerators, hazardous waste facilities, and recycling plants at the base of the mountainside. It was the closest piece of Coutts land to where I'd lived most of my life; always an untouchable, mysterious place. A large building Mom once identified as a waste sorting facility stuck out from the rock, emitting a low green-blue light shining out over hundreds of acres of waste.

To the Coutts, I was sure this seemed like a wasteland, but for us on the Outside, this was prime scavenging ground. The locals had learned there was little security over this place, leading to new work dedicated to sifting through Coutts garbage, harvesting things to be consumed or used for other things like construction work or medical care. Adaptation was essential for human survival.

The road we traveled down had once been a border — one side was Coutts land, the other side belonged to the United States. The difference was so stark it almost hurt to look at; dilapidated buildings next to a sophisti- cated waste center. I wondered how people in the sorting facility looked out over those buildings and justified the separation between themselves. Did they watch people rummage through garbage, looking for discarded remnants to keep their families alive? The thought made me seethe.

"There," Sid said, breaking me from my thoughts, pointing toward the road leading us to our destination. "We should park farther up the road and walk the rest of the way." He rummaged through the brown duffel. "Just in case." My limbs ached at his suggestion, but I knew he was right. We were being hunted, and exhaustion was no excuse to ignore safety.

We entered the small town, traveling down cracked pavement. The glow from the waste facility reflected in the building windows, making them look like alien eyes, watching us as we traveled further into the dark array of buildings.

I pulled into an old parking lot still filled with cars of days past — some in decent shape, others just a shell. A thick layer of grime covered them, but at least for the night, I could only hope our addition would not be noticed. I parked and yanked the keys out of the ignition, looking around at my weary companions.

"Everybody ready?"

Nobody answered, and I didn't blame them.

21

MAURA

AT ELI'S ORDER, the group began to move, doors creaking open, feet hitting the pavement. The truck stood in a long-ago abandoned parking lot, sandwiched between two brick buildings. Thick clouds rolled across the sky, occasionally concealing a crescent moon. But the thing capturing my attention lingered in the distance and I could not stop looking at it.

Lights from the windows built into the mountainside illuminated mounds of trash, visible through the gaps between the buildings. But it wasn't just trash. As we'd driven by, I glimpsed bulging bags of *things*, books, clothes, and boxes, some labeled as medical supplies, rife for the taking. My brain worked in overdrive, trying to find the answer to what this place was — a dumping ground for the Outsiders, perhaps? But even if I couldn't admit it outright, I knew from the lights shining through dozens of clean, modern windows it had to be part of our commune. Only, this was a part of my home I'd never seen. If I was honest, it was a part I'd never even considered.

Eli's face appeared in the car window, one brow raised as he studied me through the dusty barrier. "You coming?" he asked, his voice muffled through the glass.

I blinked, nodding, grasping for my pack on the floor between my feet. Eli opened the door for me and I used the side step to get down. The air smelled awful, like eggs gone bad, and I struggled to stomach it without gagging. I focused on securing my backpack, filled with medical supplies and extra clothes, over my shoulders.

"C'mon," Eli said, impatiently.

"Wait," I whispered, locking eyes with him. I couldn't stand it. I was so tired of wondering about everything. My world inside the commune had been small and simple. Out here, around every turn, I constantly bumped up against things I didn't understand. Against things that challenged what I'd once been so certain of. "What is this place?"

His eyes widened, then he sighed, rubbing his hand against his head. He looked exhausted. "It's the Coutts waste center."

"The waste center," I repeated.

"Where you all throw your trash." He looked between the buildings. "Why? You've never—?" He broke off, the familiar look of pity crossing his features.

But I gazed beyond him, back at the heaps of garbage. My hands clenched into fists, my anguish so red-hot I didn't hear what he said next. I thought, instead, of how Father and Andrew had told me a year ago how they'd selected me for some prestigious duty — a way to contribute to my family, to lead a purpose-driven life as someone not yet with child. How I had *agonized* over that responsibility, heading to my assigned zones, picking through rubbish and overgrowth. How I'd been chastised for not bringing back enough, as if that was the true measure of my worth. Of my godliness. Of my devotion to the Prophet.

And here sat all the discarded things. A scavengers dream. Thrown over the mountainside and left to rot. I had crossed the creek for just a *fraction* of what sat in those piles. To please my husband. A man I'd seen kill in cold blood.

I felt sick again. Trying to make sense of this through the horror of Andrew's actions was too much to bear. I leaned up against the truck behind me, the world too big, the air too thick with decay as I bent over, attempting to curl into myself. Only a week ago there had been certain things my life revolved around. The Prophet's omniscience. Andrew's holiness. The sanctity of our Coutts Family. And the glimmer of hope that my scavenging could one day be enough for Andrew, Abigail, and Joanna.

And now? I was no longer certain of any of them.

My head ached as I grappled with the reality of what I'd seen with my own eyes and the teachings drilled into me from such a young age. How could only days of being on the Outside unravel a lifetime?

I suddenly understood my sister. She had spent weeks out here before — she'd seen things she couldn't speak of, things I hadn't wanted to hear. I'd never given her a chance. I'd shut her down with the claim of wickedness and sin, told her she should ignore those things she'd seen and turn her attention to the Lord and Prophet. Had she lived the past year in secrecy? In fear? Feeling as alone as I did now? The guilt only added to my grief.

There was a hand on my shoulder, gripping me, grounding me back in reality. My hands found my knees, and I took a few deep breaths, trying hard not to gag at the smell encompassing us. I looked up. There was Eli, and behind him, Holli. Their eyes traveled over me, then back to each other — a gaze of understanding between them, and I couldn't find it in me to care. My chest was tight. I was losing everything I knew to be true, and these people did not understand.

"Maura." My name sounded distant. Eli's hand was still on my shoulder. "Can you walk?" His eyes were bright with urgency. "We need to move."

I understood. I'd have time to process these emotions later, but it was difficult. Nothing seemed real. Everything was wrong.

"Maura?" Holli approached, her smaller hand at my back. "Breathe. In through your nose and out through your mouth." We locked eyes, and I found calm in her concern. "You're okay," she said.

My breath came in irregular heaves, so I took her advice, closing my eyes, letting my breath travel through my body in quick waves that became slower each time. The tension in my shoulders relaxed, and I allowed my head to hang forward before the tightness in my chest eased and the world stopped spinning around me.

By the time I opened my eyes, it was only Holli beside me, rubbing gentle circles between my shoulder blades. I bit my lip, shame spreading across my cheeks in hot waves.

"I'm fine," I croaked, not meeting her eyes as I lifted myself from the side of the truck.

"You sure?"

"Yes, I'm sorry, I—"

Holli waved her hand in my direction. "You have nothing to be sorry for," she said, beginning to walk toward the rest of the group. "It's no surprise you're having anxiety over what's happened to you. It's all very normal."

I wanted to tell her how *not* normal all of this was, but it seemed impolite to contradict her sympathy.

We joined the others beside the lot and walked, following Sid's tall frame, the hunting rifles hung over his shoulder, shadowed by the buildings. Eli wore a hiking pack with a step and a strap to hold Mia secure. Her head rested on his shoulders, tiny hands gripping both of his arms. Holli handed me Mia's small backpack, and I hugged it to my chest, grateful it gave my hands something to do.

Chunks of pavement were missing from the deteriorated street. Trash littered the dark corners, blown across the road from the waste center, or left long ago. Jars clinked together as we walked, becoming the only sound perforating the silence between us. I was grateful for the quiet.

We passed building after building and I wondered what differentiated one from the rest. The windows were too dusty, cracked, or dark to see much inside. At last, the street ended in a U-shape cul-de-sac, two cars still parked on either side. Sid paused, edging us to the right toward a three-story brick building.

"C'mon," he whispered into the night, crossing the

sidewalk toward a shattered glass door, covered by a torn green awning. With a rustle and a click, Holli produced a flashlight and flipped it on, showering the crumbling sidewalk with a thick beam of light. Beside us, a rabbit jumped up on its hind legs in surprise. I heard a quick swish and a small whimper. Sid pulled up his knife, still inside the body of the rabbit, quivering with its last breaths.

"Dinner," he whispered, eyeing his prize with satisfaction. "Unlucky bastard."

"Come on now," Holli said, motioning toward the door. "Let's get inside."

22

ELI

LONG AGO, someone had etched a company logo in the center of the building's front door. Half of it was gone now, shattered on the sidewalk. Beyond, the dark interior mocked us. We had scoped this place out months ago in case of an emergency. Our last stop near the Coutts commune before heading farther northwest. Still, the unfamiliar territory kicked my adrenaline up a notch.

Sid led us forward, glass crunching as he pulled what was left of the door away from its frame. He turned to us, finger at his lips, the pistol clutched in his free hand. The rabbit's blood made a thick plopping sound as it dripped from where it hung on Sid's waist.

One by one, we scaled the threshold. Mia whined from my back and I reached over my shoulder, letting my fingers stroke her hair. "S'alright," I told her. "We're going to eat and go to sleep soon." She nuzzled her head into my shoulder, sniffling. If I was exhausted, I could only imagine how her little body felt after today.

We entered a small lobby. Inside, the office building

smelled stale but not putrid — a relief. There would be no fresh bodies to share space with. A black cut-out image of the logo that had once graced the front door hung behind a large, C-shaped desk. Someone had taken red ink to the wall below it and written: *SELL OUTS* in wide, angry letters. Two overturned chairs remained in the far corner closest to where we stood, beside a pair of fake potted plants, frozen in forever containers.

Together, we journeyed through, our boots muffled against a worn carpet as we approached an archway leading to a single elevator and the belly of the building. On either side, desks, chairs, boxes, and old filing cabinets covered the area in varying formations. With the only windows at the far end of both sides, the place was dark and, despite the lingering humid air, a little cold.

Mia whined again. "What's wrong?" I whispered.

"Water," she cried, mucus rattling her tiny voice.

"Here," Holli reached for Mia, lifting her from the pack and relieving the pressure from my back. I shrugged off the backpack and let it fall to the ground before rolling out my neck and shoulders. Holli bounced Mia in her arms around the room, letting her take small sips from her water bottle.

Sid pointed to the left. "Eli, take this floor. I'll take the second floor, and I'll meet you all on the third."

I nodded, pulling my handgun free from its holster. Sid jogged off toward a door in the distance with a faded STAIRS sign hung above.

I ventured to our left, finding a women's restroom dark and empty. "In here," I waved Holli over. She took my cue and, with a nod of thanks, carried Mia into the bathroom. "You too," I told Maura, "at least until we know it's safe."

She glanced into the room, then back at me. "I want to come with you."

I studied her. For the week we'd been confined to Mom's trailer, she'd been cautious to make eye contact. But now, in the dark of the office building, she met my gaze fiercely. There was an inkling of fight within her. I gave her a reluctant nod before sticking my head back into the bathroom.

"Got your gun? Flashlight?"

"Don't father me, boy," Holli shot back, shining her light in my eyes. "Be careful."

I squinted and grinned before closing the door. The lock clicked on the other side. Maura hovered in my peripheral as I reached for my flashlight.

"Stay close," I said, clicking the light on. "Since you don't have a gun. I need you to stay directly behind me."

"Okay."

I took a deep breath, situated my flashlight above my gun, and walked into the dark depths of the building. Beyond the central area, false walls separated the desks from each other in uneven rows, shielding the rest of the space from view. We walked through them, peering into each one as we went, making every step intentional. In the dark, the makeshift offices looked even more depressing than they might have when the building was still in operation.

"People worked here?" Maura asked, inspecting a desk over my shoulder.

"Yeah," I said. " A long time ago, before we were born."

"What did they do?"

I shrugged, shining my light over the dusty graveyard of office supplies. "No idea."

As we entered the third row of desks, Maura's footsteps faltered and I backtracked, finding her clutching a picture frame in her hand. I held up the flashlight to make sure there wasn't a threat behind her, but the room was still empty.

"What happened to these people?" she asked, looking up from the frame. She turned it around so I could see a faded photo of a young family, two proud parents holding their newborn, smiling. A moment suspended in time. They did not know what was to come. "Do you think they're dead?"

The question shocked me, coming from Maura. I had her pinned as a see no evil type of Coutts. The kind who knew not to ask questions you didn't want answers to.

I opened my mouth, but nothing came. Nothing to wash that harsh reality away. She pulled the frame back into her chest, cradling it as she seemed to soak in the helplessness so many of us out here felt as things continued to crumble around us. There was a part of me that wanted her to suffer, just as we did. To understand the unbearable grief we carried on our shoulders every hour we remained alive. The survivors' guilt that kept us awake at night. The ever-nagging question of *why me*?

"I... don't know." My half-hearted words felt feeble and forced. It sounded ridiculous because it *was* ridiculous. No matter what, the people in that photo were more than likely dead and rotting by now. I knew that. She knew that. There was no sugar coating it.

"I just don't understand," she sniffed, wiping away the dust on the frame.

"Understand what?"

"This!" she exclaimed, waving the photograph at me. "This!" She stuck her arms in the air and motioned around us. "How could God let this happen?"

Anger rippled through me as I listened, but I willed it to settle. "I don't blame God," I said.

She pulled her mouth taut. I was sure she knew who I blamed. I didn't need to say it. Even before the sickness, the Coutts family had stripped away everything good about living in our world. The end — this end, had always been inevitable.

———

AFTER SWEEPING THE FIRST FLOOR, we freed Holli and Mia, then swiped all the pillows from the meager selection of lounge chairs in one of the second-floor break rooms. On the third floor, Sid sat cross-legged next to the door to the stairs, skinning the rabbit. Blood and fur surrounded him, his wild eyes concentrated on making clean cuts. Against the wall he'd laid a few wooden frames beside a silver pot, stuffed full of crinkled paper.

"We good?" Sid asked, without looking up.

I nodded. "Empty."

"Good."

The third floor was smaller than the bottom two. The wide space boasted an open floor plan, with a stainless steel kitchen on the far left, abandoned cafeteria tables and chairs in the middle. A few small windows dotted the far wall, crusted over with dirt and mildew.

Holli collected two pillows and a thin blanket from her tote to make Mia a makeshift bed. She whined between the soft melody of Holli's low singing, silencing as she drifted off into sleep. Guilt weighed heavy in my gut. Mia was a good kid. A strong kid. Barely complained, always did what we asked of her. But leaving Mom's behind had been a horrible blow.

There was a low probability Neil was still alive. He would've never left Mia on her own in the woods otherwise. And if he had survived, he would've found us by now. But Mia had kept our hope alive. We couldn't crush that. It was too cruel.

But now, the chances of finding Neil were slim to none. We'd put our escape plan into action. We would not return to Mom's for a long time, if ever. The emergency plan had always been to head out over the rocky terrain behind this building, heading west — away from the Coutts, from the possibility of Neil, and everything else we'd ever known.

Maura settled into one of the cafeteria chairs. We hadn't told her our plans, but come tomorrow, she would, again, have a choice to make. Come with us, or return to her commune. And as much as I wished I wouldn't, I wondered if she'd stay. If not for herself, then for us. Another able body, another pair of eyes to help keep us alive. We'd need all the help we could get after abandoning a year of hard work.

With a wince, she stripped off her backpack, brought her knees to her chest, and massaged her calves. I followed suit, finding a spare chair for myself. Getting off my feet spread relief to my legs, and I basked in it as I turned over my hands. They had healed well thanks to the yarrow and now only a few pink remnants of skin remained on my palms.

Holli stood from where Mia lay, heading in our direction as she folded her hands and lay her head upon them to show me the young girl had fallen asleep. "I'm going to check the kitchens. See if there's any food," she said as she passed us. The kitchen had likely already been looted but I supposed it never hurt to check.

Across the room, Sid struck a match, fire catching at the end. He threw it into the paper-filled pot, then went to work on breaking the wooden frames, throwing the pieces into the catching fire. The rabbit wouldn't be much meat for us all, but it would reduce what we'd need to take from our food stash.

Preoccupied with my throbbing limbs, I rifled through my bag, looking for water.

"How are your hands feeling?" Maura asked, her voice low enough so only I could hear.

I made two fists, then released. "A little sore still, but nothing I can't handle."

She gave a knowing nod and looked down at her lap.

"I wanted to apologize," she said.

"For what?"

"Downstairs," Maura answered, shifting back in her seat. She looked off toward Sid. Smoke rose from the pot, the crackling fire a soothing backdrop. "For forcing you all to leave. And for not listening to you when you...told me what happened to you."

Turned away, I could take in her soft features, dotted with tired creases. She'd tied her curly hair up behind her head, where it bobbled as she moved, messy and unkempt, indicative of our day.

"It's not your fault," I said, following her gaze to Sid, who'd used his knife to roast the rabbit over the fire.

"You know that's not true."

I looked back at Maura. She bit her lip as her eyes scanned my face, searching for something. I sighed, exhaustion hovering. "You falling into that creek was an accident," I said. "An act of God, if you will." She tilted her head back and forth as if she wasn't sure she believed me.

"Do you believe in God?"

Her words hung in the air, our gazes fixed on one another. Mom had been a believer. Back before things got bad, she went to Sunday mass, dressed to the nines, her voice the loudest when singing the hymns. Sid and I went, but not as frequently, and less so as we grew. But Mom prayed, even after everything fell apart.

"No," I answered, looking at my lap. "Not in the traditional sense, anyway. But I can understand why people do."

Silence lingered. "And why is that?"

"The world is a pretty brutal place. It's been that way since I can remember," I said, choosing my words carefully. "So much evil, so much unexplained hatred and distrust. I think people find peace in God because it's something bigger than us. It's something you can't explain. It's easier for people to put their faith and trust in something that's not tangible. That way, when bad things happen, they have an answer — an answer to the why. They can place the blame and responsibility on something we can't fully wrap our minds around." I paused, the sadness of Mom's death threatening my chest. "It makes it easier to process. And it makes it easier to move on. I both pity and admire that way of thinking."

"Why pity?" Her tone was curious.

"Because not everyone uses their belief in God for

good," I said. "People have used religion to justify a lot of things. Hate. Fear. Sometimes people are religious because then they don't have to be accountable for their own actions. They can blame everything on God. Sometimes people are religious because they believe it makes them better than others." I shrugged. "I don't think it matters either way. Either you're a good person or you're not. Both kinds can say they believe in God."

She nodded, slowly, as if she were unraveling the weight of my words. Her brows drew together in a worried bundle. "I have a lot of questions," she said. "For Father. And Andrew."

I nodded. "I'd imagine you do." I tilted my head. "And I really am sorry for that."

Maura shrugged. "I guess I always had this feeling," she said, in a small voice, "that things weren't...exactly as Father said. Times where I questioned him. But I never expected something like what Andrew and his men did. Has done. I don't even know anymore. What to think. What to believe." She pressed her lips together, then looked up at me with wide eyes. "Even saying that out loud..."

I leaned in. "They're not listening," I reminded her.

"Yeah, but..." She looked at the ceiling.

"God?"

She nodded.

"I think God knows killing is wrong," I said as gently as I could. "If God does exist, I can't imagine you'd be punished for questioning someone who did that."

"But I'm meant to respect my husband, to follow him to the ends of the Earth and back." She glanced at me. "God heard me make vows. I promised."

"But so did he," I countered.

She shook her head. "But his vows were different. He promised to protect me."

"Has he?"

The question seemed to startle her. She opened her mouth as if she was going to say something, then closed it again, her shoulders curling forward, eyes darting across the floor.

I sighed. "Mom always used to say that God — if there is a God — would want us to be happy. That he wouldn't give us a bunch of arbitrary rules to follow. He'd want us to follow our hearts, to explore the world, to fall in love, to make mistakes." I smiled at the memory. "She said God gave us our minds and free will to explore all avenues of life. And that it was okay to question things. God wouldn't punish us for being who he made us to be."

Maura looked bewildered — some cross between curiosity and disgust. I tried to imagine how she felt. How different my thoughts might be if I'd been raised in an environment where there was no room for error, no grace for honest questions. But I couldn't. And so I was grateful when Sid interrupted by telling us dinner was ready.

After we ate cooked rabbit and stale potato chips Holli had found, we chose lookout shifts from loose straws she'd found in the kitchen. Holli and Sid took first shift, while Maura and I drew second. We slept in the cafeteria, divvying up the remaining cushions. As I lay on the floor, my gun within arm's distance, I missed Mom's bed.

"Wake you in four," Sid said before he disappeared behind the stairs door.

I saluted him, settling into a dreamless slumber.

23

MAURA

THE CUSHIONS SLIPPED against the laminate flooring as I rolled to the side, glimpsing Mia's small, huddled form in the corner. Eli's rhythmic snores echoed throughout the large room, accompanied by the occasional *thunk* from the ceiling as Holli or Sid shifted their position.

It seemed foolish to try to sleep. I couldn't pinpoint a single thought racing through my head, let alone the will to quiet them. I didn't know what was coming next. Where would we go from here? More importantly, where would *I* go? Eli had already tried to take me back home once. It wouldn't be long before he tried again.

Thinking of home physically hurt. Days ago, all I had wanted was to cross back over the creek, find Sweetheart, and race back to the ranch. I longed to see Andrew, to atone for my transgressions, and continue serving the Prophet and God. But now? The decision didn't seem as clear. What was I returning home to? I was practically forbidden to see my sister or Mother, chastised constantly by my sister wives, and working a job with no true meaning. My husband was a murderer. The Prophet lied to us, and as much as I wanted to convince myself it was for the greater good — for something perhaps we did not understand — I couldn't.

Maybe I *was* a sinner. Maybe that was why this happened to me. That's how Father and Andrew would explain it, anyway. But if what Eli said was true — that God gave us our free will for a reason — perhaps I was looking at it all wrong.

The idea froze me, and I clutched the cushion I lay on, heat washing over me in slow waves as I pushed the thought out of my mind. There was no greater sin than questioning Father. Part of me wondered if he felt my disobedience; if he lay awake in his bed knowing I laid here doubting him.

I looked at the ceiling, a fire burning in my belly, my eyes struggling to blink away exhaustion. There would be punishment and penance when I got home. There would be consequences. I could hear Abigail grumbling as I stood at the edge of Andrew's estate, the dry summer air making my throat parched.

"Look what you did," she snarled, spittle flecking my cheek. "Aren't you ashamed?" She pointed her finger into the distance and I followed it.

Father walked down the main road of Coutts Estates with an arsenal of green-suited armed men, a smoking assault rifle held tight in his hands. He approached each family at the end of their drive, raising the gun to shoot them — the men, the women, the children. No one protested as they crumpled upon each other, their blood trailing like honey through the yellow dirt. Every bullet made his shoulders shake.

He approached me, his eyes empty and unforgiving as he raised the rifle. My lips trembled, unable to release my words. I couldn't move. Andrew, Abigail, and Joanna held my writhing body back as I tried to escape. But my struggle was futile. The barrel of Father's gun touched my forehead, pressing into my skin so forcefully, I was sure I would bleed.

"For you have sinned in the eyes of God," Father recited, his finger inching toward the trigger.

"You have standards to uphold," Abigail said in my ear. "Your failures reflect on this family."

My eyes widened. I tried forcing my words, to throw them from my throat, to move against the restraints of my family.

"Pray *harder* Maura," said Andrew.

Father's finger pulled back on the trigger.

"Maura!"

The edges of my world faded. Someone shook me.

"No!" I cried, my voice finally cooperating. "Don't!"

"Maura!"

I knew that voice. Deep, a little husky, but level. Calm. I came to, swimming from the depths of my dream. Eli hovered above me, his forehead wrinkled up in worry as he scanned my face. "You're okay," he hushed, squeezing my arm. "You're all right."

My breath caught in my throat and I struggled to inhale. In an effort to root myself, I focused on Eli's fingers through my shirt, letting my heartbeat steady as his thumb brushed against the fabric. Clarity found me and I remembered the office building.

I sat up, the cushion beneath me shifting again. Light from a flashlight bounced somewhere in the distance.

The dark seemed different, the air a little colder. I shivered.

"You okay?" Eli asked.

I swallowed, coating my dry throat. "I'm fine. Just a silly dream."

"I'm no stranger to nightmares. We all have them."

I nodded. "Thanks," I said, though an embarrassed flush rose to my cheeks. I was grateful for the dark. "Did I wake you?"

He shook his head, then looked up and over his shoulder. I followed his gaze. Sid kneeled in the corner of the room, fluffing the cushions Eli had left, his flashlight between his teeth. "Our shift starts soon. You still up for it, or did you want to keep sleeping?"

I could think of nothing worse.

"I'm up for it."

Eli smiled before pushing back on his feet to squat and stand. "Alright then," he said. "I'll meet you up there." He crossed the room, disappearing behind a large metal door labeled STAIRS.

My fingers took a few tries to shake the remnants of sleep, but I laced my boots up, tucking my jeans inside my socks. For a moment, I became acutely aware I was alone with Sid. He readied himself for sleep as I stretched my toes inside my shoes to make sure they were comfortable.

Sid lay his flashlight on the floor beside his makeshift bed before climbing on top of the cushions. He looked tired, but somehow softer and more approachable in the shadowed light. He glanced up at me and before I could look away, he grunted, clicked his light off, and rolled over to face the wall. The sting of rejection Father had always promised from Outsiders was there. It clutched at my heart, but I was more surprised to find how familiar it felt. That rejection, that immediate apathy, reminded me of the painful dismissal my own sister wives had shown me.

I laughed to myself as I got to my feet, moving toward the door Eli had disappeared behind. The dream I'd had disturbed me, but it only highlighted the true feelings I'd suppressed.

The door to the stairs opened to a wide landing with flights on either side, one going up and one going down. Worn stairs led to the roof, the flimsy plastic railing held only in place by poorly wrapped duct tape. I climbed it to the top, pushing through a door labeled ROOF ACCESS, which led me into the night air.

The humidity from earlier had lifted, allowing cool air to settle around us. It still smelled of rotten eggs. The middle of the flat roof sagged under stagnant rain water, some spots worse than others. Rotting leaves decomposed in corners and crevices, eating away at the ceiling below. I edged toward Eli and Holli, who stood near the far side overlooking the waste center.

"Nothing much happening up here," Holli said, her voice strained as she turned to me. She needed sleep. "Be careful of the dips in the roof. Not sure how much weight it can support anymore. Sid and I were okay around the sides. And if you see anything, wake us up."

"Only if there's an emergency," Eli answered, placing his hand on her shoulder. "Get some rest. You've had a long night. We'll be okay up here." Holli narrowed her eyes, then nodded, before she turned to leave.

Eli stood with his back to me, staring out toward the commune mountains, their shadows looming behind the glow of the waste center. Even though this was part of our commune, it still seemed like a distant land. How could I have never bothered to question where our trash ended up?

I approached the edge where Eli stood, his focus distant. A hint of light had begun to rise. Dawn would be here soon.

"Awake yet?" Eli asked, without turning toward me.

"Kind of," I answered.

Eli gave a muffled chuckle. In his arms, he held a long gun that looked heavy and inconvenient. He played with it, clicking some things into place and then placed it flat on the ground before him.

"Should be quiet for us. I suspect the Hunters have stopped for the night and will resume their search for you in the morning," he said. "But I'm hoping the three of them can rest before we need to move again."

"Where will we go?" I asked.

Eli hesitated, looking back out toward the peak. After a minute of silence, he said, "We're planning to go west." He turned, jutting his chin at the opposite end of the building toward the rocky incline. "If we can scale this hill, get to the other side, we can put some space between us and the commune." He grimaced. "But it's risky. We don't know what's out there, if anything at all."

"You'll leave?"

He met my gaze, frowning beneath his beard. "Yes." His tone suggested it wasn't up for discussion. "And you'll need to decide what to do, Maura," he added. "I think I could convince Sid if you wanted to come with us. But I know you must want to go home."

"I—" My voice cracked, and I closed my mouth. "I have to."

Eli turned then, his brows raised. "You don't *have* to do anything," he said.

I laughed coldly, hugging my arms to my chest. "You make it sound so easy."

"It is. It's your decision. You have free will for a reason—"

"Oh, *stop* with your free will!" I shook my head. "I have the Prophet to answer to. God! Leaving means breaking my vows, it means I'd never get to see my family again. I can't just pick up and leave like you can!" The words hung between us and I wished I could've taken them back.

Eli turned his whole body toward me, narrowing his eyes. "You think what we did back there was easy? You think that was a choice we made lightly?" He scoffed.

"No, I—"

"You know what leaving is gonna do to Mia? Six years old and she's left everything she's ever known behind? Both parents gone? Sid and I left our Mother's body behind — the woman *your father killed*!" he shouted.

Fury rose in my chest. "Father is a holy man. A good man. He's the Prophet!" I said, holding my hands out to the sky. "Our mouthpiece to the Lord. He hands down his teachings, he—"

"Lies to you?"

Time seemed to stop. The rest of my sentence dissipated, curling in on the edges like paper fed to a flame. I grabbed my elbows, huddling in on myself as I looked at the floor. Eli was right. Father had lied to us — to me. Why else send a caravan of armed men into nearby towns? Why else forbid us to move beyond our boundaries? I tried to come up with something else to say, some defense to hold against Father, but none came.

But it didn't matter.

Eli turned away, one arm straight out to stop me from coming any closer. He shifted right, his gaze fixed on where we'd driven in.

"Fuck."

My heart picked up its pace as I followed his line of vision. He turned, eyes wide and filled with terror.

"What?"

"We need to go," he said. "Trucks are headed our way."

24

ELI

WITH THE RIFLE over my shoulder, we rushed from our place on the roof, through the door and down the stairs, our footfalls a loud thunder in the enclosed space. In my mind's eye, I could still see the dark trucks barreling down the main road, dust plumes rising from behind their tires in the dim glow of early morning. If we were lucky, we had about five minutes to make our move, but realistically, we had about three.

I barged through the third-story door, scanning the room.

"Get up!" I roared. "Now!"

Two shadowy figures on the floor shot up. Sid grabbed his pistol, slinging the other hunting rifle over his arm before he'd even gotten to his feet. Holli rolled to the side, rousing Mia from where she lay, scooping everything they'd taken out for the evening back into a pack.

I grabbed my backpack and the duffel with the rest of our weapons and ammo. Mia had begun to cry at the sudden chaos and Holli did her best to soothe her before scooping her up and placing her on the step of the hiking backpack Sid was securing to his chest. Maura stuffed our discarded blankets into her pack, her shadow moving fast in the darkness, and I reached down, collecting any spare food I found into my pockets before racing to the exit.

"Let's go!" I cried, moving to the stairs, pushing the door open. Mia held tight to Sid's neck as he raced forward, her face a wet, snotty mess as she struggled to comprehend what was happening. Holli came next, her gait slowed by stiff, sleepy joints, followed by Maura whose look of uncertainty made my stomach roll.

Together we bounded down the stairs, a cacophony of movement. How much time had passed since Maura and I had left the roof? A minute? Two? Did the Hunters know where we were? Had someone seen us? I knew it didn't matter. It was too late. The trucks were headed in our direction. We'd have to call our own truck a loss — walking out the front would be suicide.

We reached the dark lobby, funneling from the stairs one by one. The lobby windows were too dusty to make out anything on the street, and approaching them was too dangerous.

"Was there an emergency exit when you searched this floor?" Sid whispered, turning to Maura and me.

"Yes," Maura said before I could answer. "Down the hall, to the right."

Sid inspected her for a minute, a flicker of gratitude flashing across his face, then waved for us to follow at a low squat. Hunched and panicked, we darted down the hallway in a single line. The padded carpet quieted our footsteps through the cubicles. I heard them now — the truck engine's rumble. A distant shout. My heart hammered in my throat.

"There!" Sid whispered, pointing at a shadowed metal door at the far corner of the room. A faded EXIT sign hung above. We darted toward it in a crouched run, our only belongings in the world bouncing on our backs. I hoped the Hunters had stopped at the beginning of the office buildings and searched there. We needed all the time we could get.

Sid pushed the door open with a screech. The fresh glow of dim morning light washed over the surrounding land, but we stood in the building's shadow, facing a steep incline. The earth was rocky and uneven, overgrown with dead grass and sparse trees. At the top, a dense thicket grew. We needed to get there before anyone saw us.

I glanced at Sid, who'd likely deduced the same. He gave me a knowing nod, shrugging off the rifle, which he handed to me. I slung it over my left shoulder with the other one, feeling the weight even through my adrenaline.

"We need to run," he said, directing his attention to Maura and Holli. "Into the trees. Fast as you can."

Both women nodded, Holli's mouth a thin line, Maura taking short, quick breaths. Sid turned, keeping one hand on Mia at his back and took off, his speed both remarkable and intimidating. With one last glance at my companions, we all followed.

The dead grass provided decent traction, but the incline was so sharp none of us could run well after the first few strides. As Maura and I climbed behind Sid, Holli fell behind. I paused, waiting for her, but as she passed me, she turned her face, her gaze suggesting I better not slow down for her. Well, she'd have to knock me off the hill before that happened.

The terrain became more unforgiving with each step we took. Every muscle in my body burned, a stitch appearing on my side, threatening to stop me in my tracks. I shook from both fear and exertion. The trees seemed too far — we were out in the open, completely exposed. Someone was going to see us.

As I thought it, I heard the shouts. I hadn't wanted to turn, but had little choice now. I was our last line of defense. I reached around for one of the rifles, bringing both hands up as I swung it forward.

In the distance, between a cluster of buildings, I saw three green armored suits pointing at us. I kept my aim on them, the hill at my back.

"Eli!" Sid shouted. "MOVE!"

I glanced up the hill. Holli had put good distance between us, so I let the gun swing away from my grip, continuing upward at the quickest run I could manage. I kept waiting for the pop, the sudden pain, the explosion of blood from my chest as I ran, my back turned to our pursuers. I thought of Mom. Had she run like we had? Had she been afraid?

We continued forward. Sid grabbed Mia, throwing her over his shoulder for a better grip. They were nearly at the tree line, Maura close behind. Holli continued to climb, her wheezes audible as we climbed together.

"HOL! ELI! C'MON!" Sid's voice was urgent now. I looked back down toward the buildings. The armored men ran at us, guns drawn. Holli scrambled up the hill, grunting as she forced her last bits of exertion to get to the trees where Maura, Sid, and Mia hovered. I followed on her heels, using the last of my strength as we both reached the shadowed thicket. Momentary relief flooded me, but not before a sharp noise cut through our tired breathing.

"Get down!" Sid screamed, shifting Mia so his chest protected her. "Run!"

"Are they—?" Maura's panicked voice rose an octave.

"Shooting at us!" Sid yelled, taking off at full speed between the pines. We wasted no time following, bursting through branches and bristles, thorns and foliage, clothes and skin snagging on nature's loose ends. The smell of earth and our own sweat and grime encompassed us as we ran. We needed to reach the other side of the hill and find better cover. I wasn't sure how long they'd keep chasing us, only that they wouldn't give up at climbing a hill. Escaping the Coutts's clutches once was sheer luck. Doing it a second time was not likely.

"Go!" I shouted at Holli, slowing my pace. I looked to my left at Maura, her face a dark burgundy as she pushed herself ahead of me. I kept moving, turning to look over my shoulder, knowing the rifles on my shoulder would be no match for the Coutts' automatic weapons, but also knowing I would have to take a few of them out before they riddled my body with holes. I kept waiting for men to come spilling up over the crest of the hill, but none came.

The terrain evened out for a few minutes before it began sloping sharply downward. The hill opened into a wide valley, filled with broken roads and stretches of dead farmland. A large piece of mountain curled around the valley on either side, hiding whatever lay beyond it from view.

But a worse realization came to light. The trees ahead of us thinned. If we ran down the hill, we'd be just as exposed as we were running up. If the Hunters reached the top of the hill, it'd be like shooting fish in a barrel.

"Sid!" I cried, but I barely needed to warn him. He turned, eyes wide and panicked — a sight I never wanted to see.

"We've gotta go down," he said between breaths, his gaze traveling over my head toward the hill in front of us. "If we can get down to one of the neighborhoods, we can find somewhere to hide." I could tell he was fighting to find confidence in his words.

"They'll see us," I said. "They'll get up here and see us."

Sid shook his head. "What choice do we have, Eli?" he asked. "It's not like we can reason with them."

I pressed my lips together. Sid was right. There was no reasoning with the Coutts. We lived in a lawless land. We'd be marching to our own execution.

"I've got an idea," Maura said, breaking our silence, her gaze fixed on Sid. She threaded her arm through one strap of her backpack, grabbing it in her hands. "They're looking for me. So I should go to them."

My eyes widened as I took her in. She seemed both frail and full of fire, radiating certainty while she pushed the backpack into Sid's free arm.

"No, Maura," Holli said. "Absolutely not. They're going to shoot anything that moves right now."

Maura shook her head. "There's no time to argue. I'll announce myself. They won't kill me. Either way, I need to go back," she said. "It's where I belong."

"Maura," I breathed. Every instinct I had pushed me to convince her to stay. That we could make it work. That we could take her back when the Hunters had stood down and we were safe. But I knew that was a fantasy. Every second ticking by put us at more risk. Running or staying meant death. And even if we escaped, the Hunters wouldn't stop looking for her.

This was the only way.

"She's a grown woman," Sid said. "She can make her own choices." He turned toward me. "And right now, it's the only one we've got if we want to save our sorry asses."

Maura straightened. "I have to go to them," she said, meeting my eyes. I opened my mouth, desperate for words that fit the situation. End of the world, and I was still searching for the right thing to say. "If I don't go, they will find me. And when they find me, they'll find you. And..." Her voice cracked. "I don't want the same thing to happen to you all that happened back in town. I don't want to be the reason you all die."

"Maura..." Holli said in a tone of warning. "That's very noble of you. But..."

As I turned toward Holli, I saw the wheels turning in her head as she, too, tried to think of a potential solution. But as the silence hung heavy in the early morning air, I think we all recognized that Maura had handed us the best option on a silver platter.

I felt like someone had punched me in the gut. I had saved Maura's life, sure. But had I also damaged her by exposing her to a world she was never supposed to be in? It was unfathomable imagining her returning to her murderous husband, expected to stay quiet and pleasant. My stomach rolled with guilt.

"Maybe we can find a new place," I tried to reason. "We can make it work."

"She'll be safer in her commune, Eli," Sid said. "And we'll be safer too. You know that."

It made sense, but my muscles quivered in anger. "Stay out of this!" I growled, irritated by the softness in his voice. "You don't give two shits about her safety."

"Stop." Maura crossed her arms. "You don't have time for this. Plus, my mind's already made up. I thank you for your kindness, but I will not be responsible for any more of your pain."

Her face fell, but she didn't cry. She seemed to hug herself more tightly before taking a deep breath.

"Maura," I said, closing the gap between us so I could grip her shoulder. She looked up, her brown eyes meeting my own, and I smiled sadly at her. "Thank you."

"Thank you," she repeated in a small voice, before she glanced over her shoulder. "Now go. Quick! Before they get here."

A shout echoed in the distance — far, but still too close for comfort. We all froze, our eyes flickering across each other as reality sunk in. They were still hunting us. And I knew they wouldn't stop until they had Maura.

"Go," I hissed to Holli.

I expected her to run, but Holli placed her hand on Maura's cheek. "You'll always have a place with us," she said. "And if you ever do follow, go west. Follow our path from here — I'll mark trees as we pass them, just in case. Look for my H. And please." Holli closed her eyes. "Stay safe."

Maura nodded and with that, Holli took off toward the trees. With one last fleeting glance at Maura, Sid let a small smile cross his face before he followed in Holli's footsteps, Mia clutched tight in his grip.

"I'm sorry we couldn't help you," I said as urgency nipped my heels.

"You have helped me a great deal, Eli," she answered. "You've shown me the world for what it truly is. And I'll never forget your kindness." She nodded. "Go." She pointed to where Sid, Holli, and Mia had already disappeared in the distant shade. Guilt weighed on me like lead.

Maura straightened, then looked over her shoulder. "Go!" she urged.

"Okay," was all I came up with before I turned and ran like hell.

25

MAURA

My throat tightened as I watched Eli's broad frame disappear over the crest of the hill at a hurried jog. Once he was gone, I turned, facing the sun as it rose beyond the trees, straining my ears to listen for the group as they journeyed down the other side of the mountain.

Please God, let them be safe.

As their noise grew fainter, I began to walk. My legs seemed heavy, my pounding heart slowing as I caught my breath. My lungs hurt. The shredded skin on my arms burned. But it was all dulled by the fear I felt at the prospect of offering myself up to the Hunters. Would they hesitate to shoot? All I could do was hold tight to the hope that they wouldn't.

It was a funny thing, standing at the edge of what might be death. Faith tricked me into thinking I wouldn't be alone; that God or Jesus or the Prophet would walk beside me in my moment of need. But that morning, I felt nothing *but* alone. My whole life, I'd been an other. I didn't *fit*. And here I was, still split between two different worlds, fighting to cling to the faith I'd been so deeply devoted to, while struggling to let go of all I'd learned in the past week. I shouldn't be afraid of these men. That's what Father or Andrew would say. And yet I was terrified.

But, fear or no fear, I owed it to Eli and the others to turn myself in. I couldn't hide behind them anymore. I had to face whatever came next.

I hugged my elbows to my chest as I walked across the flat ground, weaving between the trees. My head buzzed, clouded with conflicting thoughts. I tried focusing on what awaited me back inside the borders of the commune. Dread filled me at the idea of telling Father what I'd seen out here. I had to believe he was still right-eous. He had lied, yes. But if I was returning to my commune, I *had* to trust it was for some greater good I did not yet understand.

A figure appeared at the top of the hill. Then another, and three more. I raised my hands over my head, palms facing outward, continuing to step forward.

"Stop!"

One of the green-armored men raised his automatic weapon up, aiming it at me. Part of me had expected Andrew's voice, but this was not, though it sounded familiar. I was sure my heart had stopped as I struggled to swallow.

"It's me!" I yelled out to them, my voice cracking in fear. "Maura Coutts!"

The Hunter aiming his weapon at me faltered, letting his hold go slack so the gun aimed at the ground.

"Maura Coutts?"

"Yes!" I stepped around a tree trunk, coming into full view. I was dirty and unkempt, but still very much me. I wondered how many of these men I knew. How many served Andrew. How many were killers like him.

"My God, Maura! Praise the Lord!" One Hunter pulled off his helmet and approached me, as if I were a mirage. "Stand down, men!" he shouted to the others in the distance. They lowered their weapons as I put my arms down. "Is it really you?" he asked.

I recognized his blonde hair, short nose, and round freckled face. Morgan and I had once confided in each other that we thought he looked like an oversized baby. It was Luke, one of Andrew's highest ranking men. Though he was not a Coutts by blood, he'd been one of the most devout in the commune, privy to the Prophet's private meetings, assigned to some of the most prestigious duties. Andrew, I understood coming out here to look for me. But Luke?

He smiled, though I could not detect an inch of kindness. Confusion wrapped its slimy arms around me once more. "It's me," I confirmed.

"Oh, God is good! Thank Jesus! The Prophet is *mighty*! We have been praying for your safe return!"

I forced a smile at him as he shouldered his gun, pulling a two-way radio from his belt loop. He pressed the button. "Men," he said into the static, "we've found her! Praise the Almighty Prophet! Returning to the trucks now." He glanced back at me with a wicked smile. "Are you hurt?" he asked, inspecting me in a way that made my insides squirm. "Where have you been?"

"I got lost," I told him.

He cocked an eyebrow, his grin widening. "Lost? On your scavenging route? All the way out here? Were you alone?"

He knew. How could he not? There had been five of us. The chances of them not seeing that was practically impossible. I thought my heart would burst. Every single one of my muscles tensed. I hoped to the Lord my inner turmoil wasn't as obvious as it felt.

"Yes," I said, meeting his eyes. "I was alone. I fell in the creek and tried to find my way back."

He nodded as he listened, but I knew, even before what he did next, he wasn't convinced.

"Well, come on then," Luke said. "Let's get you home."

At once, I realized I wasn't returning home under the same conditions I'd left. Luke urged me forward with a flick of his hand and as I began walking, Hunters flanked me on either side. Two more stood beside them with their backs turned, their weapons aimed into the thicket, as if expecting an ambush.

For a moment, I worried more would head behind us, looking for the group. But so far, it seemed, they were only interested in me. Good. Even if they deployed extra men to go after Eli and the others by the time we got down to level ground, they'd be long gone.

We descended the hill, walking around the office building and through a narrow alley, emerging back out on the street that ran through. In the approaching daylight, the decay became even more obvious, the stench even more overbearing. Seven black trucks were parked across the street, looking out of place. Their cleanliness stained the dirty world I'd walked through with the others. They didn't belong here. Luke and the other Hunters, they didn't belong here either. And me? I wasn't sure where I belonged.

Luke approached one of the trucks, opened the front

passenger side door, and threw his helmet inside. His radio crackled, and he brought it up to his mouth, having a conversation I could not hear. The wind picked up, and I glanced up and down the street, where more men emerged from between various alleyways. Father had sent an army after me.

My stomach tensed. I wanted to believe he'd sent his men after me because he'd feared for my safety. If I hadn't seen him turn a blind eye to Morgan when she'd run away, I might've stuck with that thought. But a sinful thought nagged me. Perhaps he wanted them to find me because he knew I'd seen too much.

"Your father wants to see you, Maura." Luke had turned toward me, his tone sharper.

"He knows you found me?" I asked with surprise, realizing how stupid it was the moment it came out of my mouth. Of course he knew. He'd likely have his ear glued to the radio for any word that they had found me. Father had eyes and ears everywhere, even here, on the Outside.

"Yes," Luke said. "We'll go straight up to the church."

I shivered at the thought. What else had I expected? To walk back into Andrew's house and be welcomed with open arms? That Father would come for a cup of coffee and we'd discuss Eli's existence over Andrew's kitchen table?

Luke said nothing else. Instead, he opened the back door of the truck we stood near and made a motion with his hand, telling me to hurry inside. Though I was familiar with these trucks, I'd never been inside one, and as soon as Luke opened the door, I knew why.

A solid black partition patched up crudely with what looked like metal welding separated the back space from the front seats. The windows on each side were blacked out, making it impossible to see out or in. There was no trunk to speak of, sealed off again, by welded metal. And the worst part of all? There were no seats — just a dark, carpeted floor.

I froze outside the vehicle, hesitating as I held onto the door for support, afraid I would lose my cool and faint right there.

"Is there a problem?"

I looked up at Luke, who smiled at me, as if he were offering me something I couldn't refuse. I wanted to scream at him. Of course there was a problem! He was throwing me into a black, windowless cell, without explanation. But I couldn't try to fight my way out of this. I had to obey. That was what I was best at, after all.

"Come on!" Luke said, as if I were a disobedient dog. He nudged me forward with his elbow and, with no other option, I slid into the truck. I turned to ask how long it would be, but before I could speak, Luke closed the door.

"Wait," I croaked, turning toward where the light had gone out. I pressed my palm against what I assumed was the window, spots swimming in my vision as my eyes adjusted to the darkness. "Luke!" I said, louder this time, my neck muscles straining in panic. "Luke!"

He didn't answer. Dark overwhelmed me. I fumbled around, startled at the sudden shock of losing my sight. My fingers trailed over the carpet, studying the stitching, the cool metal where seats had once been. I let my fingers trace over my body, my worn jeans, the hair on my legs, and my shoes, spongy and wet from the dew-covered grass we'd run through.

But it wasn't enough to keep me level. Hysteria rose

from my belly, erupting in my chest. I couldn't breathe. I curled up on the hard and unforgiving floor, scraping my bruised and battered body against the itchy carpet, as I tried to calm myself. It was useless. I tucked my head to my chest, unable to suck down breaths fast enough. Disorientation clouded everything before the tears came, hot and heavy, in thick streams. It seemed impossible for any more of my emotion to come unraveled, but it did. Grief. Loss. Betrayal. Sadness. Fear. In and out they went, slamming into me like bullets in a body.

I thought of Holli. How she'd told me to breathe. In through my nose. Out through my mouth. How her hand had felt at my back. It calmed me momentarily before the ground moved beneath me.

I was going home.

26

ELI

THE APPROACHING sun disappeared as we descended the hill. Now behind us, Coutts Peak and its surrounding mountains seemed to watch us as we went, scurrying like ants toward the unknown. As much as I hadn't trusted her when we'd first met, I was confident Maura would do what she could to protect us. But she couldn't control the Hunters. We still ran the risk of getting shot at from behind.

Going down the hill was easier than going up, we just had to be careful of our footing. It took only a few minutes for us to reach the bottom and there were only two directions to go. To the south were the dead farmlands. To the north, more hills and forest. Sid paused, considering both directions, then moved toward the trees. We'd agreed a long time ago to travel northwest if we ever left Mom's. The weather would be more moderate than down south, where temperatures often reached over 120 degrees in the summer. Northwest also meant we had stronger winters to contend with, but that was a problem to tackle later.

We hurried along in silence, our breathing labored. Beside me, Holli's face was purple from exertion, her eyes bloodshot. She held her ribs, limping as she continued at a half-run.

"Almost. There," I wheezed, hoping to encourage her.

She nodded, gaze focused forward. I took a chance and looked over my shoulder back at the hill. I half expected to see a stampede of those armored suits scrambling down toward us, but was relieved to find it empty. Finally, our feet found flat land, and we headed toward the tree cover at a slow jog.

Holli fell to her knees the minute we crossed beneath the foliage, rolling over so she lay on her back, crushing her pack under her weight. Sid released Mia, and she hopped off onto solid ground, her thumb stuck firmly in her mouth, clinging to his arm. He used his fingers to wipe the thick layer of sweat from his forehead.

"Everyone okay?" I asked in a hoarse whisper, glancing out at my weary crew. Everyone's eyes found me and though no one responded, I took it to mean no one was mortally wounded.

But even though it seemed like the Hunters had gotten what they came for, it didn't mean they wouldn't follow us. We needed to keep going, cover our tracks, and put some distance between us and them. If Maura falling into the creek was a sin, as she'd said, I hated to think what they thought of us exposing her to the other atrocities they'd committed in the name of God.

Holli sat with her legs splayed out in front of her, gulping water from one of her glass jugs, wiping the moisture from her lips with the back of her hand as she handed it to Sid. He downed a few healthy swigs before handing it to me. The water was warm but glorious, coating my dry throat, filling me with my second wind.

"We can keep going," Sid said, peering up at the lightening sky through the trees. "We'll walk until we absolutely need rest. Okay?" He directed the last question at Holli.

She looked up at him, eyes narrowed in determination, and nodded.

"Good," he said, turning, his hands on his hips. Mia tugged at his arm, and he leaned down so she could whisper something in his ear. I took advantage of the distraction, squatting beside Holli as I held out the nearly empty water jug.

"What you said to Maura about marking our path. Are you really going to do that?"

Holli's eyes met mine, and she brushed her sweaty hair away from her brow before grabbing the jug. "I am."

"Do you think that's smart?"

Holli took a small sip of water, her eyes darting toward where Sid stood with Mia as she relieved herself between a pair of bushes.

"I think it'd be cruel to condemn her to that place forever without some kind of hope."

"She won't follow us," I said with certainty. I thought it was crueler to promise hope to someone who would never benefit from it.

"I wouldn't be so sure."

I raised my chin. "What's that mean?"

"Did you see her face?" Holli's eyes studied mine. "She was terrified to go back." She shook her head and looked at the ground between her legs. "We shouldn't have let her. God knows what they'll do to her. So, yes, I'm going to mark our path. It's the least I can do for her after what she just did for us."

My cheeks flushed. I thought of Maura after she'd watched those men murder innocent people in broad daylight. Her visible relief when I'd told her she could come with us.

"She's strong, Eli," Holli continued. "She's going back now, but it doesn't mean she'll stay there. She's had a taste of freedom. It's going to change her."

"Are you going to tell Sid?" I glanced at my brother, who was approaching us again.

"What do you think?" Holli whispered. I offered her a hand to get to her feet, and we both straightened, converging as a group once more.

"Let's move." Sid waved us along, and we all began to walk.

TREES COVERED the hilly land we traveled. With no evidence the Hunters had followed us, we took things at a slow pace. Every so often we'd stop to relieve ourselves or rest, and every so often I'd find Holli, somewhere off to the side, her small pocketknife in hand, making small carvings in the tree. The rational side of me knew Holli was only marking our path to make herself feel less guilt, but there was another side of me that wondered if there was a possibility Maura would, at some point in the future, follow us to wherever we were going.

The trees and hills seemed so endless, I found myself

wondering if we were walking in circles. A few times it looked as if we were nearing flat land, only to end up in a small clearing with another hill on the other side. Finally, the terrain began to level and both the trees and earth fell away, revealing a lake, the tips of the green water shimmering like diamonds in the sun, now on its descent in the west.

A small dirt trail led to a beach of rock and sand. Huge pines that seemed to touch the sky surrounded the area, reflected against the still water. On the left, a wooden dock with a capsized boat was green with algae, with only a few planks remaining, like an old man's smile. We were silent, the only sound the lapping water on the sand. For a moment, I was certain what we were looking at was a hallucination — a trick my brain was playing to satiate my needs.

We began to undress, kicking off our boots and socks, laying our weapons on dry rocks, shedding our jeans and backpacks. Sid ran through the shallows, disappearing beneath the surface, emerging some twenty feet away in a deeper part of the lake. Mia held Holli's hand as they carefully stepped over stones and branches to soak their feet. I waded up to my knees, using my hands to cup water to wash over my sunburnt face, arms, and back before submerging myself. My hair soaked in the water and as I brushed it through with my fingers, I was pleased to see the dirt and grime I'd accumulated wash away. I couldn't help but think of it as a cleansing. A new beginning.

Mia giggled near the shore, her eyes wide as she glimpsed fish swimming around her ankles. She splashed, eliciting a laugh from Holli, who splashed her back. I grinned, laying back, straightening my body so the sun washed over my face as the water massaged my aching muscles. We were free from burden, free from running, free from fear. It would be short-lived, I knew, but the hill where we'd left Maura was a day's journey through the woods away. We were within safe range, at least for the night.

We spent the rest of daylight in the lake, floating on our backs, dipping in and out of the cool surface, helping Mia make little sandcastles on the beach. As the sky turned from blue to a hazy pink and orange, Sid pulled on his boots and pointed toward the dock.

"I'm going to check out over there." He secured his pistol to the holster he'd fastened over his hips.

"I'll come with you." Our tension had not subsided completely, but near-death experiences have a funny way of reminding you what's really important. Sid nodded, rolling his left shoulder as he walked. I grabbed my handgun and holster and followed.

We took slow, careful steps through the mud around the overgrown edges of the lake, approaching the dock. As we neared, the ground firmed up, and I saw small wooden steps built into the side of the earth. We climbed them cautiously, and I held my breath on each one, sure our combined weight would splinter them.

The stairs held, leading to more overgrowth. At the top, a shingled roof was visible through high grass and we moved toward it, hands on our weapons as we approached. But there was no need for caution. Someone had clearly abandoned the old hunting cabin long ago. It was made of large cypress logs, notched together at the edges. Greenery covered most of its foundation, curling up the sides between the wood. The front door and a shuttered window both hung open.

Inside was a single room that smelled like mildew. A stove, ice box, and a countertop covered half of the left-side wall, next to a flimsy, moth-eaten curtain which we found hid an old pull-chain toilet. Against the far wall sat a small stone fireplace covered in cobwebs. A couch, which was damp to the touch, filled the center space of the room, and a twin-sized bed was pushed up against the right side. It would be a cozy fit tonight, but miles better than sleeping on the forest floor.

After we collected Holli and Mia and brought them up to the cabin, the four of us sat together, eating some of the food we'd brought with us from Mom's. Outside, the sun sank below the horizon, covering the sky with a blanket of indigo. As we ate and talked, it was almost hard to remember we'd been running for our lives only a few hours ago.

Holli fell asleep first, sprawled out on the couch, with Mia curled up beside her chest, their arms draped over each other. Sid and I played three rounds of rock, paper, scissors, determining I'd take first watch. Though I was tired, I didn't mind a little quiet to unravel a few of my thoughts. But Sid lingered, hovering behind me as I settled in on the front step of the cabin. I looked up.

"You glad we're alive?" I asked.

Sid laughed. "I guess. And I've gotta give credit where credit's due."

I cocked an eyebrow. "What do you mean by that?"

Sid shrugged. "The girl," he said. "She went back even though I don't think she wanted to. She did it for us."

I rolled my tongue over my teeth. "I never wanted to put us in harm's way. I only did what I thought was right."

"I know." Sid shifted, moving toward the door. "I wouldn't want to be here with anyone else, you know," he said, pausing before he opened the door. "You're my brother for life. No matter what."

I smiled at him. "Likewise."

Sid disappeared behind the door, pulling it closed, leaving me in the fading heat, the sounds of wildlife growing louder by the minute. I leaned back on my hands. My arms ached, my legs felt like lead, but relief blossomed in my chest.

I felt guilty about it. Maura had sacrificed her safety for us. She had walked right back into the belly of the beast and Holli seemed to think the Coutts would punish her for it. I didn't doubt that. I hoped she was as good a liar as she was a Coutts loyalist when I first met her. Above all, I hoped she stayed safe. And though it would take me some time to voice my thoughts aloud to Holli, some part of me hoped she'd return to us when we were somewhere safe.

There were still obstacles ahead of us. Leaving Mom's was only the first step in a long journey. We were starting over in a world unknown to us with dangers that rivaled the Coutts. We would need food, ammo, and shelter. We would need to figure out how to survive another brutal winter. And we would need to make sure we were hidden well enough from those green-armored Hunters, so they could never find us again.

But those were tomorrow's problems.

27

MAURA

I BRACED myself against the wall of the truck in the all-consuming darkness. Upon further inspection, I realized they'd stripped the inside clean of any type of handle or button, deliberately turning it into a prison. Without something to hold on to, I was at the mercy of the driver, who made sharp turns and abrupt stops. I kept my hands flat on the carpeted floor, trying to keep my nausea at bay. I certainly hadn't expected a warm homecoming, but I definitely hadn't expected this.

I wasn't sure how far we were from the commune, but it hardly mattered. No span of time would be enough to prepare me for Father. I feared punishment awaited me, but that concern fell to the wayside. I was more preoccupied with how I would tell Father about Andrew. In our commune, going against your husband or superior wives was a sin. They were righteous and just, no matter how much you didn't like their commands. But what Andrew did was different. Wasn't it?

I tried shaking away my doubt. This terrible accusation of a man so close to Father must come with some level of certainty. I had to be confident. I had to be sure.

But there was still a deep-seated defensiveness within me. One that emerged by surprise, nagging at me like lingering guilt. Maybe Andrew had to kill that man. Maybe he had no other choice. Perhaps I didn't understand the whole story. Andrew had always been a good man. I'd never had a reason to question that. I struggled to wade through the murky uncertainty that surfaced.

What I saw in Eli's town had been the most certain thing I'd seen in a long time. I could make excuses and attempt to justify the murder, but deep in my gut, I knew that whatever the reason, it was wrong.

Father would understand. He *must*.

After some time, the truck's turns grew sharper. I had no way of knowing for sure, but I thought we were getting close. My beating heart refused to calm, and I'd given up trying. I had been brave enough to return to the Hunters, to allow Eli and the others to escape. If I could do that, then I could confront Father with Andrew's actions.

We took a few more turns and traveled down one long stretch of straight road before the truck stilled. Someone cut the engine, and a door slammed. Within seconds, light filtered into the caged section of the car and I raised my hand to shield my eyes. White light blossomed across my vision, blinding me, but I didn't have time to adjust. Luke reached into the truck and grabbed me by my ankles, forcing my head to crash backward against the truck floor. Stars blossomed in my vision as he dragged me toward the open door.

I yelped, humiliated by the action, instinctually trying

to kick him away. I thought he might shout or reprimand my response, but he only dropped my legs at the edge of the truck, so half my body hung out the back door, my shirt pulled up, exposing my back. My body shook from surprise and anger, and I struggled to sit up. I blinked, hot tears running down my cheeks, still half-blinded by the sunlight.

"Let's go," Luke barked from somewhere outside the truck.

I inhaled, trying to steady myself. My vision returned in pieces and as I gripped the sides of the door, the unmistakable handcrafted structure that stretched to the heavens came into view. And though I couldn't see it, I knew at the very top, the highest point of the commune, was where Father would be. And that was where Luke would take me.

Spots danced before my eyes and I squeezed them shut, scooting myself forward until my feet hit solid ground.

"Come on, Maura," Luke urged.

I needed a minute. I was weak from my emotional eruption, exhausted from the past week, and mortified at the way I was being treated. But I would say none of those things. Instead, I got to my feet in the humid heat that lingered like fog.

My surroundings came into view. We stood at the edge of the paved parking lot, the truck in front of the marble steps leading to the church. Once a beacon of hope and pride, I was horrified to find myself fearful at the bottom of the steps. This was *home*. Despite what I'd seen and experienced, part of me had been eager to come back to the familiar. But now that I was here, I wanted to run.

Sinner.

I shook the thought away as my vision adjusted. A crowd of people stood outside the church, lining the short walk to the stairs. That was strange. Church mass would not be starting this late in the day.

"Maura!" My mother's voice seared through my heart and when I turned to find her face in the small crowd, it almost brought me to my knees. She looked like she hadn't slept in days, lines creased across her face from worry. Beside her stood Morgan, her hair stringy from being unwashed, staring at me furiously. Against my better judgment, I reached out to them. I wanted to be close to them, to hug them, to let them know I was okay. That I hadn't meant to worry them. That this was all a mistake and I could fix it. If I could only…

"I don't think so," Luke said, gripping my shoulder. I looked up at him in horror as his fingernails sunk into my flesh, stopping me in my tracks.

"Your Father wants to see you," he growled.

My face warmed. I was not welcome to question commands from Hunters. And I was then certain Father brought Mother and Morgan here as a punishment — to remind them of their status. And what happens when you disobey. Still, I looked back toward them, certain my heart was cracking open in my ribcage, bleeding for them with regret and guilt. I gasped as I turned, surprised at the warm tears rushing down my chin.

"Maura!" This voice was just as familiar as Mother and Morgan. Andrew's six-foot frame hurried through the parting crowd, stopping Luke with a stern stare.

"Maura!" he said, sounding out of breath. "Oh, thank

God you're alive! The Lord is mighty and good!" But his gaze suggested anything but — he was cross, holding his anger between a furrowed brow. "Where have you been?"

I met Andrew's eyes. I had not been mistaken that afternoon as I watched him kill the old man. Of course it had been him — only my obedience convinced me I could've been wrong. There was no mistaking his cold blue eyes that seemed to hold no life behind them. He was a murderer. A sinner. And I had married him in what Father told me was a blessed union. Could that have been a lie?

Before I found words and formed them into some semblance of a sentence, Luke spoke with purpose. "I have strict orders from the Prophet," he said in a low voice, so the others didn't hear.

"Don't speak to me that way. I'm her husband," Andrew growled. "I lead the Coutts Peak Hunters. You report to *me*." His confidence came across as anger. Luke tightened his grip on me.

"Those are not the Prophet's orders," Luke spat. "He told me your judgment may be clouded and instructed me to take her straight up to him. Now. Move out of the way."

Andrew's face purpled and his hands clenched into fists. In one swift movement, he straightened his shoulders and stepped up to Luke, almost touching his nose with his own. "You dare disrespect me?" he hissed.

Luke didn't flinch. "You dare disrespect the Prophet?"

The words softened Andrew, and he blinked as if he just realized what he was doing. He took a step back and looked at me. "Maura." I looked at him warily. "Just let me know you're okay. I've done nothing but pray for your return."

Done nothing? I wanted to scream. I wanted to call him out on his phoniness, tell him he was lying to me and all those around us. That the Lord knew. God saw it all. He knew what he had done, and he knew it was wrong, and yet he still tried to stand here and be a righteous man. He might as well have spat on Father. But I stayed still, letting my thoughts and emotions roll around within me like a raging storm. My tongue jolted in pain and I felt confused until I realized I was the one biting it. I focused on unclenching my jaw. I hadn't experienced anger like this before. It seemed impossible to hide it.

"Let's go."

For a moment I was grateful for Luke's command until his hand found my bicep and he yanked me along with him, as though he were leading an animal. I was shocked. To be so blatant with his force seemed so bold, but as we brushed past Andrew and I heard my Mother cry out, I knew he meant to make an example out of me.

We began to climb the stairs. I heard Andrew grumbling in the distance and I knew what for. I was his. His property, his responsibility. Father was making a clear statement by not including him in this conversation we were about to have, and he must've had his reasons. A glimmer of hope found me. Maybe Father had some idea of what I was about to tell him.

Luke and I climbed the stairs, one at a time. I tried to use the opportunity to steady my breath, to find a sliver of confidence to cling to.

You know what you saw. Just tell him the truth.

But that was easier said than done. I needed to reveal the truth diplomatically, without seeming like I was going against my husband. I would need to apologize for my disobedience first. Show how loyal and devout I was. Remind Father that I was a loyal Coutts daughter.

We reached the top of the stairs. Without releasing the grip on my arm, Luke opened the door to the church and together we walked through the doors, letting the heavy wood seal us inside.

Though there was little of it, the doors shut out the noise from outside. The air was thick with sage and smoke from lit and extinguished candles. The smell was comforting, reminding me of time with family, of time with others in this community where I felt safe. I inhaled, hoping to cherish the memory, for whatever awaited me in these next few hours was so unknown.

Luke and I turned right, our footsteps echoing off the high ceilings and rose glass windows. The glistening sun created long rays of light that shone across the wooden pews and the intricate detailing of the floors. We reached a double door, which Luke pushed through, guiding me toward the next set of stairs. We would climb it to the top. Father had once said being closer to God made it easier to hear the words the Lord handed down to him so he could distribute them to us.

The wooden stairs wound round and round, floor after floor. I clung to the polished banister, straining my tired muscles to keep going. By the time we reached the top, my entire body trembled. We pushed through the only door, spilling onto a small landing with two doors. One led to a small bathroom, and the other to Father's office. A rich red carpet lined the floors, leading to ornate wooden walls with framed photos of Coutts leaders in generations past — our founder, Michael Coutts, my grandfather, John Coutts, and Father.

We reached an unremarkable closed door on the right with a small golden plaque nailed to the front that read *Peter S. Coutts.*

Filled with uncertainty, I recited what I planned to tell Father. How my disappearance was an accident. That there were others outside this commune; others who needed our help. And my husband, Andrew, had been out there with his men and his guns and I think I saw... no, I *know* I saw him shoot an unarmed man. An unarmed man whose children begged for his life. Andrew hadn't hesitated. He had gone against our teachings, against everything we'd ever been taught. And he needed to be punished.

Luke knocked. And we waited.

28

MAURA

"COME IN."

Father's voice stirred anxiety within me. He was usually calm and level, even in anger, making it difficult to anticipate his reaction. I hoped he would listen to me; that he would allow me time to explain what happened and would sympathize with my plight. I inhaled.

Please. Lord God, please help Father hear me.

"Go ahead," Luke prompted, glancing at the handle.

I hesitated, swallowing hard. I had been to Father's office before, but under very different circumstances. The first time was when I had been late to purpose training as a young teenager. Morgan and I had run off to one of the nearby parks and she had fallen and hurt her knee. We hobbled back quickly, but the damage had been done. Morgan's knee still hurt when it rained, and they gave us a month of cleaning duty inside the church.

The next time I had come to this office was when Father had announced my marriage to Andrew. Mother had been with me then, as had Andrew, Joanna, and

Abigail. I had tried to hide my shock while my two sister wives hadn't bothered to wipe the hatred from their faces. Mother had elbowed me to give my thanks and show my gratitude at the opportunity to join their family. And I had pretended then, like I would now.

I turned the handle. Everything moved too slowly — my breathing, the turn of the knob, the creak of the door. I let it fall open, swinging inward. Father's beautifully crafted office was made from hand-cut wood, each side boasting ornate, stained-glass circular windows. Custom-made bookshelves covered the walls, filled with scriptures and teachings from Prophets before Father, and many of his own.

In the center of the room stood a massive desk cutting the space in half. Father sat on the other side of it, looking down at papers in his hand. Two empty seats preceded the desk. Today, Father wore his work clothes: dark jeans, a faded denim jacket, and a t-shirt underneath. His skin had tanned in the summer sun, freckling his nose and knuckles.

He looked up at me as I took another step forward. His blue eyes narrowed, standing out against his skin, twinkling from the heavy sunlight pouring through the windows. Father had a sharp nose, cheekbones, and chin. His thin lips pulled into a frown.

"Close the door, Maura," Father instructed.

I obeyed, pulling the wooden door closed to leave Luke outside before I approached one of the chairs. I looked at Father, asking permission, and he nodded, showing it was acceptable to take a seat.

I sat. The chairs were made from handsome leather, sewn together by men in our commune. They were comfortable too, the kind of furniture you wanted to sink into and stay for hours.

"It's good to see you alive," he said, breaking the silence. Father put his papers to the side and brought his elbows up to his desk. He steepled his fingers, pressing them to his lips, his eyes glued to me.

"I am glad to be alive," I answered.

"Praise the Lord," he said, locking eyes with my own.

"Praise the Lord."

"Indeed." He sat in silence for the next few moments, forcing me to look anywhere but at him. "So," he said, as if we were discussing the weather. "What happened, Maura? Why have you been gone for so long?"

"I fell. Into the creek," I began, just as I'd rehearsed. "The water... well, the current, was so strong, it swept me right up into it. And then I hit my head—"

"Why were you in the creek?" he pressed. "I looked at your boundary area when we were first notified of your disappearance. Even if you were just on the edge, it would be difficult to get swept up into the water, wouldn't it?" His feigned curiosity hid his true intentions. I knew this trick well.

"I...went in to get a drink of water," I lied, suddenly feeling very defensive as I stumbled over each word. "I guess I went in too far..."

"Well," Father interrupted, "we found your horse running through the forest. Spooked Marta over in Z18." He narrowed his eyes at me. "And how did you get out of the creek?"

"Someone saved me."

Father's eyes widened, then returned to their narrowed place. It was so quick, if I hadn't been staring at him, I might have missed it. He seemed surprised. This was my in.

"It was a man," I continued. "He wasn't part of our commune. I'd never seen him before. He had dark hair and a dark beard, and his name was Eli. He couldn't be much older than me. Father, there are others out there!" I rambled. "There were more with him! A whole group!" My heart thundered as I found confidence in my words. Father would believe me — of course he would! How had I doubted him?

"A whole—?" Father laughed.

"Yes!"

"This is a very big commune," Father began.

I shook my head. "No," I said. "They weren't from our commune, Father. They were…Outsiders." I whispered the last part.

Silence hung between us for a moment and then, without warning, he raised his hands and brought them down, slamming his palms against the desk. Everything on it shook, from the pens, the papers, to the picture frames he had situated on each side. "Enough!" he cried, looking at me with absolute disdain. "Lies! There are no survivors outside of this commune! You know that!"

I recoiled in my chair, sinking into the comfort but completely at odds with the man I had grown to idolize over my youth. His reaction confused me. Perhaps he didn't understand.

"But Father," I said, as calmly as I could manage, leaning forward into the desk to make sure he heard me. "There *were* people out there. I saw them with my own eyes. Honest! Just as real as you and I sitting here. Father, they're out there and they need help. They even have a little girl. We need to help them."

I expected his face to soften, for him to nod with understanding. Instead, rage burned behind his eyes. They no longer twinkled like water in the soft summer sun. There was no comfort in his features. No rationality. I thought of how dark Eli's eyes had gotten that first morning before we'd visited the graves. There had been such a distinct sadness behind them. Father's stern stare felt like pure hatred.

"Maura," he said. His mouth looked like it was moving in slow motion.

"Yes?" I asked.

"The Devil has tricked you. You did not see anyone out there," he told me.

"But—"

"Do you understand me?"

"Father, I *did*—"

"DO YOU UNDERSTAND ME?" He screamed so loud I was sure everyone down below heard him. His face turned a deep red and he stood with such force that he knocked his chair to the floor with a heavy thud.

I nodded, knowing acceptance was the only correct response at this point. "Yes, Father. Yes."

"You *wicked* girl," he growled, nostrils flaring as he continued to stare at me. "You have the Devil inside of you."

I squeezed my eyes closed, any glimmer of hope I had of his understanding, shattered. If Father had reacted this way, how might he react to my next revelation? I considered staying quiet, keeping Andrew's awful secret to myself. But how could I? How could I ever face

Andrew again? My stomach turned as I pushed myself forward.

"Father?" I said, chewing my lip.

"What?" he asked, turning to pick up the chair he had knocked over.

"There's something else."

He stopped, lowering his hands to the top of the desk. Slowly, he raised his eyes to meet mine, his blue irises a colorful contrast to the pink shade his face took on. His lips were pursed, the vein on the right side of his forehead protruding.

"And what could that *possibly* be?"

"I saw Andrew... do something. While I was out there."

As I spoke, his expression changed again. There was something there, in between the fury. Fear? Uncertainty? Could he, perhaps, be opening his mind to what I had to share?

"And what was that?" he asked.

"He... did something. Something terrible."

"Andrew is a follower of the Lord, Maura. Whatever it is, I am sure he is still in good graces with our gracious God."

"He hurt someone," I whispered, knowing I was downplaying the entire incident. He'd *murdered* someone. I searched for Father's adverse reaction. Surely he was disgusted?

Instead, Father sighed, sat back down in his chair, and crossed his arms. "Well, *if* that's true, he must have had good reason to."

"To hurt an innocent person?"

"How do you know they were innocent?" he snarled suddenly, his lip curling.

"Well, I…"

"You're assuming, Maura." He clicked his tongue in disappointment. "You are too quick to judge! Making up stories in your head!" He flicked his hand upward as if swatting a fly. "The Devil is putting sinful thoughts into your head! You have soiled your reputation in this commune!"

"He killed someone," I said, my frustration arming me with false confidence. "I saw him with my own two eyes. This was no hallucination. It happened. I'm sure of it. Killing is a sin." I was confident he would understand that.

He scrunched up his nose and glared at me. The sides of his mouth moved, as if he was trying to find his words. "If what you're saying is true, then Andrew had good reason for it. Did you think perhaps he was helping you? Sometimes we need to make hard choices to protect the ones we love."

"But I wasn't in danger, Father. I'm not even sure Andrew knew I was there!"

"And yet," Father said, "you're here, behind his back, telling me something that might not even be true."

I straightened in my seat, disappointment seeping into every crevice of my being. "Father," I tried again, "I didn't mean to go behind his back. I just thought I should come to you with what he'd done. You are so righteous and fair. I couldn't go to him. I was scared. I'm sorry—"

"You do know Andrew is your husband?"

"I… Of course, I know," I said. "But—"

"Well then, you should know your place as his wife is to *support him*. Lift him up and fight for him. Your immediate assumption is that he harmed someone intentionally? Maura," Father chided, shaking his head in disappointment. "When God called for you to be Andrew's wife... a wife of the Coutts, he expected *better*. I expected better."

Relentless guilt flooded through me. Being a wife was an honor, but being the wife of a Coutts man was a privilege. I knew this. It had been the topic of many conversations throughout my short marriage. I was expected to be better. I was expected to obey. But this? How could Father refuse to hear this?

"I'm sorry," I breathed, lowering my eyes. "I didn't mean to go against him. But what he did, Father. What he did was unforgivable."

"Don't you *ever* question your husband!" he hissed. I shook with a horrible mixture of humiliation and terror, fearful he would slam down on the table again. "You are lucky to be part of such a prestigious family. Joanna and Abigail have shown you *nothing* but kindness, and Andrew has taken you under his wing, despite your barren womb. He has never *once* complained." Father's nostrils flared as he spat his next words, "and yet...here you are." He looked me up and down with pure hatred. "Ungrateful and dishonest. My own daughter."

I held my tongue.

"You have disobeyed this family. Your family. Your husband. Your sisters. Mother. Siblings. *Me*," he shouted, fueling his frustrations at me. The floor spun as I desperately tried to push away my confusion and anger.

"Father," I pleaded, the warning signs of tears prickling the inner corners of my eyes. "I'm sorry."

"You are filled with sin. And you will repent by serving penance."

The word elicited a shudder. People feared Father's

penance across the commune. If I thought cleaning the church for a month was bad, it wouldn't hold a candle to the punishment he was about to hand down to me.

"Penance?" I choked.

"Yes," he said, not bothering to meet my eyes. "The Outside has filled you with lies and fairytales. You must prove to me and your family that you are truly committed to your mission here, Maura. Your time out there," he said, pointing out the window, "has harmed you." His features softened as he caught my gaze. "We need you to do your duty," he stressed. "Become a mother. Give Andrew the attention he deserves. Scavenge materials for your family. Those are the things that matter. It seems you need a reminder."

"Please don't take me away from..." I caught myself before I said Mother or Morgan's name, "... my family."

"You don't deserve that family, child. God is frowning upon you."

I hung my head.

Father opened one of his desk drawers. "You will stay in solitude until you figure out how to right your wrongs. Until you understand that you did not see what you thought you saw out there. Until I decide you are worthy to return back here to be with us. With the righteous ones." He flipped through the files in the drawer, producing paper after paper and, finally, a thick, white envelope.

"No wonder the Lord has not rewarded you with children," he spat, shoving the papers inside the envelope, his eyes narrowed in on me. He took little care with organization, his hands trembling with anger as he looked at what he held in his hands with satisfaction. "This," he said, waving the envelope at me, "will teach you obedience again."

I gaped at him. I shouldn't have been afraid of a few pieces of paper, but it was fear of the unknown that undid me. I wasn't sure how long I sat in that seat, turning Father's words over in my mind. Repentance for something that wasn't even my fault. I had been a devout follower of the Church and the Prophet for my entire life. Never stepped a toe out of line. I'd been loyal. The perfect role model of what Father's children should be. I knew he held disappointment for Morgan. But for me?

Sadness and frustration bubbled into my chest. I couldn't cry here, though. I'd have plenty of time for that later. He had sent Morgan away to repent when she'd left the commune all that time ago. For months she'd been alone, isolated from the rest of the world. No communication, except between her and Father. She had to beg for his forgiveness. When she returned home, she was not the same woman she had been when she left. She had refused to talk to any of us about her time there, but I still heard her muffled sobs when she thought I was asleep.

Now, it was my turn.

"Stand up," he ordered, coming around the side of his desk. "Away from the chairs." He pointed to the middle of the room.

I moved, refusing to meet Father's eyes as he inspected me, hands on his hips, as though he were studying an animal for slaughter. He stepped forward until our toes almost touched, hunching his shoulders so his face was level with mine. I looked down at the pointed toes of his boots — darkened with wear and creases.

"You disobedient girl," he spat, his breath like curdled milk. "You are a sinner."

I stood in silence.

"ANSWER ME," he bellowed.

"Yes, Father," I said, working hard to control my shaking limbs. "I am a sinner."

"And a liar," he added. "Making up stories of what you have seen outside these borders."

"Yes Father. I am a liar." I glanced up. His lips curled into a sneer. In one swift movement, he brought his elbow back, hand at his ear, bringing his palm down upon my cheek with surprising force. The pain startled me, my stinging skin making my eyes water.

"Do you know what happens to sinners?" he asked.

"They are denied entry to the Kingdom of Heaven," I gasped through my pain.

"What else?"

"They must repent."

He nodded. "And what did you see out there, Maura?"

With a shuddering breath, I said, "I saw nothing, Father."

His shoulders softened. I held my breath, using every strength I had left in me to hold back tears.

"I don't believe you," he spat.

Father moved away from my line of vision and I looked up. He grabbed the envelope from his desk, then walked toward the door of his office.

"Luke!"

I thought of the man who stood outside the door and panicked.

Please, God. Please don't let him do this.

As Father disappeared from the room, I stared at his

desk, desperation morphing into loathing. It was sinful, but any control I'd had left was gone. I was tired, dirty, and disoriented. Hatred seemed to be the only emotion I could feel. I was powerless against it.

"Maura," Father spoke with finality. I looked up as he pressed the envelope into Luke's hands as they entered the room together. "Go with Luke."

"Father…" This man had given me life. He'd taught me morals and showed me how to be an obedient servant of God. I trusted him. And I so desperately wanted him to protect me. If not Father, then who? If I had fallen out of Father's grace, did that mean I fell from God's grace, too? It was nearly too much to bear.

He turned his back on me then, walking toward the windows to stare out into the distance; beauty he didn't deserve. I wanted to scream at him, to lunge at him from behind the desk and shake some sense into him. But there was no way I could.

I had no choice but to go.

29

MAURA

I CLAMBERED down the stairs of the church, desperate for a breath of fresh air. The office had been so stifling, so constricting, and so unbelievably disappointing, it almost felt like a dream.

I did not know how long we'd been inside, but the small crowd that surrounded the truck when we'd first arrived had dispersed. We were a busy commune, but my absence and return home would be a welcome subject of gossip for many. The Prophet's daughter had gone missing and returned a week later. There would be talk of sin, of straying from the flock, of running away. They would bring up my sister's journey to the Outside, how there was never only one bad apple. They would bring up my barren womb, a sure punishment for my disobedience. They would blame Mother for her upbringing, for her ungodliness, and her skin color.

The paved lot wasn't empty, however. Mother and Morgan still stood by the truck, their gazes fixed on me and Luke. He'd grabbed me by the arm again, as we left

Father's office, the envelope in his hand. Mother and Morgan would know what that meant, too. I hung my head in shame as we reached the bottom step. I couldn't bear to look at the disappointment washed across their faces. Perhaps that made me a coward. But I was well past the point of caring.

I heard Mother crying; her agonized sobs reminding me my adventure hadn't only impacted me, but her and Morgan as well. Against my better judgment, I looked up. Mother's hands covered her face, but my sister watched me, nodding at me as her eyes flicked to the envelope in Luke's hand and back. In her own way, she was telling me I would be okay. If she could make it through, I could too.

Luke yanked me toward the car, pulling open the rear door to the dark prison. I stilled, staring at the belly of the darkness, nausea making me want to gag. He shoved me forward, but I grasped the frame of the door, the claustrophobic fear bundling at the base of my throat.

"Get in the car, Maura."

"I need—"

"I said, GET IN THE CAR!" A sudden pain spread like fire across my lower back, shooting up my spine. I crumpled against the door from the force of Luke's blow, still clinging to its frame as I yelled out in surprise.

"Stop!" Mother yelled from somewhere in the distance.

The sun blotted out Luke's face, but I still saw the glint against his white teeth as he smiled down at me. How had I ever thought this man holy? How had any of us? He was cruel. Sadistic.

I got to my feet, determined not to give him the satisfaction of my tears. My confidence was shaken and the last thing I wanted to do was climb into a cold, dark box, but the threat of another hit to my back kept me moving. I entered on my knees, like a wounded animal about to meet their death, turning to look at my captor.

He didn't give me the opportunity. The door slammed shut before I got one last look at the church or my family, choking out the daylight, shrouding me in darkness. I made no effort to sit up. Instead, I laid my head on the carpet and wept.

I wept for the others, the ones I'd left out in the wilderness, who had left their home behind. I wept for the innocents out there in the world, navigating the treacherous terrain without the resources they needed. The resources our commune so greedily kept to ourselves. I wept for Andrew, for his cruelty, and for his defiance of God. I wept for Father, for his ignorance of what Andrew had done, for his desire to protect the men around him, regardless of if they were holy.

I wept for Mother. For Morgan. For the rest of my siblings. For my sister wives. But most of all, I wept for myself. For the secrets that had unraveled me.

For my future.

For my soul.

THE RIDE to the Island of Repentance happened in a void where time seemed to not exist. At first, I tried studying the truck's movements to maintain some sense of direction. There was no reason for it, of course. The island was an island for a reason. I thought of Holli, how she might be carving an *H* for me at that moment, and wondering if she knew how pointless her effort would be.

Eventually, I lost track of where we were and how many times we'd turned. At one point, I became certain Luke was driving in circles to disorient me on purpose. Time crawled by. I closed my eyes and tried to sleep, but every bump or turn sent me rattling across the back seat. After some time, the tires found flatter terrain, and we drove on.

As the drive persisted, my muscles began to ache from the uncomfortable floor. My bladder urgently needed to be emptied. I tried to remember the last time I'd eaten — dinner with Eli and the others? The thought made my stomach cramp with hunger. But on we drove.

I was sure a day had passed. Every bump made me sweat, for fear of vomiting from hunger or accidentally wetting myself, and finally, when I thought I'd have to relieve myself on the floor, the truck rolled to a complete stop. I sat up, my hair stuck to the back of my neck and forehead with sweat, scrambling toward where I thought a door might be. It opened. Light flooded in, blinding me. I gasped in relief, eager to escape from my prison. I didn't care that I was going to the islands. I didn't care what happened next, so long as I got out of the godforsaken truck.

"Let's go," Luke said, pulling my arm.

"Bathroom," I croaked, and he scoffed, inconvenienced by my request. All I saw were white spots of light, but I could feel the bush he threw me in. I fell, the sting of pain radiating from my skinned knees to my back. Thorns poked at my skin, tearing across my legs and arms, jabbing through my shirt. I squinted, watching as he turned his back to me. I knew I should've been embarrassed by the lack of privacy, but urgency allowed me to do my business quickly.

Before I'd even done up the zipper on my pants, he yanked me alongside him as he walked away from the truck. My vision returned in pieces. I glimpsed tall trees in the distance — massive white pines that stretched to the sky, swaying back and forth against the clouds. They blotted out any distant landmark, enclosing Luke and me in a foreign landscape.

The heat had worsened, the only indication I had that we were closer to sea level. The overgrown grass at our feet shot up so tall in some places, it reached my middle.

As we moved, the grass overgrowth thinned, making way to pine-needle covered ground, shadowed by the trees above. We walked on, Luke's grip still tight on my arm, bruising my flesh with his meaty fingers. There was no need for that, but I didn't dare tell him. I had no idea where I was. I was starving and exhausted. Even if I could've run, where would I have gone?

The arch of my foot began to cramp, seizing up as we walked. I pushed forward, gritting my teeth, wondering if it was Father or God punishing me and if it even mattered. Finally, the trees cleared, leading to a wide dirt path that led us down to a crescent-shaped beach. The sand curved around the edge of a body of water stretching into the distance, where it met more tree-covered hills. At the center of the wide expanse was a small island, dotted with the same tall white pines, a small dock visible at its edge.

Gentle waves lapped at the beach, but the water was otherwise still. Luke dragged me along, our feet sinking as we approached the sand. At the farthest point of the left side of the beach sat a wooden post to which a small, motorized boat was attached. Its bow came up onto land, keeping it still.

"Get in," Luke said, pushing me forward into the water. It splashed into my shoes and up my ankles. I waded forward, inspecting the small wooden structure. It looked like it could barely hold me. But Luke?

Still, I was nothing if not obedient, so I pulled myself up and in, where I took a seat on the closest wooden seat. Luke followed, looking out of place in his green uniform. He'd left the helmet in the truck, it seemed, but he kept one hand on the gun slung across his chest as he gathered the rope, before stomping through the water to join me.

I had never been on a boat, so I watched curiously as Luke sat on the farthest plank, using a pull cord to start the engine. The sour smell of gasoline filled my nostrils, and I set my hands out on either side to steady myself as Luke navigated the boat with a loud rumble.

We approached a dock at the edge of the island. Luke guided the boat beside it, securing us with the rope before instructing me to get out. I stepped out onto the dock, trying to swallow my dread as I looked out at what was my new home.

Overgrowth spread across the cut of earth, but there was a clear path from the dock into the trees. Luke grunted as he joined me on the dock and I winced, expecting his grip, but he brushed past me, taking the dirt path. I guessed he assumed there was nowhere for me to run, and he was right about that. There was nowhere to go but forward.

The massive pines parted like the Red Sea, the path

widening into a circle as we entered the tree shadows. Six A-frame homes stood around the dirt circle, each the same. There were no windows, only a single door with a light, a number, and two individual steps leading up to each of them.

The Homes of Repentance.

I had known of their existence for most of my life. These homes had been used as veiled threats when we were children — a place we should never hope to visit, for they were for the wicked. I had thought, over the years, that I must've known people in our community who had visited here. But aside from unreliable gossip, we never truly knew. It was common for families, especially of Andrew's stature, to lie about these things. Solitude was a cruel punishment meant for the very worst of sinners.

Luke pointed to the home in the middle with a faded number 3. "That's you," he said.

The structure loomed above us as we took the stairs, before Luke pulled a keyring from his pocket to open the door. I swallowed. There would be no people, no sunlight, and certainly no scavenging. This was my prison until I could convince Father I'd reformed.

Luke opened the door, letting the stench of mildew out before flipping on a light switch to illuminate the entire place. It was a single room, painted beige. The high ceiling met at a point in the middle of the home, a skylight on either side, and a single light hanging from the middle.

I scanned the room. A small kitchen with a refrigerator, counter, and sink was to my left. A door on our right led to a cramped bathroom. The only other furniture in the room was a ratty loveseat with a blanket draped over the back, a coffee table, and a knitted rug. A small wood-burning stove with a pile of wood beside it hugged the right wall. Above it hung a framed photo of Father. Even higher on the wall was a large digital clock with red numbers.

"The couch pulls out," Luke grumbled, shifting his weight as he answered a question I didn't ask. "You will stay inside at all times," he continued as he closed the door behind us. He pointed above the wood-burning stove. "You are expected to pray for ten minutes at the top of every hour, from sun up to sun down. The clock will beep and not stop until you kneel here." He pointed to a white square set into the floor.

"Failure to follow this procedure will result in additional days of repentance." He handed me the white envelope Father had given him before we left. "You will answer the questions in this envelope at the end of every day. When the next person comes to deliver your food, he'll bring your answers back to the Prophet, who will determine if you've shown enough repentance to be granted additional privileges.

"There is firewood beside the stove. You will receive food every two days. It's your responsibility to ensure your food lasts. Water is meant to be used sparingly, no more than twenty minutes per day. When you have down time, you will make scarves and hats for the winter. Those materials will also come with your food. And, as punishment for your disobedience, you will not receive your ration of food for the next two days," he said. I opened my mouth, but there was little point in protesting.

"You must complete your penance and repent for your sins," Luke continued, ignoring my horror. "Do what you're told, return home sooner. Do you understand?"

"I do," I said, not meeting his eyes.

"Do you have any questions?" he asked.

"What happens if I get hurt?" I asked. "Can I call you on a radio?"

"No," he said. "Anything else?"

I shook my head and crossed my arms. I knew Luke would not have the answers I wanted.

He nodded. "Good. Remember, be good and obedient, and God and the Prophet will reward you," he said, before walking to the door. "I leave you in God's grace and pray you are protected from his most holy wrath."

I should've responded, should've asked God to bless him in return, but my defiance was all I had control of in that moment. He shrugged and pulled the door closed behind him, leaving me alone.

30

MAURA

As Luke turned the key in the lock, I ran to the sink, throwing the handle up. Fresh water flowed freely from the spout and I nearly cried in relief. I cupped my hands beneath the water, brought them to my mouth and drank. Water sloshed down my front, soaking my shirt and chin, but I didn't care. I cupped and gulped, over and over again.

When I'd had my fill, I shut the faucet off and stilled in the home's silence, hands gripped against the sink. The door to my left was locked. I would have no food for two days, that was, if anyone ever returned at all. My stomach roared at the thought and I yelled in frustration, using what little strength I had left to kick the cabinet beneath the sink.

All I had focused on when I chose to return was Eli, Holli, Mia, and even Sid's safety. It had been my mistake to correct. But I hadn't thought farther than that. I was blind, still hoping Father would see Andrew's evils for what they were. Instead, he protected him and chose to banish me. To force me into obedience. I had lived so long trying to be obedient and steadfast, knowing in the depths of my soul that Father was always righteous. As long as our Prophet was righteous, all was right in the world. We had sacrifices to make. We had jobs to do. We didn't complain, because the Prophet was hard at work with God.

I had learned in the many teachings with our Matri-arch, that there would be times we were unhappy. Times we had to surrender the will of our bodies and minds to allow the Coutts' men to fulfill their righteous duties. And I had done it time and time again. Like a fool.

Clarity hit me, and it was sudden — the world seemed to flower open, revealing the very thing that had been hidden for so long. I'd been hiding behind my faith, behind Andrew, Father, and my family since the day I was born, convinced others knew better. That others had the answers. That my only duty was to follow obediently. And where had that gotten me? What had that done for me?

The digital clock buzzed — a relentless screaming alarm that broke me from my thoughts. I hurried from the sink to the living area, sinking to my knees against the patch of white. It was a thin platform, covered in a white rug and as I kneeled upon it, I felt a spring beneath. My weight pushed it to the ground, and the buzzing ceased. Above, the red numbers switched to green, counting down from ten.

I think I prayed during those first ten minutes, but not for the reparation of my soul or anything else Father would've wanted. Instead, I prayed for a sign from God. I prayed for another chance to make a choice. I prayed for strength. For peace.

When the ten minutes was over, I retrieved the envelope Luke had left on the kitchen counter, settling on the floor in the main area. Turning the thick collection of papers over in my hands, my heart pounded at the mere thought of what was inside. I knew the protocol — if I didn't comply with these instructions to a tee, Father would keep me in solitude. Only until I was obedient would I be allowed to return to my home. And even though that wasn't ideal, either, it was miles better than this.

After a deep breath, I pulled the seal apart, opened the lip, and dumped the contents out onto the table. A clump of paper and a few pencils fell from the open mouth. I inspected them — I would answer the same questions every day: *How did you show service to the Lord today? What sin did you commit? How will you make up your transgressions to God? What have you learned from your disobedience?* There were twenty in all, each a different deviation from the last, meant to remind me of my inexcusable defiance. I pushed them away, across the coffee table, then climbed up onto the couch, sinking into the cushions, where sleep took me away.

THE ALARM WOKE me and I scrambled from couch to white carpet, too exhausted to do much praying. This went on three more times until the alarm silenced for the night. My sleep was black and dreamless until I woke some time later, my neck stiff.

The room was dark. I hadn't turned off the light before I'd fallen asleep, so I sat up, confused. A pitter-patter of hard rain echoed against the roof of the A-frame, disorienting me as I peered through the skylight, thick with running rainwater. Time seemed strange, just like it had in the truck. I glanced at the clock, for its proud digits it'd shown when Luke and I had walked inside. But it was blank — a black box hung upon the wall.

A deafening clap of thunder shook the house, one that rattled my bones. A splash of lightning followed, brightening the room for a few seconds, before it left me in the dark again. It washed me with fear, reminding me of being trapped with the others in the trailer. Luke said food would come in two days, but what would happen if a storm ravaged the area? What if I remained here for a week or more without something to eat?

I tried standing, but the room spun and I steadied myself on the couch before I returned to the sink for more water. It eased my hunger cramps some, but I knew they were bound to get worse over the next day and I didn't trust anyone to return if the storm raged on. The Homes of Repentance were here for punishment. It would not be high on Father's priority list to send his men out into dangerous weather to feed us.

Desperate from the thought, I reached for the handle of the front door. Maybe the key hadn't turned all the way in the lock. Maybe Luke hadn't checked. I let my hand curl around the thick brass knob before twisting. My wrist caught against the lock and I strained, the muscles in my forearm tightening. But it didn't budge. It wouldn't budge. Thunder clapped again.

In the dark, I tried inspecting the hinges, the space between the door and frame, but nothing suggested the door wasn't solid. Wind howled on the other side, teasing me, as if reminding me how trapped I was.

I could admit defeat. My exhaustion was too great to keep trying, and so I pulled myself away, too tired to cry, too tired to do anything but push the coffee table away from the couch, and pull the mattress out. It was already made with crisp white sheets and I climbed beneath them, using my hands as pillows. I thought of Eli and the others, where they might be by now. Were they safe? Had they made it away from the hill and into the trees we'd seen on the other side? Were they heading north?

Each one of them swam into my mind's eye and I lost myself in the delusion, comforted by the idea that I had saved them. That this all might be worth it, if they were safe. I imagined them somewhere else, somewhere where they couldn't see Coutts Peak, where the sun was warm and the grass was soft, where Mia could play and Holli could plant and Sid could shoot and Eli could tell us stories of better days. Sleep carried me off as I joined them, barefoot and carefree, the idea of Father's punishments so far away it was laughable I'd ever even worried about them at all.

A deafening crack startled me awake, so loud, I shot upwards, one foot still wrapped in the sheet, the other leading me away from the noise. My ears rang, and I tried looking upwards, realizing I could no longer see the skylights. Something obscured the windows and the ceiling, and as I shook off the blanket and backed away from the couch, I realized what it was.

Horror gripped my throat and though I wanted to, I could not scream. A massive pine tree sat in the middle of the living room, its long branches reaching so far down, they touched the couch and coffee table. The trunk hung over what had once been the A-frame roof, the beams splintered by the weight, drywall and insulation hanging from the destruction like innards of an animal. Rain dripped from the sky and roof, down branches and pine needles, into the room, soaking the furniture and rug. Everything smelled wet, earthy and fresh and in the distance, thunder rumbled, louder this time, with no walls to suppress the sound.

Another loud crack and I screamed, pressing myself back against the solid wall. The tree shifted downward, stray branches ripping Father's photo and the digital clock from the wall as it found its final resting place on the floor.

My limbs shook as I took in the sight. The tree had shattered the skylights, glass visible near the fireplace and side of the couch. The mattress I'd been lying on only moments ago was now obscured by thick branches and pine needles. Lightning brightened the room. The wider part of the trunk sat over what used to be the bathroom, the walls crushed like crumpled paper. Water spurted up from somewhere in the distance, gushing from some broken pipe.

I wiped my mouth against my hand, crouched and frozen to the wall. I couldn't think. I had no idea what to do. There was no one to contact, nobody who would even know this happened.

Nobody would know this happened.

Nobody.

I straightened, breath unsteady, palms flat against the wall behind me. Nobody would know. At least, not until the storm ended and they returned with food. Hadn't I asked God for a sign? For another chance to make a

choice? Was this what I'd been asking for? Was God
calling out to me? Asking me to fight through my fear?

I watched the storm from my place on the floor,
frightened at the wind and unrelenting rain, by the way
the thunder rolled and rumbled, by the cracks of lightning
in the sky. Rain dripped through the house's broken
cracks and I feared too much would flood the home. But
as the night wore on, the thunder began to drift and
silence. The lightning faded. The storm began to move on.

Despite the hunger pains crippling my energy, I felt a
rush of excitement as the pouring rain turned into a drizzle. Morning peeked through the dark, gray clouds, and
before I picked myself up, the rain ceased completely.
Dawn brought a fresh blue sky, which I saw from my spot
on the floor. Faith blossomed in my chest. God was
leading me in the direction I was meant to go.

In the morning light, I saw the tree stretched almost
across the entire length of the structure. The tip of the
tree was the lowest point, laying beside the far side of the
couch. I moved toward it, testing my weight against it,
pleased to find it sturdy. The base of the trunk was somewhere outside, but I might be able to climb to it through
the broken wall.

I went to the kitchen, throwing open the cabinets,
urgency nipping at my heels. The heaviest thing I found
was a cast-iron skillet. I stood on my tip toes, reaching for
the highest branches I could, nestling the pan between
them. Next, I took two rubber gloves from beneath the
sink and filled them with water, tying them closed at the
end. I gathered a few eating utensils and a matchbook left
in one of the drawers, stuffing everything in a spare

garbage bag. Then I pulled the drawstrings together into a makeshift pack, which I tucked beside the skillet.

I inspected the climb I was about to take, reminded of Eli and my journey down the river, holding tight to the dead tree that saved my life. I climbed on top of the arm of the couch, using a thick branch to hoist myself up and over the saturated trunk. Pine needles scraped at my exposed skin, sap sticking to my clothes and fingers like glue.

I inched forward, careful to keep my balance. At the middle of my climb, I looked down. The floor seemed foreign and far, darkened by the rain that was never supposed to enter. As the trunk thickened, I got to my knees, using them to continue my climb. Drywall gave way to the thick trunk on my left, where the bathroom had once been.

Through the crack to the outside, sunlight poured through the trees that were still standing. Mist rose from the ground as the last of the storm disappeared. I longed to be out there, in the sunlight, the damage behind me, but I still had a climb ahead of me. The wall split into a V, but there wasn't enough room for me to squeeze through. I hoisted myself up further, to the branch where I'd tucked the filled garbage bag and cast-iron skillet. I took the skillet first, feeling the weight in my hands as I scooted further up the trunk.

Wet and splintered drywall was the last barrier between me and my prison. I lifted the skillet with two hands up to my right ear and swung down at what was left of the wall. My weak muscles struggled to maintain strength as I hacked away at it, using my fingernails to tear bits away until they bled.

Finally, I dropped the skillet from where I sat — it was too heavy to consider taking — letting it fall to the floor with a loud clang. My fingers grasped for the pack and I launched it over the opening in the wall. I'd only widened the space slightly, but it was enough room to wiggle myself through. Using the remaining drywall, I lifted myself from the trunk, gritting my teeth, tearing the flesh on my hands. My toes found balance against the trunk as I pressed myself up on my arms.

The wood tore at my chafed skin and I winced as I scraped my knee against something sharp. But I had come too far to give up now. I hoisted my torso, then my legs over the side of the house. My fingers gripped the top of the wall, feet dangling over the ground. I swallowed hard, looking over my shoulder at the drop. It was farther than I liked it to be, but what choice did I have?

I let go.

My body hit the ground with a crash and spots appeared behind my eyelids — bright and blinking, like stars. I lay still for a moment, internally assessing my body. My legs seemed to work okay, ankles twisted fine, my feet sore, but uninjured. My arms and shoulders ached from exertion, but all seemed in working order.

I opened my eyes to look up at the sky, cloudless and blue. The pines swayed, dancing in the breeze, as if the storm had never even happened. To my left, I glimpsed the large broken roots of the tree, stretching skyward like twisted fingers. Beyond that, the lake rippled, beckoning me.

Even then, I hesitated. I could stay. Figure out how to survive the next few days, find things to eat, even try to make my way back into the commune to enlist the help of a kind Coutts follower. But too much had happened to return now. In my moment of need, God *had* sent me a sign. He gave me a choice, a way forward, a way back to the others. And I wasn't going to let it pass me by.

After some time, I got to my feet, my hair caked in mud, skin bruised and battered. I picked up the mud-slicked garbage bag pack and secured it to my belt loop, then turned to one of the large, broken branches of the pine tree. As I dragged it toward the edge of the water, I looked back through the trees at the demolished home. God had given me the tools to escape. And I'd had the strength to do it. It filled me with pride and an unrelenting fire. I turned back toward the water, my chest tightening as I unlaced my boots and secured them to another belt loop.

The calm lake spread before me. The other side surely looked closer than it actually was. But this time, I was prepared. I took a deep breath, pushed the buoyant branch out into the water, and began to swim.

TO BE CONTINUED

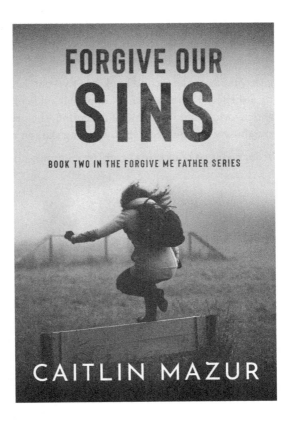

I thought we were the last survivors on Earth. Now, I know better.

After fleeing her commune and leaving behind everything she's ever known, Maura Coutts may never be forgiven for her sin. She embarks on a dangerous journey to return to the group that helped her survive once before. But as she travels deeper into the unknown, she finds the world is more brutal than she could've imagined.

Just when she thinks all hope is lost, Maura finds an old friend in dire need of medical care. But with the odds stacked against them and her limited survival skills, she's not sure they'll make it out alive. Can Maura save herself, her companion, and find the group she's looking for? Or has she sacrificed her comfortable prison for certain death?

Forgive Our Sins is the second book in a five-part series following a sheltered woman facing impossible odds in a post-apocalyptic world. After a lifetime of deception, she's ready to show those who doubted her how strong she can be.

Order today at books2read.com/forgive-our-sins

ACKNOWLEDGMENTS

An endless thank you to the people who helped bring this book to fruition. I could not have done this without a massive support system and a variety of incredibly kind individuals who allowed my book to take up their time.

To my WPC Coven: Michelle, Jennifer, Debbie, Monica, and Jason, who let me vent, cry, and celebrate. To my Belgrade Wordsmiths, especially Keith, who provided some of the most valuable feedback I could've asked for. To Lindsay, who provided deep insight into what it was like to survive a cult. To my incredible team of beta readers, who saw the things I couldn't. To my family and friends, who have supported every step of this journey.

Thank you.

THANK YOU!

Thank you so much for reading **Forgive Our Ignorance.** If you enjoyed this book, please consider leaving it a review on your platform of choice. Reviews significantly help indie authors like me increase visibility and boost credibility for future readers.

ABOUT THE AUTHOR

Caitlin Mazur is a multi-genre author whose works span science fiction, speculative fiction, horror, and supernatural genres. As a transracial adoptee, Caitlin's work often touches on themes of found family and self-discovery.

Caitlin co-founded the Writing, Prompts & Critiques (WPC) Facebook community with over 11k members, named one of Reedsy's 50 Best Places to Find a Critique Circle. She helped develop WPC Press, a spin-off independent publisher that publishes anthologies with stories from WPC group members. When she's not writing fiction, Caitlin is a freelance writer, wife to an incredibly supportive husband, and mom to two amazing kids. Caitlin holds a degree in English Communications with a minor in Marketing from Saint Joseph's University in Philadelphia, PA, and is now living her best life in Central Maine.

Follow Caitlin: https://linktr.ee/caitwritesstuff

facebook.com/caitlinwritesstuff
instagram.com/caitwritesstuff
tiktok.com/@caitlinwritesstuff

Made in the USA
Middletown, DE
24 August 2024